Swimming with Jonah

D0062856

Audrey Schulman

BARD

AN AVON BOOK

AVON BOOKS, INC.
An Imprint of HarperCollins*Publishers*
10 East 53rd Street
New York, New York 10022-5299

Copyright © 1999 by Audrey Schulman
Cover design, illustration and computer imaging by Amy Halperin
Interior design by Kellan Peck
Published by arrangement with the author
ISBN: 0-380-80086-1
www.harpercollins.com

Library of Congress Cataloging in Publication Data:
  Schulman, Audrey, 1963–
  Swimming with Jonah/Audrey Schulman. —1st ed.
  p.   cm.
  I. Title.
  PS3569.C5367S95   1999   98-42111
  813'.54—dc21   CIP

First Bard Trade Paperback Printing: February 2000
First Bard Hardcover Printing: March 1999

BARD TRADEMARK REG. U.S. PAT. OFF. AND IN OTHER COUNTRIES, MARCA REGISTRADA, HECHO EN U.S.A.

Printed in the U.S.A.

OPM 10 9 8 7 6 5 4 3 2 1

Also by Audrey Schulman

THE CAGE

My gratitude for the kind support,
editing advice, and continual patience of:

Erin Belieu, Chuck Brodsky, Scott Campbell,
Beth Castrodale, Achmad Chadran's mom, Elizabeth Graver,
Jennifer Hershey, Allison Hill, Karen Jersild,
Pagan Kennedy, Anne Keniston, Nicole Lamy, Richard Parks,
Anne Whitney Pierce, Lisa Poteet, Donald Powers,
Katrina Roberts, Bill Routhier, David Rowell,
Dr. Yvonne Schulman, Lauren Slater, Bob Steinberg,
Cammy Thomas, Wayne Wilson, and of course
Andre Dubus's Thursday nighters.

Swimming with Jonah

Prologue

At her age, Jane's father had been in Vietnam. He told the story frequently, the bare bones of it. Jane, knowing him, had elaborated. Over there, he had said, for the first three weeks, tramping through the jungle, all he'd thought about was the first time they would engage the enemy. He waited for it. Jane imagined him: raised a quiet and unassuming boy, grown up in Des Moines, always picked last for any team. He'd never been sicker than having a cold, never broken a bone or had stitches. He'd once mentioned he'd had a cavity drilled out and as the smell of watery burning tooth raised to his nose, he'd fainted clear away. She put this boy in Vietnam, tramping through the jungle, backpack strapped on, rifle slapping against his ribs, humidity wrapped tight around him. He thought about death, about pain and fear.

Three weeks into the jungle it happened. A rocket-propelled grenade landed in their midst. His friend Jed, standing a few inches from him—Jane's father is quite specific about this, he said Jed was standing so close he could have touched Jed with his shoulder just by leaning a little to the side—Jed is disembow-eled. Jane could see it, Jed falling over on the ground, the top *of his torso turned away from the bottom in a way that suggests two different men standing near each other with very different things on their minds. Gunfire stutters, all of them throw themselves to the ground, to the level of Jed. The rookies fall with their hands over their heads, guns forgotten. It is their first action. Jed is in such pain. Such pain. He is begging and pleading and his hands trail through the leaves around him making rustling noises. Jane knows her father wants only to run away. He looks at his buddy and sees nothing there he recognizes, not the grasping hands, not the distorted face, certainly not the way the base of the chest caves in toward an unnatural diet. He is filled with a fear that this surprising thing twisting in front of him might reach out to touch him, might call out his name. He scutters away on his knees to get morphine from the medic kit. He gets a lot of morphine, two tubes, maybe three. There's been some suggestion among the men that one tube would probably not be enough, not for a normal-sized man with any real pain. Jed is six feet four. Jane's father wants Jed quiet. He jabs the needles into the muscle of his friend's arm, squeezes the tubes all the way down to the needles. His friend changes. His hands gentle in their movements, then stop. He turns his face up to Jane's father and his breath slows. His expression goes blank with surprise.*

"Ahh," he says, "ahhhhh."

A silence falls. Pure chance. A sudden complete silence as sometimes occurs anywhere, even in a jungle, even during war. No one happens to fire, the birds happen not to call, no one yells. Jed's "ahhhhh" hangs in the air. And in that unaccountable quiet moment in that foreign jungle, staring at what remained of Jed, holding the used needles in his hand, Jane's father understood for the first time how the world worked. It felt like someone passing a hand over his face.

He was very concrete about this detail, mentioned it several times, in different retellings. He said, "a hand passing over my face."

He stood up straight then with surprise. The guns started

again. Hanging there for a moment, he looked down at his new world, his friend's face still motionless, cocked, listening to something far away; the rest of the men, living and dead, spread out beneath him on their bellies. His hair prickled with pity for them. One bullet passed close enough to brush a perfect hole through the slack material of his sleeve like a cigarette burn. Jane's father felt his power.

After that his gestures changed, his voice. Within a month he was leading the squad. And when he returned from the war, he went through medical school with a single-mindedness of purpose that left nothing to chance. He specialized in anesthesia. He patented the Augie Pump as well as the Halodine Delivery System (HDS) which was bought by 3M. He got a percentage of the money anytime HDS was used anywhere in the world, in births, in deaths, in gallbladder operations. He married a beautiful Bostonian ballerina, Jane's mother, and was now the seventh richest man in Connecticut, 128th in all of New England if you didn't count Boston. He never stepped down from an argument.

His friend during the war had died within five minutes. Jane knew his wounds were lethal on their own. Jed had been bleeding to death, exsanguinating as they called it. There was always the chance his death hadn't been from what Jane's father mentioned once was an overdose of morphine.

One

↝

The day Jane got into Queen's Medical School her parents took her out for dinner as congratulations.

Of course the application procedure for Queen's hadn't actually encompassed a rigorous screening of her transcript and college activities, her MCAT's and two recommendations. She hadn't had to write an essay that explained her vision of medicine's future, as well as her weak grades in Organic Chemistry. No, to get in, her father just had to write out the check, place it in the dean's hand. Eighty-three thousand dollars for year one, not refundable even if she left on the first day of school. Her father signed it in front of the three of them, Jane, her mother, the dean. He used his Mont Blanc pen, his heavy even hand, the rasp across the paper at the final stroke. Looked right up at Jane then, and smiled.

That night her parents congratulated her repeatedly, gave her a gold watch, an off-white linen safari suit they imagined appropriate for the tropics, and a guidebook to Indonesia. Her father took them out to Hattie's, the most expensive restaurant in Greenwich. Her mother brought along the school syllabus and brochures to have something to talk about over dinner. Still, even after her mother discussed with Jane each class and what it might entail, what vaccinations Jane would need, what clothes she should pack, even after dictating a list of all Jane had to do in the three months before she left, their conversation petered out by the main course. After that all three of them were pretty much silent, the clinking of forks, the gnawing rasp of knives through meat, the chewing.

After that only her mother spoke occasionally in order to critique the efficiency of the waiters, the restaurant's decorations, the crispness of the salad. She worried about the traffic to the airport on the day Jane was to leave three months from now. She asked them if they knew that human feet sweated an average of three quarters of a cup a day, she'd heard it on the radio. She said they would have to be sure to leave early enough in the morning, on that day, three months from now. Between each sentence, minutes passed. She didn't look over at her husband during any of this. He didn't say a word back. She sat up very straight. One thing was obvious, he was mad at her. Jane figured it was about the dean, that her father thought her mother had been flirting with the dean. After some of the parties they attended he would be angry for days, freezing her out. He once said to her, in Jane's presence, that his anger meant he loved her. For the longest time Jane had thought of that as a kind offering, an apology, to all of them.

Jane slouched embarrassed between her parents, her smile wide and hopeful. She watched her manners, knew either one of them could switch their anger onto her with a single blink. She didn't risk starting any conversation on her own, but nodded mechanically to support each of the short comments her mother made. She methodically swallowed every bite on her plate to show her gratitude for the gift of the restaurant, the gift of their support. She smoothed her napkin flat across her lap and sucked on her teeth after each bite. Small things could enrage them too. She fully realized her own shame.

She hadn't made it into any medical school in the U.S., not even wait-listed. Not that she'd applied to every one of them, not all 123.

She'd had hopes at least for the state school, hoping her father's name would carry some weight. He'd lectured there on occasion. He'd donated money. There was a bronze statue in the front courtyard in his name. The statue was to Ether, the first type of anesthesia, showed a patient lying back, the doctor leaning over him pressing the mask in place, reminiscent perhaps of the position of a mugger. The statue was all bronze too, not covered nickel. Still, the rejection from the state school just took a week longer than the others to come.

Each day, for those weeks between when the first reject arrived and the last, she tried to get to the mailbox before her parents. She hadn't always succeeded. In their unhurried efficient way they'd beat her at least twice that she knew of, the time she was in the bathroom and the time her bio lab ran over. Both times the medical school envelopes were just laid out on the front table where the mail was always placed. Neither of her parents said anything to her. There was no need. The contents of the envelopes were obvious from their light weight, from her grades and from what she'd done last fall. Her parents did not once allude to next fall and what she might or might not be doing then. That was the way they were with bad things. Silence was the weapon.

Other families, they yelled and gestured, they slammed doors and called each other fools. In Jane's family, the unwilling creak of a chair, the lonely clatter of ice in a glass echoed louder than any argument. Jane had never tried to describe this silence to anyone. She thought there was no reason to try; if you hadn't grown up in a family like this you wouldn't understand how damaging silence could be. In loud arguments someone yells at you and you know exactly what was said and how it was meant, how your actions should change. But when Jane's father sat beside her all evening with his neck so stiff he couldn't look at her, only her imagination could tell her the extent of his thoughts.

At Hattie's, Jane's mother made one last effort toward conversation. "I've been playing around," she mentioned, taking another sip of her water as though relaxed, as though not angry, "with the idea of organizing a program to bring dance classes to the elderly. Increase flexibility, get them exercising."

Her husband just sat there for a moment, then nodded once, firmly. In approval? To stop her from saying anything more?

And Jane, so hesitant, glancing from her father to her mother, started to mouth some bland affirmative. Her father sent her a slow turn of his eyes. She shut up, midword, pulled her head in.

Her mother sat there afterward, in the fresh silence, in essentially the same position, essentially the same expression on her face. The only changes, her so-exactly-enameled nails were tucked in a little more toward her palms, her breath a little more shallow.

Jane's father continued to chew his steak, methodical, a clicking sound each time he moved his jaws to the side.

Jane grinned skittishly down at her plate and dug her thumbnail into the side of her finger, hard.

On a visit to the States, the dean of Queen's had travelled to Greenwich to meet with Jane and her parents that morning. Jane wasn't sure if it was so he could interview her, or vice versa. She felt pretty certain the school wouldn't reject anyone who could pay tuition. That, she realized, was the point. In spite of this she was nervous, wore her best suit, used mouthwash and brought along the Italian leather briefcase her parents had given her for her birthday. Unfortunately the suit had become a bit tight across her hips and belly, and there was nothing she could really think of to put in the briefcase but the Greenwich telephone book. Still, she thought the material of the suit made up for how it fit and the briefcase added to her appearance, especially with the impressive bulge of the book inside. Her mother had always said looking your best was very close to actually being your best.

Jane thought she looked best sitting down, or at least standing still; not walking into an interview, her hand out. Because she had a limp, a congenital birth defect. Not, her parents always rushed to point out, *genetic*. No, it was something else, perhaps from her mother gaining only ten pounds through the entire pregnancy, perhaps from her father's Vietnam exposure to sundry chemicals. Jane's limp was not obvious. You might not even notice it watching her walk toward you for a few steps. Not one of those limps where a shoulder humps up and down and the hips swivel unsteadily, exposing movement for all its work. It was just a small limp, from her left ankle being a bit inflexible, her Achilles tendon a trifle too short for her height. A limp that put her stride off-balance, canted forward, as though she was just about to break into an eager trot toward you. It gave many people the feeling she liked them more than she did, that she liked life more than she did.

This small limp was one of the central ways she thought of herself, one of her main attributes. This was understandable given that her mother had been a famous ballerina and moved with a silky grace. "Janey Guy" was how Jane categorized herself. "Daughter of Dr. Augie Guy. Overweight, wants to be a doctor. Limps." She believed the limp was also one of the central ways her parents thought of her. Not that they said so. In fact they said the opposite. At least once a week her mother repeated the limp was hardly noticeable anymore. Every week. She asked if Janey was still doing her stretches.

In any case, Jane had been worried about walking into the interview. She needn't have. Entering the room, her parents got all the attention, her father's serious voice in greeting, her mother's straightforward beauty. By the time the dean turned around to Janey, she was sitting down.

Looking back, from the time after Queen's, Jane could see she wasn't, as she believed at the time, all limp and rounded thigh, weighty flesh. She understood now other people looking at her would have noticed she had a serene kindly face, straight white teeth and blond heavy hair that rustled with a sound like distant rainfall, hair that fell so smooth and shiny and filled with health it was possible to see simple reflections in it, the dark loom of the dean's desk, the glitter of her mother's canary-yellow dress, the patient wait of her father's pink skull. Jane always kept her hair long, down to the middle of her back because even she recognized its uncontested beauty. She hid behind it, washed it daily, hoping people would think of clean blond tresses and not of her. In the interview she scooped hair forward over her shoulder to cover more of herself up while the dean talked.

"Let me start off," Dean Craigy said, smoothing his tie down with his thick fingers, "by mentioning that since 1987, the number of people applying to medical school has just about doubled. The competition for medical school, never easy, has gotten worse than perhaps ever before. It has gotten away from who would make the best doctor, who would care for a patient well. If a student gets just one C, in French Composition or Phys Ed, she can't get into medical school. If she doesn't play a third musical instrument, doesn't read Cyrillic. We're talking bad luck, a different set of priorities, or the unfairness of affirmative action. It doesn't matter. Queen's exists to even out the score."

He smiled wide and reassuringly at all of them, Jane's

parents first. "I think I can say quite confidently Queen's is the best in the world at what it does. Two Rockefellers have attended, a Kennedy, recently one of the Bronfmans.

"I don't want you to think," he said, "Queen's is easy. It's not quite Club *Med*," he said and laughed a little at his joke in a way that made Jane think he was pretending he'd just made it up. She thought from the smooth beat of his laugh he must've been using the joke for years. He did not look like the school would be easy. He was one of those sun-worn rangy Brits she associated with the colonization of Africa during the last century. His skin was permanently creased and reddened by the sun, the hair across the back of his hands and wrists bleached and bristly as a caterpillar's fur, fingers knotted with strength and age. He wore a pinstriped suit and school tie, looked unnatural as a dog in it.

"The curriculum," he said, "is even more difficult than at most medical schools. We have to push students who don't have all the . . ." He paused here, thinking. ". . . natural gifts of other medical students. We have to get them through all of med school, on top of teaching them any pertinent information they might've missed in college." He faced her parents more often than her in his swivelling chair, turned to them each time he gave one of his wide smiles. From the side, she noticed when he smiled, his whole face moved back a bit on his head, pushed back his hairline, as though the skin of his face was only loosely connected to his skull. He had very white teeth and clear blue eyes, surprising through his leathery mask.

"Of course, it might end up Jane won't have to stay with us for all four years. The top ten percent or so of the school are able to transfer back to schools in the States after second year. Queen's wouldn't have to appear at all on her diploma if she could manage that."

Jane's parents made no comment on the likelihood of

that. The dean looked from one to the other, then continued.

"We chose Indonesia for the school's locale in order to help defray the overhead, as well as to isolate the students as much as possible from previously disruptive influences. We use the latest educational techniques and equipment, a one-to-four ratio of teaching staff to students. We have no . . ." Here he pulled his lips wide while he searched for his next words. ". . . fear of discipline. I think I can say quite confidently, if Jane decides to attend, Queen's will be the hardest thing she ever does." He paused then and intoned the school motto. "We are the boot camp of medical schools."

Her parents were the ones to smile at this.

"Jane," he said, abruptly turning to face her. Her parents followed his lead. She jerked on her grin like a shoe. She saw his eyes flick down over her. She began to blush. Her hands were crossed on her too wide lap. Her feet crossed beneath her, the straps of her good pumps cut into her ankles. Her whole body crossed.

"Jane, do you," Dean Craigy asked, "foresee any problem with that?"

She stared at him, the blush obediently heating up her face. When they'd come into the office, the dean had greeted her father first, clasping his hand with both hands, eight or nine pumps up and down, explaining how honored he was to meet him, how often he'd used the Halodine Delivery System during operations back when he was still actively practicing medicine, how much HDS had helped the world, removing its pain, quieting its patients. Her mother had smiled at the dean's praise, awaiting her moment, her long neck extended, her stance automatically shifting to first position, her smile carefully held, personal and charming. While Jane snuck behind them to her chair.

Now Jane's parents waited for her response, smiling at

her, seeing her changed by the school, becoming knowl-
edgeable, aggressive. Like them. She wanted that too. She
imagined it like a promised bed she could lie down on at
the end of a long day. She imagined herself confident, successful. Acceptable.

In the end she did not speak, but only shook her head
soundlessly, renouncing any problems at all.

Two

About the blushing—the blushing Jane did at the interview—it was a habit, a habit she hated. She blushed a lot. She'd been blushing ever since she turned eleven and found out from one of her father's medical textbooks all her parents had to go through in order to have her. Her parents never even held hands that she could remember, not at home, not around just her. In public, sure. For photo ops with reporters or during the entrance to a large party, her mother would drape her arm through her father's, cross her other hand around the front of her body to rest it against his chest, walk swaying right against him, like their hips were connected, their rib cages, their souls; smiling out at the people. Her man.

In private, around no one more than Jane, she never touched him unless it was time to give him his medicine, unless it was time for bed. Then she would sometimes touch the fingers of her hand to his shoulder, alight her fingertips as gently as in the game Slap where the other person might try to catch her hand there napping. He would turn his slow head toward her, focusing. Sometimes then,

Jane snuck a look over, from the edges of her eyes. When she was eleven she thought the fact that they had to touch so much and so extremely in order to give birth to her explained why they had such high expectations of her.

They were not very physical with Jane, either. Those times Jane tried hugging her father, he would stand there for a moment in her hug, holding her, standing there until he felt enough time had passed, then he would pat her shoulder. He didn't pat like some people did, slowly, cupping with the whole of the hand to offer reassurance, to hold the other person close. Her father instead rapped with the flat of his palm, the tap a farmer gives a domesticated animal to move it to the side. She would know then to let go and back off from her dad. The only times she minded this declared time limit were when she was emotional, when she forgot. When someone had done something bad to her at school or her grade on a test hadn't been all that high. She hugged him then, too tight, too long. She rested her face in against him, his smell of meat and medicine. She breathed in. She sighed out, started to breathe in again. He patted. Thwack, thwack. Surprised, she jerked her head back, stepped away abruptly, remembering.

So, for that first year with this new knowledge of what her parents had done in order to have her, she blushed each time someone looked at her because her very existence was the uncontestable proof of her parents' actions. After that year she blushed partly out of a fear of blushing again. She would meet a new person, reach out to shake hands and think, this would be a bad time to blush. The blush would obediently roll its slow heat up her cheeks. She ducked her head, tightened her mouth. Her mother, standing next to her, snorted delicately out her nose in irritation.

Even now, as an adult, Jane couldn't imagine her mother having sex. This is not to say she didn't think her mother was sexual, for her mother was always sexual. She was always flirting and being desired, running her fingertips along her exposed collarbone to the edge of her shirt as though tracing an old touch there, shrugging her shoulders so slowly and fully it seemed part of some completely different action, laughing with an almost inaudible smack of her lips at the end, the nearby men's eyes looking at her lips kissing together, her father watching the men. Yes, she could be sexual, but Jane couldn't imagine her actually having sex. Because at least from what Jane had seen so far with Bertie, sex was red-faced with wet swamp sounds and awkward twisted limbs and no one could remember to keep their bellies sucked in concave through all of it. In fact, it seemed to Jane the exact opposite of how it was described in books and movies. Sex, which was supposed to be about the highest human emotion possible between two people, was actually about a lot of internal concentration and repetitive slamming, similar to video games. There wasn't half as much preliminary hugging and emotional kissing as she'd wished for. At least with Bertie, all this resulted in the mild desire that he'd just disappear afterward so she could stretch out and not feel ashamed of how she smelled. Of course she'd only done it fourteen times with him—not that she thought she should be counting, but she found it impossible not to. After each time he would fall asleep on top of most of the blankets with the condom still on like a little plastic nightcap, and in her mind the meter would roll over by one.

She tried not to think like this, different from how others seemed to think. She watched other people and saw no suspicion in their faces while they watched romantic movies. After one of the harshly silent dinners her mother held her head just as high when she followed her husband up the stairs to their bed. And Bertie's face never twitched when he rolled off and murmured, "Love you," in the same mechanical undertone Jane used saying, "Thanks," to the bus driver as she got off at her stop.

She tried not to think of her father in bed at all.

Jane had had different people—journalists, other doctors, and her classmates—ask her what it was like, what it was like to have Dr. August "Augie" Guy for a father.

He acted so different from most other fathers, not soft and relaxed, not filled out with puns and beer and football trivia. He stood tight, upright, looked at people intently, like the sights on a gun never straying from the target, blind to all else. He didn't make small talk, didn't laugh or relax. The nearest thing he did to joking was to guess a person's weight within three pounds, usually closer than the person could guess. He would announce how many c.c.'s of Halodine it would take, touch his fingertips professionally to the best vein on the person's hand.

He also looked different from others. Because of the baldness. It happened during the war. All his hair fell out, not only the hair on his head, but across his whole body. His eyebrows, eyelashes, beard, pubic and armpit hair, the transparent down along his fingers and face you'd never notice except sometimes with the light behind him. This complete hair loss is called alopecia. No one knew much about it: perhaps the unlikely outcome of the common flu, maybe a genetic predisposition. It happened most commonly to pregnant women. It happened to Jane's father when he was twenty-two and he never wore wigs or pencilled in eyebrows or reacted in any way aside from putting on a hat when he went outside during the winter. His stern gray eyes peered forth from the hospital brochures, stamped out above magazine articles, his smooth pink head duplicated without distraction or artifice, as hairless and certain as marble.

He was different from other fathers, but he'd raised her with firm moral standards, with a lack for nothing material.

When people asked Jane what he was like as a father, she responded she couldn't imagine any other.

Jane had always assumed she was going into medicine, that she would try to be like her dad. She believed in medicine. Aside from four outpatient operations on her ankle, the only time she'd spent in a hospital was walking down the halls to pick her father up or delivering his dinner on nights when he worked late. She'd seen the doctors bustling by, lab coats flapping. She'd heard the intercom crackle urgently for Dr. Blue, Dr. Blue, and imagined the doctor whirling, running for his patient. She imagined that behind each of the office doors she passed stood a doctor—a figure in white, bent over, tired, laying a reassuring hand on a wounded child's head, loving the child like a parent. The doctor held an important instrument in hand. The instrument might be a thermometer, or a clipboard with the patient's history clearly outlined, or a scalpel. The child in any case was looking up, in great need.

With the operations on her ankle Jane hadn't met this type of doctor. She'd only had doctors who looked more at her father than at her, who when they did look at her looked only at her ankle, who never wound the bandages on slow as she'd imagined, never held her hand and told her it would be all right. Never asked her if she had any questions and waited, waited there for her stuttering fears and hopes. Still, she believed in each individual doctor, regardless of how the last one had acted, she believed in her idea of doctor. She imagined herself behind each office door—not as the patient looking up at the doctor, as had been her experience in the past. Instead she saw herself as the doctor looking down at the patient.

When she was thirteen she told her father over dinner she wanted to be a doctor. He nodded. She remembered his exact words.

"A useful profession," he said. "Pass the pork chops. A

solid income. Respect." She never knew if he meant useful for the patients or for the doctor. She knew he took pride in how he helped his patients, in keeping them from senseless pain, easing the fear from their faces until the only emotion left was the blue plastic respirator pursing their wet lips out into a slight surprise. He also took pride in his possessions, in their Connecticut home, the beach house in Florida, the condo in Aspen. She thought he looked at his continually growing belongings as a way of judging his assistance to others. If you piled all his possessions on top of each other to form one mountain of houses, swimming pools and cars, you'd get an idea of the size of the mountain of his white-gowned unconscious patients.

Those four operations on her ankle hadn't helped much; in fact, they'd mostly just scarred it more. With her fingers running light along her tendon she could feel the scarred lines and tissue within, bumpy and hard as bone against the tender Achilles. A hidden secret, an iatrogenic writing on her body, trying to communicate. It was like the flesh of the girl's stomach in *The Exorcist*, spelling out her troubles. In Jane's flesh rested hard nodules of stubborn material, material that would not stretch out as desired no matter how often she did her calf stretches, no matter how many times the surgeons recut.

It sometimes seemed to Jane in all the attempts to construct the ideal ankle, her own imperfect ankle had been killed, and she swayed around the lump of its stiffened corpse, overusing her foot and calf in an effort to pretend everything was fine.

In a way, she'd begun to realize that rather than being the broken point, the weak link, her dead ankle was the strongest point, the one aspect that could not change, not even if she wanted it to, the one point that would not stretch to accommodate.

Three

Two weeks before her acceptance at Queen's, the last of the letters addressed to Jane had arrived from the medical schools, the envelope from the state school containing a single sheet of paper with the paragraph that began, "Regretfully."

After Jane had read the letter all the way through, she put it slowly down on the mail table. She thought hard about what to do next: lunch, TV, perhaps a long walk. It was a sunny spring day. Beside her the grandfather clock clicked. Outside a lawn mower hummed closer, then away. A single fly buzzed and rapped its head again and again against the windowpane. She couldn't think of anything in the world she wanted to do. She couldn't think of anything in the world she could do.

While she thought, she went to her room to lie down, dragged the covers slowly up over her. Sank her head onto the pillow. She lay there for the whole of that day and then that night. Nothing existed to motivate her. She wasn't even sure when to go to her bathroom four feet from the side of her bed. There seemed no better time or worse. Twice that night she abruptly found herself on the toilet, staring down at her feet. Then it took her a long long time to get back to the bed. In the end she lay on her bed for the whole of the second day, looking from wall to wall, tracing the wood trim along the floor with her eyes, the repetitive wallpaper violets entwining upward, the wide white expanse of ceiling, pure and plain as snow. She might have been thinking, but if so, she did not know of what. She lay there for the third and fourth days, looking at anything but her mirror or out the window to the open space of the road where all sorts of things could happen and anyone, anyone could look at you to see what they pleased.

She didn't eat the food her mother left in the hall, didn't step out of her door. There was a family rule against locking doors, but she kept her door locked, didn't answer her parents' calls, their knocks. She'd never done this sort of thing before. In her actions she was generally a very practical and undramatic child—only sometimes fantasizing about running away from home or maybe dying in a traffic accident, imagining how her parents would miss her then, how they would learn to value her through memory. Now she found she didn't think all that much about anything. She lay there, her eyes moving repetitively over the walls. She felt no embarrassment about her actions, did not think directly of her parents at all. Simply her room existed, it occupied her mind.

Downstairs, her parents must have known she was alive only from the occasional flushes of her toilet. Within four days, her mother, always efficient, had found out about Queen's, got her father to agree to send her there. It was a school meant for the rich, for those who didn't make it into any of the others.

Her mother told her about Queen's through the closed bedroom door. She said they had a meeting set up with the dean next week. She said it was another chance. Jane could go to medical school. Her mother spoke loudly, carefully enunciating from the diaphragm as she had given her thank-yous to the crowd outside the stage door. She asked if Jane could hear her.

Lying in bed, Jane did not respond.

"Janey," her mother asked, "Jane, Janey?"

Jane could hear her mother. Jane was listening. There was a tone there she didn't recognize. She listened to it from deep inside her bed. She listened to it hard.

Actually she'd heard that tone, she remembered now, a long time ago, when she used to run into the backyard sometimes and hide under the rhododendrons just before lunch. She must have been around the age of six, loving the disobedience of it all, the novelty as an only child of being chased, the thrill of being missed. At lunchtime her mother called her quietly, calmly from near the door, never raising her voice for fear someone would hear her: the gardeners, the weekly cleaning woman. For fear they might think something wrong. The only suggestion of emotion was the slight tension in her voice, a catching at the end of the name. "Janey" was cut off a little too fast, a little high at the end, "Jane?" And Jane, grinning up at the blue sky visible through the leaves, sucked in every word of it, every moment of her mother's concern. Enjoying it all, until the time she'd rolled over to peek forward under the bushes, hungry to see her mother searching for her also. And instead her mother was just standing there, no more than eight feet away, perfectly still, on the inside of the honeysuckle trellis, screened—she must have thought—from others' view. She, who never stood gracelessly, was balanced heavy on her splayed feet, her knees slightly bowed like an old man, one hand resting against the base of her throat as though her spoken words were actually screams.

Jane had run straight to her, held her tight, feeling her mother's fears as her own. She had never hid again.

Now through the bedroom door her mother asked if Jane

could just respond. Just say something. She said Jane could get into Queen's, Augie just had to write the check.

Jane waited, distant as light, listening to her mother's voice. She realized her mother's face must be quite close to the door. She must be leaning into the corner the door made with the frame, staring at the thin line that could open up into an entrance, leaning close like it was a face she could intimidate or convince.

"Janey?"

Jane didn't move. She wasn't smiling, but her lips were spread enough to show her teeth.

She heard fabric rustle, a knee pop, then her mother flicked something under the door. It slid a few feet into the room. Her mother's heels clicked away. On the bed Jane let her head roll over toward it. A brochure. It glittered shiny and colorful from her floor. In the cover picture she could see brick buildings and palm trees, smiling students arm in arm on the way to class.

Within the hour Jane came out, her hair combed, her smile clear and embarrassed.

In the living room when she saw her, her mother stopped in midstep, touched her lips, composed her face. She did not move toward Jane.

"You must be starving," she said. "You must have lost so much weight." She turned around, led the way to the kitchen. She walked methodically ahead. Jane limped along, following hesitantly, running her hands over her hair, then hiding them in her pockets. Her mother served her a bowl of tortellini, moved away to the other side of the kitchen to lean against the sink, fidgeted with the clasp on her bracelet. Jane picked at the food at first to please her, then began to eat faster, mechanically, remembering. It kept her hands and mouth occupied. It kept her eyes down. Her mother filled up her bowl again, gave her ice cream for dessert. She said she didn't want her daughter to fade away, people thinking she was a bad mother. Obediently Jane ate it all.

So it was only afterward, rinsing the dishes in the sink, no door between them, just her back to Jane, that Jane's mother began to get mad. In a way Jane felt relief. The world was still recognizable. Her mother said Augie and she had had to cancel dinner out two nights in a row on the chance Jane had decided to come out. She said she hoped Jane had gotten a lot of reading done in there. She added that Queen's cost almost half of a million for all four years counting interest. Only seventy percent of the students passed the American medical boards at the end of the four years, and if Jane didn't pass the boards the degree was worthless.

Jane listened over the clinks of the plates to the tone of her mother's voice. She could not hear anything different anymore. Her mother was speaking clearly, no words cut off. Things were back to normal. Even with her mother's back to her Jane nodded several times, her eyes closed. Her head hurt. She touched a fingertip to each eyelid. She would do, she said in a voice breaking from lack of use, her best. She smiled, blind, at her mother's back. Outside of her room she realized again her own shame.

Her parents and she assumed it would be worth it. She would pass. She would make good for her four mediocre years of college, what her parents now referred to as her childhood weaknesses. She would succeed at Queen's. No other choice existed.

"Maybe," Jane said abruptly at her congratulations dinner at the restaurant. "Maybe, at least in one way I'm ahead of Dad at my age."

Her parents glanced at her startled over the dessert. No one had spoken in almost ten minutes now. Jane and her father had been eating faster and faster. Her mother as usual was just picking at the food, moving it around. The waiters hovering a few tables away, uncertain if she was finished, uncertain if she'd even started. After each course Jane's father finally waved them in, impatient.

Now Jane's parents stared at her. As soon as she'd spoken she felt surprise she'd said anything at all. "Umm, ah. Whatever," she mumbled.

"No," said her father, "please continue." He raised the skin over his eyes where his brows should have been. He waited, his mouth pursed. His skin had a way of shining in the light more than other people's. Sometimes she felt she was talking to a Halloween mask.

She smiled nervously, continued, "I mean, ah, Dad, when you were my age, you didn't know what you wanted to do with your life, did you? Weren't you still in Vietnam?"

He looked at her. For a moment she thought he wouldn't respond. Then he nodded his head slowly, the light tracing its path across his scalp.

"At least I know that much." She smiled, hopeful, waiting for some sort of encouragement. "I mean I know what I want to do. I know what I want to become."

Her father nodded one final time. Her mother turned back to her espresso. No conversation ensued.

Jane stretched her lips in a fierce smile down at her apricot truffle cake, like at a guest she was embarrassed for. She ate the last bite fast, made a show of chewing with appreciation, wished she could order a second slice.

Partly, she guessed by mentioning the war, she'd hoped to coax her father into telling his Vietnam story again. She liked to hear her father talk about his change. She liked to contemplate the extreme situation that made him switch from someone unremarkable to the father she knew. Weeks of black nights, leeches and the constant weight of heavy packs and guns, the whistling drop of bombs into that single moment of peace before the explosion. She liked to hear the story because now her father seemed so different, so powerful. It was hard to imagine anyone thinking otherwise. Newspaper stories were written about him, hospital wings named after him. He stood differently from most people, with his feet wide apart like the floor might suddenly shift. He had a presence. Even when people didn't know who he was, they looked over toward the thickset bald man with the disturbingly bare gaze.

Jane liked to hear that story because she thought if he could change like that, just by thinking, maybe she could too. She'd been trying for years to change and it hadn't worked yet, but perhaps one just had to be in an extreme situation to have that happen.

Maybe all she needed was to be pushed.

Four

The small island plane bounced to a halt at the end of the
runway. Looking around, Jane saw her classmates still
gripped the armrests hard and even the stewardess kept her
eyes closed for a moment with her head back against the
seat. Jane thought it couldn't have been all that dangerous
a landing because the school's plane had to do it all the
time. She thought there must be legal standards for landing
fields here in Indonesia, the same as there were in the
States.

Two years ago she'd travelled a bit in Europe with her
parents, and there the airports seemed safe: long lit run-
ways, control towers and people in matching coveralls waving the planes in. She'd never thought of landing in Europe
as any different from landing in America. Her family had
travelled first class, stayed in Ritzes for all three weeks, and
to her disappointment, there never seemed a need to speak
anything but English. She'd been looking forward to trying
out her high-school French, her first-semester Italian. However, the waiters and receptionists at each hotel had only
to watch her family walk up before knowing enough to

greet them in English, speaking English so much better than her parents or she spoke their language. Jane did not know how it was the hotel personnel figured out her family's language simply from the way they walked, from what they wore and carried. She tried for a while to fool them, wearing a variety of different costumes: a beret, or tighter pants as the Spanish did, or carrying several guidebooks in her hands like the Germans. Still, everyone greeted her in English without hesitation. In her bathroom in Marseilles she tried walking up to the full-length mirror again and again, looking for clues, smiling confused at her reflection, her pink-cheeked health and big-boned height, her large beef-fed teeth, her face open with innocent assumptions about human equality and good service, limping forward in her earnest wide-country stride.

She'd realized seeing the world was a surprising thing and she looked forward, here in Indonesia, to being surprised. To becoming more worldly, eating ethnic foods and maybe seeing some sights in between classes. She'd always secretly dreamed of travelling to places like this, to Vietnam, to China and Malaysia, to places where people carried fire-wood on their heads and children on their backs, their arms hanging empty at their sides. Places where food consisted of entirely different categories from steak and potatoes, where a car was not waiting in any driveway. Places where the spirits were so active and determined that houses had sharp spikes on the roofs and mazelike entrances to discourage them. Places where everything she'd ever believed irrefutable and commonplace was turned completely upside down.

Indonesia, she'd learned from her guidebook, was made up of over a thousand islands, different customs and languages on many of these, bound together by the aggressive Javanese government and army.

Unfortunately, on this island it didn't look like there would be many sights to see. When the plane had circled for the landing she saw the island was only three or four miles across, thick jungle surrounded by white sand, the sea clear as a chlorinated swimming pool. At the center of the island the school's roofs stuck out above the jungle. There were no other buildings visible from the air. The sea was empty except for one square-prowed fishing dhow, the men on board invisible under their swaying domed hats.

Now, on the ground, Jane could see jungle out the window. Two Land-Rovers labeled "Queen's" were parked near the plane and some Indonesian men were hunkered down on their haunches wearing chinos and T-shirts which declared them "Queen's" also. They looked like they had been there for a while, squatting just that way. They did not look up at the plane.

Even before the plane's door opened, the other students pressed impatiently forward in a line to exit, their carry-on bags already packed. It had been a long trip, over twenty hours for most of them, on three or more different planes. They all looked exhausted, clothes rumpled, hair sticking up. The boy across the aisle from Jane had white flaky drool along the side of his cheek. Personally, Jane would have done the whole trip all over again right then so long as it ended here, with her at medical school.

She was the last one up, which was fine with her for then no one would see her limp. The stewardess popped the door open. The air-conditioned temperature sucked out and the humid heat hit them all. For most of them that had been the last time they would feel air conditioning for four whole years.

"Shee-hit," said the woman in front of Jane and shouldered her bag a little higher. Looking out at the palm trees and brown-skinned men she said, "Check it out. Disneyland, all expenses paid." Several of the others smiled.

When Jane stepped out of the plane onto this island, she wore all white for the tropics, safari-style, and a big straw hat. In her purse was the guidebook to Indonesian customs and official language, a bottle of sunscreen and a wallet with a picture of Bertie, the man her parents assumed she'd one day marry. When she stepped off the plane onto the metal staircase she felt cheerful and ambitious. She held her face up to the tropical sun and breathed deeply of the sticky air. Closing her eyes for a moment, she could hear the foreign birds calling in the jungle, as well as the fast chatter of English and other languages. Bahasa, she'd read in the guidebook, was the official Indonesian language. Sasal was this island's dialect. Dutch had been the trading language here for a century. The Land-Rover engines started. She felt such joy, such optimism. Her greatest wish in the world had a seventy percent chance of being answered. She might be a doctor. She might use her life to solve other people's problems.

Her eyes still closed, she took her first step down onto the metal staircase. She stepped forward fast, excited. There was a thin slick of moisture on all metal down here, the humidity. There was her limping left ankle to consider; it was harder to get her whole foot to the ground for all the traction needed.

With that first step on the plane's stairs, her foot slipped. Right out from under her. Her arms started rolling, the bag went up in the air and she bounced sideways down that entire iron staircase, knocking over three other classmates in the process and dislocating her left shoulder. She saw her shoulder get dislocated. She was reaching for the railing and missed, her arm there between the metal posts. She continued to fall, saw her arm jerk, and there was a muffled pop.

Lying on the cement, half on top of the woman who'd been in front of her, Jane stared straight up at the tropical almost-white sky, a single seagull hanging up there, looking down at her. For a moment it felt as still as her bedroom at home for those five days she'd lain in her bed.

Then the woman wriggled out from under her. Her classmates got up, furious, examining their cuts. Several had bad scrapes. They were all exhausted, irritable, jet-lagged. They gazed down at Jane with disgust. At first, with Jane's arm beneath her, she looked unharmed, soft and heavy, the creamy complexion of a ripe peach. None of them tried to help her up.

"That really hurt," said the woman Jane had fallen on, brushing dirt off her cut knee.

One man snapped, "We could have hit our heads, broken our necks."

"Sorry," Jane said, looking around at her new classmates. Her lips seemed a bit thick, so the word sounded mumbled. She tried to speak more clearly. "I'm so so sorry." She sat up too quickly then and heard the heat pulse heavy in her ears. She blinked into the light, listing slightly to the side. Belatedly she realized her left arm hadn't moved. She looked down at it, asked it to move and it still didn't respond. Her arm hanging slack as a sleeve by her side.

Using her right hand she picked her forearm up, put it in her lap. The familiar outline of her shoulder was gone. Instead, at the end of her collarbone, on the front of her body, the knuckle of her arm sat, its outline stark and white outside its familiar joint. The pressure of something new pushing out from under her skin.

Five

~~

The examination table was the first vision Jane had of the inside of her new school. One doctor held her wrist, the other her neck and waist. The doctor with her wrist was the type of tall man whose thin tendons and skeleton were always exposed by lack of flesh, so that even now in his fifties he looked like he'd never outgrown adolescence. He seemed the one in charge. His name tag said Dr. Egren. Later she would find out he was the Physiology teacher. The other doctor behind her stood a foot shorter, thick with muscle and fat, his white lab coat highlighted the blotchy heat rash across his face, from sweating too much. He was sweating now, his face shining uniformly. His name was Krakow. He taught Histology. Krakow's hand on her waist lay a little high, sort of close to the bottom of her left breast, but she said nothing for he was a doctor.

Sitting on the exam table, she eyed the tall doctor in front of her warily. Her thick hair was plastered down upon her forehead from the sweat and the pain, but already the ends were rising in the humidity of the island, curling up slowly like ghosts who had never lived. The pain seemed the color of metal scraped back and forth within her mind. She waited, obedient.

"One," said the tall doctor, locking eyes over her shoulder with the red-faced one. She looked away from their silent communion to the stainless steel sink and began to pant.

"Two," the doctors intoned together. Something rose like a ball in her throat.

"Hey," she whispered. "Hey please . . ."

"Three." The doctors jerked and twisted and a flash of light exploded up from her shoulder and into her mouth and she vomited over their hands onto the clean tiled floor. Leaning over like that, she could see the last of the pink ham her mother had cooked as a good-bye dinner. At the dinner her parents and the gardening staff had sung "Happy Birthday" to her four times in a row for the years they would miss.

"Shit," said the red-faced doctor, as both men looked down at their shoes.

At first when Jane was younger, she had at first wanted to be a nurse. Medicine to Jane had always seemed an act of grace, a benediction. To care for another's wounded body, to take away their pain, to bandage, hold and care for. At the age of seven she had told her mother her career wish. Jane's mother was working on her exercise bike. Each morning she worked on the bike, and each afternoon she went into The Body Clinic where she had her own personal trainer named Greta. Greta was an iron-hard Swedish woman who wore brightly patterned Lycra like a superhero and referred to Jane's mother's body as her own, patting it on the still-quivering stomach after the third set of sit-ups and saying, "Gut, gut. My abs are getting ripped."

Jane stepped up to her mother, watching her legs pump round and round on the bike, the sweat darkening her leotard along her back and breasts. She was watching a TV show devoted entirely to stocks. Normally, no matter what

Jane said during this show, her mother wouldn't even look at her, not away from the charts of cut-up pies and growing bars. So Jane felt safe in saying over the announcer's voice that she would be a nurse when she grew up. She held out her doll with the bandaged knee for her mother to see.

Her mother stopped pumping, turned away from the TV and asked why.

Her mother was beautiful. It's the first thing that would strike you about her, a strong kind of beauty that looked better unadorned, like a mountain or a knife. She had black straight hair that shimmered each time she moved her head, green eyes and her white skin pulled sharp around her bones. Her neck arched so bare of flesh the tendons seemed rigid with emotion even when she dozed in front of the fire. And the way she moved. The way she walked and reached and laughed, with an erect back and a ballerina's duck-toed sway, so slow, so smooth. The slightest shift of her weight rolled deliberately out from her center, like something much bigger than her thin frame, something weighty and possibly dangerous.

As an adult Jane noticed each time her mother turned to look directly at Bertie (the only man Jane had ever brought home), he tightened up like a spring, ready to do whatever her mother said. And when Jane's mother looked that way at one of Jane's few female friends, Jane could see her friend shrink inside. Jane knew she herself huddled down into obscurity from the moment her mother walked into the room, even those times she was holding Bertie's hand in her own. Perhaps especially then.

Once a few weeks ago when Bertie, in his eagerness to please, asked her mother if she needed her car washed, Jane had pinched the back of his hand, hard, with her nails. His head had jerked back, his neck boneless as a puppet's. In a way it had been funny. His motion had been funny, the way he had turned to look at her so stunned, the way they immediately covered up with the story of his hiccups.

The way, alone with him, she denied any idea of where the impulse had come from.

That time with the doll, her mother regarded Jane straight for several seconds. Jane let her doll fall back down and then wrapped it tight in her arms while her mother asked again, "Now why would you want that?"

Jane looked down at the rug, around the corners of the room, and then to the bandage on the doll's leg before she responded, "To help people," in a small voice.

Her mother breathed out her nose, then said, "Janey, if you're going to aim, aim high."

She turned back to the TV. "Be a doctor. Doctors help people much more. More efficiently."

With her arm in a sling against her belly she was dropped off by the school ambulance at her new home. The pain medication they'd given her made her mouth feel very dry. She was supposed to keep the sling on for two days as a precautionary measure. Her whole body felt sticky and slow from the plane. She felt as though she'd been wearing the same rumpled clothes for weeks. She wasn't sure how many hours ago she'd eaten. It had been in a different time zone, and since then she'd reset her watch. She thought perhaps it had been over China. Her stomach alternately clenched grinding, or lay as slack as something quite close to death.

Her bungalow was built right on the beach, twenty-five feet from the surf. Palm trees hung high over the terra-cotta roof. The sand glared white, the water shimmered the blue of plate-glass windows, foam danced along its tips. Except for two weeks during freshman year she'd never lived with anyone but her parents, in any house but her parents' brick and hewn-stone three-story home on Potsdamn Road. On this island she'd also have a housemate, someone she'd never met before. She walked slowly up the front steps of the house, holding with her one good hand to the railing, placing each foot carefully.

Inside, the windows had no glass, just screens. The furniture was made from bamboo, ceiling fans in each room. Mosquito netting draped down from hooks over the beds, the ends tucked in tight under the mattresses like sheets. Malaria was common here.

Her trunk had been dropped off in one of the bedrooms by the school staff. Using one hand she awkwardly opened it, thinking she should start to unpack. Pushing open the top released the scent of her parents' house, cedarwood and heavy drapes, lemon-scented Pledge and the cold of all that stone. She froze, half-leaning over the trunk, sucking air in until a gust came in from the window. The scent evaporated. Instead she inhaled the island: sea air and baking sand, damp earth and the undersides of bushes. The sweet weight of decomposition. In the midst of these, even when she picked up several shirts and pressed them to her nose, she couldn't recapture the scent of her family's home.

On top of the trunk was a canister of tacks and a photo of her parents. When she'd packed, she'd thought this way she could make her new home more familiar as soon as she got here. Tacking the photo up was difficult to do with one hand. It took her three tries. The wall was made of some type of hand-trowelled plaster. It was uneven and crumbled a bit under the tack. In the holes where it crumbled, some type of grass was woven through the material of the wall. She touched the grass with curiosity, thought of Tarzan movies, anthropology classes. The photo leaned askew, her parents standing at a slant by the Porsche on their way to a party. Her shoulder was beginning to hum. She thought the pain might start soon.

The doctors had given her a bottle of Percosets with instructions to take one every four hours. She'd taken her first pill at the clinic forty minutes ago. Her father always claimed he had a low pain threshold. He had no idea why people would maintain otherwise, he knew of no value to experiencing pain, nothing redeeming in it. He would go white with the pain from headaches after work. Jane tried not to look at her father when he seemed weak like that, when he reached for his special pain-reliever pills and they chattered like teeth inside the bottle.

Jane had always asked for aspirin as soon as she felt the slightest twinge of pain. She thought if it scared her father so, she would crumple at the first whisper. She figured since she'd never crumpled she must never have experienced real pain. She'd only had the four ankle operations as well as the scraped knees of childhood and the dental operations of adolescence. And once, at ten years old, she'd sliced the palm of her hand open to the bone on a piece of glass she'd fallen on. At the time she hadn't felt any pain at all, just abrupt numbness. Later she'd taken so many pain relievers she was not sure what she felt at all, except fear. Her fear was not of accidents that might happen to her in the future, but of what had already happened to her, what she could not understand. For years afterward she'd had nightmares of that moment, not of the fall itself, but of just after, of standing up with her hand cupping all this red. At first she'd thought she'd fallen on a flower, that slow understanding rising.

Rather than reassuring her, this lack of what she had considered real pain worsened her fear, her anticipation. She thought real pain would flatten her like a rock, transform her human spirit into a whimpering cur. Her father said she was wise in this. He said she was obviously his child.

Dislocating her shoulder was the worst injury she'd done to herself since falling on that glass. She still felt no pain, only a slow heat opening up in her shoulder like a fist. She listened to that heat intently, focused, did not let the heat fade from her mind. She thought if only she was at home, her father would make sure she felt no pain. He would understand her fear.

She missed him suddenly, his certainty, his solidity, his confident world view. Impulsively she took two Percosets, tossing them back fast without water. As soon as she swallowed she felt guilty. She hadn't needed them yet. They were against doctor's orders. She thought of herself as weak. She worried she might cause some liver damage.

She lay down on her bed to wait for her housemate to arrive. The school had tried to match students up according to habits, likes and dislikes. Jane knew her housemate's name was Marlene Diemer. Marlene had wanted a non-smoking roommate who liked to go to sleep before eleven. Marlene tended to study most of the weekend. After five minutes of trying to sleep, the drugs started enlarging the sound of Jane's heart until her body jerked forward with each beat and her lip itched with sweat.

She didn't hear Marlene enter. Perhaps Jane had fallen asleep for she simply opened her eyes and there Marlene stood in the doorway of her room, holding a pink child-sized suitcase. She stood there suddenly whole and without noise like a warning vision, the ghost of Christmas past or future. She wore a sleeveless black dress that showed her slender arms and she chewed gum, snapping it lazily. Round her head to hold back her hair, she had on the kind of nylon blindfolds stewardesses sometimes hand out to help people sleep. Unlike Jane and most of the other students from Jane's flight, she looked fresh and untired.

After a moment the noise came back, Marlene's Walkman blaring loud enough for Jane to pick out the horn section. She didn't know how she could've not heard Marlene come in. Marlene slowly surveyed the bungalow: white plaster walls, the bamboo furniture, in the hall the bathroom wall that didn't quite reach the ceiling. For the rest of the year they would hear each other pee. Shutting off the music, Marlene dropped the bag at her feet into the sudden silence.

She examined Jane from the espadrilles lying by the bed to her crumpled linen safari suit with sweat stains along her armpits, collar and in rings around her belly. She looked at Jane's arm in the sling. Sitting up heavily, Jane began to tug her rumpled clothing into place. The blush soaked slow and hot up from her neck. Blushes came easier in this heat.

"Doctor Livingston, I presume," Marlene said. Over her shoulder hung an entirely transparent plastic purse, seashells and sand and dyed blue water sloshing around in a pocket on the side of it. Pulling a cigarette from her purse, she lit a match. She didn't take the gum out of her mouth. Between inhales, she chewed. Her movements were sleepy and very graceful. She watched with mild interest Jane's blush progress, looked over her clothing one more time. "Taking this tropical thing a little too seriously, aren't we?" With Marlene's left hand up like that Jane noticed the large diamond on her ring finger. It caught the light from the window.

"You're smoking," Jane said. The Percosets made her see everything clearly, but she could only concentrate on one thing at a time.

"Shit. You caught me." She exhaled. The smoke obscured her face for a moment, then the wind from the window blew it away in a rush. The diamond on her hand glittered, shivering delicately in the light. Jane narrowed her eyes at it, unable to look away.

"Did you just start?"

"Now why would I just start a habit which has been proven to be so bad for you?" She noticed the direction of Jane's gaze, glanced down at the ring. Then switched the cigarette to the other hand.

"But the form—you said you wanted a nonsmoking housemate."

"Hey honey, haven't you heard secondhand smoke is almost worse than sucking it in yourself? I don't want to increase my chances for lung cancer any more than they already are." She looked at Jane, exhaled again. She held the cigarette 1940's style, as a fashion accessory, as close to the body as possible, limp wrist, fingers long. When she exhaled, she tilted her whole head back to show her neck.

"Besides, I fucking hate the way cigarettes make my clothes smell."

Jane snorted in surprise, uncertain about how to react, and Marlene smiled back at her with the left side of her mouth. That was the way she always smiled, the other half of her face waiting and heavy like it wasn't there at all, couldn't care less about Jane or herself.

Marlene tapped the ashes into the palm of her hand. When she didn't find a trash can, she bent down, opened her suitcase and flicked the ashes in there. Jane thought she wasn't meant to see, but Marlene wriggled the ring off and tossed it in also.

"Let's make like a banana and peel," she said, standing up.

"What? Oh, where to?" Jane asked, reaching for her sandals. This would become a pattern, later. When she was with Marlene, it never occurred to her not to obey. It took her a moment to get her shoes back on using only one hand. She fumbled, trying to hook the straps over her heels.

"The brochure says the school runs some bar. We can catch dinner there and some drinks. It's probably some shitty cafeteria with plastic trays and the beer in Dixie cups, but it's the only place to drink unless you want to head back to Singapore."

"OK," Jane said, her shoes finally on, standing up heavy. Marlene led the way out, with Jane following, off-balance.

When they stepped into the sunlight, Jane wondered what hour it was. The sun hung low in the sky but she had no idea whether it was rising or setting. Only after asking Marlene did she realize they were going to get dinner and drinks before noon.

Six

~~

At first in the wind from the beach, the heat didn't feel so
bad, but the moment Jane and Marlene stepped under the
weight of the trees, the air hung down limp. When Jane took
a breath it tasted as humid and hot as if sucked directly from
another's mouth. In her lungs it felt as if all the nutrients had
already been taken from it. She breathed a little faster, opened
her mouth a bit, figured it was the jungle breathing the air.
This jungle had a presence to it, a weight and a heat to it,
like someone leaning in too close. Jane had always thought
of the tropics as bright open sandy areas with a few palm
trees leaning scenic in the background. Here, though, even
the light, filtered through so many leaves, fell murky as underwater. The birdcalls echoed through the trees, muffled and
from all directions. There was the slow sound of dripping, the
background hum of long-term heat.

Seventy feet above Jane's head, at the surface of the trees
the leaves shimmered in waves. The wind through the fur
of something huge. Everything smelled wet and rotten and
rank, like the pelt of some aging animal, an animal
crouched motionless, for now.

Back at home, in Connecticut, the light shone bright and factual as the light from a spotlight. You could see out over the lawn curving smooth as a slide down through the ornamental trees and exact rectangular shrubs to the black cut of the road, perfectly straight. The only smells were fresh mulch, overly sweet pesticides and tar hot from the sun. The only sounds were the regular whisk-whisk of the sprinkler turning its endless circle, the pool's filter clicking on and the muffled voice of a newscaster listing tragedies somewhere inside.

Here the road was red clay dust, eight feet wide and rutted. It curved, obligingly, around every big tree or rock. The trees hung high above her. Nothing was straight, nothing was bright and Jane couldn't see more than forty feet through the foliage in any direction except straight up. There was not a house in sight, no concrete, no mailboxes, no reflective road stripes, no 7-Eleven. Just a dirt road, like the path animals would make if they had wide enough feet. Thinking about it now, she realized even in visiting the state park last summer with Bertie, she'd never been any place where she couldn't at least see brightly colored plastic trail markings and metal plaques designating rare arboreal species. Her whole body sweated. She tried to move her feet quickly, to keep up with Marlene, but her legs only swung around each other with great effort. Her shoulder swayed beside her, heavy and swollen as a separate bag filled tight to the seams. She felt conscious of the sea sway of her limp, tried to minimize it whenever Marlene looked over at her. This led to a frequent hitch in her stride.

"Shit," Marlene said, "this heat's unreal."

"Isn't it exciting?" Jane asked.

Marlene looked at her, raising one eyebrow.

Jane half-stumbled. "I don't mean the heat. I mean that we're here at all. At medical school. Seeing the world." She gestured out with her good arm to the jungle. She tried to smile. Sweat trickled down her sides, especially under the sling.

"You always so happy?" Marlene asked.

"I try to be."

"Good God," muttered Marlene, turning back to the road. "I've got Doris fucking Day as a housemate."

After that they walked along for the most part in silence.

About half a mile later they reached town. No warning. The trees continued right up to the first house. Parked along the road were a few mopeds and one flatbed truck. The road was too rough for normal cars. The buildings had thatched roofs and whitewashed walls that gleamed against the jungle. Two emaciated dogs loped businesslike across the street, looking neither right nor left, disappeared between the houses. Forty feet away a group of six men squatted in the shade of a tree laughing and talking. Each man held a rooster to his chest. The men wore brightly colored sarongs and no shirts. Their bodies were bony and coffee brown. Squatting, their limber knees rose up almost higher than their heads. Something about their articulated raised knees reminded Jane uncomfortably of insects. None of the men appeared to be sweating, while Marlene and she had large V's of moisture plastering their clothes along their backs and beneath their arms.

Each of the men had long hair and nails, smooth brown arms like pretty women. The roosters they patted were as brilliantly colored as flowers: yellows, reds and greens. They rustled with health and fury in the men's grasp, flicking their heads around to stare at each other in popeyed indignation.

One of the men pointed toward Marlene and Jane and all the men turned to look at the women's legs which were bare to the knee. Jane knew from the introduction to the guidebook that the prevalent religion here was a version of Islam. The sarongs the men wore covered them almost to the ankles. The men stared at Marlene and Jane's legs, at their bare arms. Strangely enough, they looked at Jane more—she assumed it could only be because she jiggled exotically, chubby and pale. The men were skinny in a way she associated with very old men, their muscles and bones bare beneath a paper-thin sheath of skin. As she and Marlene walked closer, the men lowered their heads slightly into their stares. She was not used to this kind of attention, but there was no other way through town but the one road. Jane began to edge off to the far side of the street, turning her foot slightly sideways to minimize her limp, her gaze averted. Marlene plowed straight on, smiling back at the men.

With her gaze averted like this, Jane noticed, off to the right, a square shrine about the size of a gardening shed. The shrine had a pagoda roof and carved ornate wood panels showing the head and hands of a god with bared lion's fangs, dog's ears and human outstretched hands with sharp manicured fingernails. Small lumps of food had been set out in front of the shrine, for those hands, on plates of intricately woven leaves. Looking around, Jane now spotted this god carved over several of the doorways and windows, this god always reaching out with those nails, its mouth opened wide. Its expression angry or jubilant, it was hard to tell.

The door of a house to the right showed the full body of the god, standing upright with knees spread in a ready stance and a sword zigzagging like a thunderbolt in one hand. The creature seemed to be laughing. Jane slowed down to look. Except in anthropology classes and museums she'd never seen a deity shown in any other positions than riding distant and bemused on top of a cloud, or nailed and slumped on a cross. This god stared out at her, direct, violent and sexed, connected to this life and very hungry.

She noticed ten feet now separated her from Marlene and she hurried to get closer.

"S'lemat pagi," one man yelled, breaking the silence. The

men all laughed and began to call, to gesture the women closer, but not like Westerners gesture people closer. Here, they cupped their hands down and paddled with their fingers, like they were digging in the earth. Jane blinked slow at this. Her shoes made no noise in the soft dust of the road and she felt almost like she was dreaming of a different world, floating, her shoulder inflating slowly beside her.

One man flickered his tongue out at Jane, fast and graphic. The roosters sensed the change, cocked their small heads to peer about for something to fight. They spotted the strangers abruptly. Flinched and shimmered, rustled their feathers out around their necks and cocked their heads back in readiness.

"Cockfight," said Marlene amused. "They're getting the roosters riled up by holding them close to each other. Men all over the world are the same." She flipped back her hair from her face and smiled at the men. "I'm going to buy a moped from these assholes. Walking is for losers."

Jane stopped a few feet back. As Marlene reached the men, they all stood up. Their roosters hissed and clapped their wings, striking out at the air with their beaks. Marlene stood three inches taller than any of the men. Even slender as she was, next to them, her body looked padded with health. Where they were all hard with immediate need, her muscles were softer, her body had curves. She looked elegant. They appeared desperate.

Marlene tried to talk to them in English. When it was clear none of them understood, she threw her leg over one of their mopeds, pantomimed driving away and then pulled out her money. The men had been looking at the outline of her thighs through the dress, but when she pulled out the money they looked at that instead. They were barefoot.

"Hey," Marlene said to Jane once the bargaining was finished and she'd handed the money to the man who reached for it fastest. "You know how much these guys earn on average per month according to Amnesty International?"

She gestured impatiently for Jane to get on the moped behind her. "Thirty-five American dollars."

"But . . ." Jane drew her head in, in surprise. "You can't even eat on that."

Marlene snorted, started the engine. "Jump on, Doris."

It took Jane three separate tries to swing her leg over the seat with Marlene already on it and her own arm in a sling against her chest. Finally settled, she put her good arm awkwardly, lightly, around Marlene and was jerked back when the moped shot forward. Jane clutched tighter with her arm and pressed her chin into Marlene's shoulder, leaned her body in. She could feel the tight sheet of Marlene's skin over her shoulder and stomach, couldn't imagine the islanders being skinnier than this. Looking back she saw one of the men holding his crotch and rolling his hips after them. The others were laughing.

The wind felt good, cooling Jane down. Marlene steered fast around the potholes. Once she hit a root by mistake and they bounced a little into the air while the moped grunted. Jane heard a click from her shoulder and her vision went gray at the edges, but she didn't say a thing. She didn't feel she had a right to ask Marlene to slow down.

A troop of monkeys chattered at them from the sides of the road, showing their bright dogs' teeth in old men's faces. The heavy sunken green of the jungle breezed by. A lizard ran across the road with the speed of a cat. Jane watched it all, her mouth open. They reached campus quickly. The whole island was on a hill. The town was halfway up, the school at the top. All uphill roads headed for school, all downhill roads headed through the islanders' town to the students' bungalows.

Near the school the road abruptly changed to gleaming white gravel, then the trees stopped. Blinking in the sudden bright sunlight, they drove through the tall brick gates with iron grillwork and the gold-painted school crest. On either side of them spread an enormous manicured lawn with

many rectangular color-coordinated flower beds, irises, tu-
lips, roses and gardenias; flowers Jane didn't think would
grow here naturally. There were tennis courts and a pond
with pure white geese paddling listlessly around, fat and
gleaming in the haze of heat. Jane recognized some of the
buildings from the pictures in the brochures she'd looked
at in Connecticut. In Connecticut the buildings had looked
like just what she wanted, just what she'd imagined medical
school to be, solid serious brick, a displaced Oxford or Yale.
The buildings looked different now, against the backdrop of
this jungle. Some island men crouched low over the flower
beds, heads bent as they weeded. On the school grounds
they wore chinos and those T-shirts labelled "Queen's."

Marlene pointed upward with her chin. A vulture hung
up there, stretched heavy and tired from the tips of its pin-
ions, its naked pink neck and bald head swivelled to watch
the geese.

Teachers and assistants in lab coats strode along the
gravel paths between the buildings, setting up for tomorrow's classes. The wind from the sea blew in gusts up here
at the top of the island, but no shade existed. Once Marlene
stopped the bike, the sun was a weight Jane felt in each
strap of her foreign clothing. She breathed out her mouth,
kept her eyes wrinkled into slits against the light, looked
around at the buildings. Even over the gold dome of the
main building, she could see the jungle, stretching up its
heavy arms.

Marlene found out from one of the teachers the bar was
down on the beach and she gunned away from campus
quickly.

The bar turned out to be a three-sided building right on
the beach with the fourth side completely open to the wind
from the sea. Its roof was thatched, its walls cool white
plaster. It had a hand-painted sign over the doorway saying
"The Bar." Above it someone had added in what appeared
to be pink nail polish, "One and Only." Inside twelve or

thirteen students sat around playing checkers or looking out at the beach. They wore tank tops and small shorts like they'd just been running; some of the men had no shirts on. There was the impression of much tanned skin and little movement. A ceiling fan turned lazily through the air. Several bony dogs skulked between the tables, quartering the ground systematically for scraps while others waited along the walls, watching everything with their bright yellow eyes.

In the whole school, Jane knew from the catalog, there were only forty-six women, fifty-nine men. In the middle of a weekday morning a tenth of the class sat at The Bar.

A red-haired woman spotted them first. She jerked her head up. "Hey," she called, her voice tight with excitement, "new students." Everyone turned around.

Even Marlene was taken aback. The students stared, as hungry and shocked as tribes first contacted. None of them seemed interested in breaking the silence or looking away. Jane nervously began brushing her hair forward over her shoulder.

Marlene spoke first, rather awkwardly. "So when's this fucking heat wave breaking?"

Their eyes widened, then the laugh burst out of them. They all laughed long and hard, sort of high in the throat, like before they'd been a bit frightened and this was a relief. The redhead's mouth stretched wide; her tongue swung about inside, pink and lost.

"Better get used to it," she finally choked out. "This is August, the end of winter." She pressed her fingertips against her chest, the point of her elbow out. "Summer's still ahead."

Jane looked out at the sea. The light cut off the water sharp as mirrors.

"How do you take it?" Marlene asked, her voice quiet. She wiped her hand along the bottom of her chin.

"You m-m-m-m. Move less," answered the thin man sitting next to the redhead. He gestured to the seats on the other side of the table. He gestured in the way Jane was used to, palm upward. Sitting down next to Marlene at the table, she glanced around at all the people still staring. Here, the eyes were fixed on Marlene.

"Summer," exhaled Marlene.

"It's OK," said the man. "Summer only gets about three degrees hotter. Basically there are no seasons here except the w-w-wet one. That doesn't come until M-M-M . . ." He paused, closed his eyes and breathed in, determined to find the word.

"March," said the redhead easily. "You mean March, honey." She put her hand on his arm, leaned forward conspiratorially toward Marlene and Jane. "He gets worse when he's nervous." She was one of those people with a direct level stare who was always being told she should go into sales, the kind of person who worried less about what sort of impression they were making than if they were getting their way. She breathed through her teeth, emphasizing the amount of air she used, making her seem wider and fleshier than she was.

The man opened his eyes to look at the redhead. He was bony as a bird. Beneath the crew cut even the outline of his skull was visible, its dips, its protuberances. His cheekbones swung wide round his narrowed face so Jane could almost see what he would look like as a normal filled-out man. His face had a bared nervous character to it, attractive in a needy way, the kind of bony man each woman thought must be weak with a hunger that she alone could satisfy. He had looked at the redhead when she said, "March," and his lips stopped shivering. His mouth slowly loosened into its normal position, still empty.

"Christ," said Marlene, "I can't imagine it. It's hot enough down here, but up there on campus . . . Fuck!"

"What about in town?" Jane asked. The three of them turned to look at her. She felt the heat rising to her face and forced herself to continue. "I mean, does it get a lot cooler there at night?"

"God, no," exclaimed the redhead, exhaling. "It swelters up there."

"Why'd they choose up there?" Jane asked. "I mean, why'd they build the town halfway up the hill where it's hot?"

The man looked at her for a moment. "You kidding? They built down here on the beach in the sea breeze as any m-m-m-m-." Each time he stuttered, he closed his eyes, breathed in, paused, then exhaled the word soft as a breeze. His stuttering had a rhythm to it.

"Mammal," prompted the redhead quietly as though he might not know the word.

"Mammal would," continued the thin man, "but when the school came, it wanted the beach. The school had the support of the government, which wanted its business and bribes. The Indonesian army's not exactly beneficent. The islanders m-m . . . Moved up the hill." It seemed to Jane his pauses were getting more rushed.

"It's OK anyway," the redhead added, turning her straightforward eyes to Jane. "They're meant for this heat. It doesn't affect them like it would us."

Behind the bar stood three islander men. They wore chef's shirts, the kind that were crisp and white and had a double row of buttons. The men looked out at the sea. Jane's guidebook said for a thousand years they'd lived on the island, mostly off of fishing. The only interruptions in their solitude had been a few Dutch trading ships and some determined tourists, until the school arrived twenty-five years ago.

When the redhead said in a normal voice over her shoulder, "Four more beers," the closest islander reached down smoothly into the ice chest and walked over, without a pause. Beneath his shirt he wore chinos—pants Jane had always associated with blond families summering in Maine.

Inside the chinos he moved his hips as though he were still in a sarong.

"Hey," Marlene asked the islander, "what kind of chow you got here?"

"Try the steaks," said the redhead before the islander could speak.

"Steaks?" asked Marlene. "Not Indonesian gado-gado or something?"

"What's that?" she asked. "Naw, it's just real stuff here. Steak, eggs, french fries, burgers. The school runs this place."

Marlene snorted. "OK, then," she said to the islander. "Make it two steaks, for me and Doris here." He turned back to the bar, never having spoken.

"Actually, my name's Jane," Jane said to Marlene and the rest of the table, to the bar in general. "Jane Guy." She waited for their recognition, for them to ask if she meant as in Dr. Augie Guy. It happened all the time. She parted her lips slightly to start the words of family deprecation.

"Whatever," said Marlene. She took a cigarette out and said to the redhead and the thin man, to the rest of the students quiet and listening, "Marlene Diemer."

Jane closed her lips and looked around at their faces, wondering for the first time how well her father was known outside of the hospital community, outside of Connecticut.

"Keefer C-C-C-C . . . Christiane," said the skinny man.

"Christiane, as in the newspaper magnate," the redhead declared. Marlene blinked in surprise. The redhead smiled, ran her curled fingers under Keefer's jaw, then touched a single knuckle to his lips. It struck Jane as a strange gesture. The woman touched him as easily as a person touched her own face, or the way a mother might spit on a tissue to scrub it across her child's mouth. She didn't look at him while she touched him, but rather straight at Marlene with her direct measuring stare. Keefer didn't jerk his head back with surprise, didn't move at all. He sat there, still, obedient.

After a moment he waggled his eyebrows at Jane. She realized she was staring. She looked down, shut her mouth.

The redhead took her hand away, added, "I'm Claren Gruenman."

"Hey," said a woman at another table. "You didn't bring any magazines with you? *Vogue, Harper's, Newsweek?*" Jane turned toward the other table with relief, away from this couple.

Marlene and Jane shook their heads.

"Who's ahead in the California polls for governor?" asked a man at another table.

"How're the Red Sox doing?" piped up a third table.

"Why the fuck don't you just call home and ask?" responded Marlene. She grinned her half-grin again, one side stretched wide, the other side of her face just watching, no more amused than a rock.

"You haven't tried yet," said Claren. "When you can get through, which is unusual, you have to listen to your mother through New Zealanders jabbering about wool prices. The whole line sounds like it's made of paper and someone's crumpling it."

"And of course we aren't allowed to get to a d-d-d-d . . . Decent phone system or newspaper stand, not even Singapore," added Keefer. "Any newspapers we get are at least two weeks old."

When the school first started, Jane knew, it had allowed the students off the island at Christmas and for summer vacation, but after a few years it became obvious too much had to be learned in four short years by students not good at learning. Also, too many students never returned from vacation, never returned from cool temperatures and no studying, from old friends, TV and all those new people to meet. Now there was just a single week of vacation between each of the three semesters per year. The school expelled any student who left the island, even during vacation. Some students still left and were expelled, but the dropout rate had lowered and the percentage who passed the boards had gone up significantly.

Five more people stepped into The Bar and Jane could see from the way everyone sat up in their seats that these were new students too. Two of the men sat down at Jane's table, as close as they could get on the bench to Marlene. Jane caught a glimpse of the man who sat closest, on the other side of Marlene: black hair pulled back in a ponytail, and as the back curved to sit down, the knobs of the spine were visible even through the T-shirt. He raised his arm to order more drinks for the whole table and for a moment Jane wondered if it belonged to the same man, for his arm was thickly roped with muscle.

When the drinks and steak arrived, Jane asked Claren if she could drink alcohol while she was on Percosets. She figured Claren would know the answer because she'd already finished at least a year of Queen's.

"Oh sure," said Claren, leaning forward in her certainty. "It'll dull the pain more."

Quite thirsty, Jane took a gulp of the beer. It was so cold a small thumb of pain pressed into her forehead between her eyebrows. She rubbed her forehead and took another gulp. She could feel the chill spread slowly out from her stomach. She sighed.

Jane tried to cut up her steak using just the knife in her right hand, sawing it across the meat. The fingers of her other hand hurt too much to hold the fork, or even to press lightly onto the slab, and the steak kept wiggling across the plate away from the knife. She wished she'd brought the Percosets along with her. No one offered to help her, no one even looked at her. Like she wasn't there. All the men at the table talked to Marlene. The women watched the men talk to Marlene. People kept buying rounds of drinks. Two more beers were set in front of Jane.

After a while a man sat down on the bench next to Jane. He placed his hands palm down on the table in front of him and sat very still without shifting or making any gestures. Mostly just his eyes moved, watching the people laughing and drinking. He didn't appear tense as some people might sitting that still. Instead he seemed somehow calm, as though he'd edited out all the extraneous static of other people's nervous habits. His hair was deer brown, fine and shiny in a way that reminded Jane of children's hair. He was quite tall, six foot two or three, and rather than slouching as many tall men did, he sat as though he thought the way to deal with this height was to keep it closely in check, in perfect alignment. He seemed to her too cautious to be handsome.

Because the table was so crowded, he sat with his thigh right against hers. She could tell from the way he sat so precise and tall he would not do this unless necessary. She thought he looked like it might even offend him a bit, so she crossed her legs and shifted a little closer to Marlene who shoulder-butted her and said without looking, "Back off, ya lesbo."

Into the silence that followed the man asked, "Want me to cut that up for you?" He gestured down at the steak and then to Jane's arm in the sling.

She nodded gratefully, already feeling guilty for his kindness. He cut the steak up precisely into inch-wide cubes, first slicing the steak lengthwise into five strips, then quartering the strips into squares. Before he made each cut, he held the knife against the meat and judged the distance. When the waiter went by he asked for water to drink.

"Drinking alcohol," he said to Jane, "makes jet lag last longer." Something about the confident way he said this made Jane think of the proclamations of her father. "I'm Michael."

"Jane," she said, "Jane Guy." He showed no reaction to her last name either. The first bite of meat in her mouth tasted heavy and sweaty in the heat and she only swallowed it by chewing energetically for what seemed like an exceptionally long time, then drinking the rest of her beer. When the waiter came back with Michael's water, she asked for water also, but the waiter didn't seem to hear, just put the glass down, and looked over Michael's head to the sea. A lot of the students didn't seem to see her. Perhaps, she thought, she just didn't speak loudly enough. She knew she did tend to mumble when uncertain. And she slouched, her mother was always telling her she slouched. Her ears had begun to ring, but she didn't know if this was the pain, or the Percosets and beer, or the noise of the bar, which had filled up completely, the waiters walking back and forth between the tables, looking only out at the sea or at each other, never down at the tables except when they reached for the money.

Jane caught Michael glancing down at her plate, at all the untouched steak he had cut up for her, and she valiantly put the next piece of meat in her mouth. Another beer glass was taken away—she thought it was only her second—and two more put down. She normally didn't drink anything except maybe the occasional glass of wine with dinner. She nodded at everything Michael or anyone said, even if she didn't understand it. Her dislocated arm felt heavier and heavier, the weight moving to her mouth and then her eyes so they watered and she had to blink frequently. She wasn't sure if this was pain or the Percosets working. Because Marlene and she had taken a roundabout route here, Jane wasn't even sure which path was the one back to the bungalow. She didn't know how far it was. She didn't want to interrupt Marlene's conversation. She took another sip of her beer.

Something bumped against Jane's back and she looked behind her to see a skinny dog sniffing up at her steak. She held out her hand to pat it but the dog backed away, lifting its lip to show its very white teeth. Its pelt was stretched tight over the knobs of its shoulders and hips. Its yellow eyes watched her wary and slightly sideways like a fish. Eyes, Jane thought, never looked like they were truly part of a starving creature, like they suffered at all. On all those Oxfam commercials she'd always thought the eyes themselves looked quite normal, fatter if anything by comparison to all the shrunken structures around, like a normal creature had just pressed its face into the bony mask when the photo was taken, the eyes glancing up at the camera, surprised.

She picked up a piece of steak from her plate and held it casually out.

The dog's whole body shot forward. Incisors clicked shut, grazing her fingers, and then, from nowhere, three dogs grappled in a tumble by her feet. Fast tangled movement. She distinctly saw one dog, in an effort to grasp the meat, sink all its teeth in around the other's face, near the eye. There was a fast yipe, a convulsive jerk, the flash of open flesh. The one dog streaked off down the beach, the others chasing.

Jane sat there dumb, looking down at her hand. Drops of dog blood lay sprinkled on the sand floor.

"Jesus," Claren exhaled, leaning forward with her direct stare. "You didn't try to feed one, did you?"

"You're lucky to have all your fingers," Michaèl said. "Those are not domesticated animals."

"Think of them as raccoons or foxes," explained Claren. "They'll rip your hand off as fast as a knife. The same goes for cats around here. They're all wild. No one feeds them. The only pets the islanders have—that they hold, you know, and talk to—are their roosters. And they pit those together in fights to murder each other."

Claren continued to enumerate the inhuman ways the islanders treated their animals while Jane propped her head up on her good arm, the pain from her other arm creeping into her shoulder and neck so even nodding at what Claren said got painful. She hoped if she held her head exactly still, the pain would go away. She kept a smile on her face, drank more beer, kept her feet tucked in under her, away from the dogs. The laughter got wilder. The remaining dogs scavenged beneath the tables, and outside the sun beat down on the white beach.

By the time Marlene felt ready to go it was three in the afternoon and Jane had to push up twice before she could stand. Although Jane denied it, Marlene said Jane was crazy drunk, chanting it all the way back to the bungalow. And outside of their new home Jane did fall to her knees and vomit for the second time that day, from the jet lag and her shoulder, from the Percosets and maybe a touch of the flu. As she started to heave, back arching, Marlene sighed and stepped forward to scoop Jane's hair up and out of the way. Her fingers pressed cool and patient against Jane's neck. Jane sprayed beer and tattered chunks of steak onto the white sand, her eyes open wide in surprise.

Marlene dropped her hair as soon as she finished.

"You're embarrassing, Doris dear," Marlene said, walking wide round the mess and up to the house. "A real dork."

"Jane," Jane whispered to the vomit. "My name's Jane."

Still, she could feel Marlene's fingers against her neck for a while afterward. She thought Marlene wasn't half as harsh as she seemed. And that afternoon, falling back onto her bed, the room swaying even when she lay so cautiously still, she thanked God she was here. She recognized this island as her last chance.

Seven

DAY TWO

Jane arrived fifteen minutes early for her first class, Physiology taught by Dr. Gene Egren. She wanted a seat up front. This was the start of her learning the information she needed to become a doctor. Most of the class drifted in over the next ten minutes. Jane found from that single afternoon in The Bar she could recognize a lot of the faces. Keefer came in with them.

"Hey," she said, "Keefer."

He leaned down and gave her a fast spontaneous hug. She felt the bony top of his shoulder press into her face, his hand gripping her back. She blinked, surprised. Her hand raised belatedly to respond, to touch his back. Under the damp material of Keefer's shirt she felt the bare hull of his ribs. Then he pulled back, his face open, smiling.

"Why . . ." She stared at him, wanting to ask him why he'd hugged her. The touch of his ribs still on the tips of her fingers. She could feel the start of her furious blush. Instead she asked, "Why're you here? In a first-year class?"

"I failed this class last year," he said. "Have to r-r-r. Repeat." He smiled wider then, almost too wide and looked away from her, over her head to the jungle outside. "Don't ever fail anything here. The teachers aren't so nice about it. It's better just to leave." He looked fast around to the clock behind him.

"Another piece of advice, Doris," he said. "Don't sit in the front row. Come back here with me." He grabbed her hand and tugged her toward the back of the class. Half-laughing, she followed, happy to have someone to sit with, happy to feel accepted, not bothering to correct him about her name. At college she'd only lived in the dorms for two weeks, scurrying from one class to the next, studying out of confusion about what else there was to do, going to freshman orientation parties and standing against the wall, clutching her cheese wedges and smiling rigidly at nothing. The second week her housemates persuaded her to smoke some dope with them. She thought if she did as they asked, they might talk to her more. The dope had the effect of pinwheeling her right into slack-faced sleep. When she woke she was draped across the couch in the common room in her bathrobe, long trails of baby-blue toothpaste striping every limb. She moved back home after that, drove half an hour to her classes each day, never lived in a dorm again.

She didn't have that many friends, not real friends. She sometimes went to parties and played tennis and spent weekends at summer houses in the Hamptons with the children of her parents' neighbors, but mostly around others her age she clutched her cheese wedges again or tennis racquet or whatever was the object of the hour, her brow furrowed. Her nervousness was just accepted more easily because they all knew her parents. "Baby Guy," was what they called her and talked to her mostly to confide in her. To these people, her friends, she simply said, "Uh-huh," and "Oh-oh," and her face showed each of the other's emotions as they were presented, for she could imagine herself in every situation and it was as though she'd done it. Not as though she'd imagined doing it, but as though she'd actually done it. So when the other person finished talking and got up—a woman, for they were almost always women—when the woman got up, much lighter, Jane slouched there slack and heavy for a moment after the other left. Each woman felt quite close to Jane for a day or two until she began to remember she'd learned nothing about Jane in return and to wonder why she'd chosen Jane to reveal herself to. Sometimes, feeling exposed, she got angry at Jane. Other times she'd just ignore Jane until she needed her again.

Dr. Egren arrived ten minutes late, hurrying in after the last student.

"Welcome, welcome, welcome to medical school," he said. He was the tall doctor who'd relocated her shoulder. He leaned forward toward the class, waif-thin with an earnest voice and bushy old-man eyebrows that grew like some type of animal-hair transplant out of his brows. One dark strand of brow hair, Jane could see all the way from her seat. It ran halfway across his left eye. She wondered if he even noticed this hair bisecting his view of the class. He moved much more energetically than he had when he'd relocated her shoulder. His voice was loud and exaggerated, his movements wide with excitement.

"I am your very first class, am I not?" He swung his arms out, narrow shoulders hunched up almost to his ears. His shrug would have been visible to anyone from seventy feet away. The farthest student sat only ten feet off to the side. Egren reminded Jane of an aging male cheerleader, silly with enthusiasm. She could not help smiling.

"Sorry, I am so sorry I am late," he continued, plastering one palm flat against his chest, fingers splayed. "I should treat this with more honor. Your arrival here. I mean this is medical school. This is an honor. I hope I'm not the only one who thinks so. At this school you'll get to learn the secrets of the human body. How each of us maintains life. How we give birth, how we die, how we eat and move and reproduce." Leaning forward he talked, his head cocked, looking at each of them in turn earnestly. When he looked at Jane, she sat completely still, not breathing. Beneath his thick eyebrows he looked into her eyes as intimately as though no one else existed. As though the whole speech was for her alone. Because she'd met him yesterday she risked a small smile. His expression stayed exactly the same, his lips didn't pull out any wider. Thinking about it later, she was not sure he remembered her. His eyes stayed on her, on each student, for longer than eyes were supposed to stay on another, his breath fast and his lips slightly wet. She felt he was coming to some conclusion about her. He turned to look at the next student.

"At school here," he said, "you will look at humans on chemical, cellular, systemic and species-wide levels. You'll learn to cut into human skin, to open up a dead body and study its organs. You will handle matters of life and death. What a sacred profession!" He popped his hands out like exclamation marks by his face and exhaled through his nose. He froze for a moment staring at the wall over Jane's head, as though suddenly struck by the sheer power of this thought. Jerking into motion again, he offered out his next words on one palm.

"And society certainly realizes this. Doctors are respected perhaps more than any other professional. Well paid. Portrayed constantly on TV."

One of the students pulled out a sandwich, unwrapping it. The paper crunkled. Several students glanced over. Egren looked, his expression still stretched in a smile.

"At most medical schools," he continued, "once you get in, it's hard to flunk out. Here, it is the opposite. Here, you have already flunked out. It is difficult to pass. The curriculum is even more challenging than normal med schools. You have to learn more information, all that you've missed in the past. You have to fight to be called 'Doctor.' "

Jane looked over at Keefer in excitement, smiling—this

teacher was saying everything she believed, was so elo-
quent—but Keefer had his head down, facing the desk with
his mouth narrow and tucked in.

"I know," said Egren, and here he lowered his voice, got
more serious. He looked at them honestly and deep from
under his brows. "I know you have not proved in the past
to be what you might call great students. You have not done
all that well at school until now. At least not well enough
to get into the competitive American med schools. Here,
that will change. We will help you become good students.
Great students. We will give you study materials, assigned
tutors, practice tests for the medical boards. Instead of five
or six students sharing a single cadaver as it is in a lot of
other schools, each student here will dissect three separate
cadavers over the span of first year. Repetition helps recall.
And to create an atmosphere where you can be the most
productive, there are no TVs here at Queen's, no video
games, no city nightlife. Nothing to do but work and learn
from each other.

"We will help you in every way we can, and"—he held
up his finger at this point—"and we assume, in return, you
will work as hard as you can. We assume, here, you will
finally be motivated. That, simply put, you weren't before.
That you didn't yet know what you wanted to do. Not with
all your heart."

He paused here, and looked down, a little embarrassed,
a little awkward. "Perhaps there are a few of you—I hesitate
to bring this up—but perhaps there are a few of you who
still aren't completely motivated, who aren't so sure medicine is your profession." He sucked his lower lip in between
his teeth in nervousness. Some of the students leaned forward, wanting to help him continue. "Generally in the past,
up to thirty percent of the class has been at least partially
pressured into this profession, into this school, by their parents. That's part of the reason why they hadn't gotten the
grades until now. This true of anyone here?"

From the back row Jane couldn't see how he chose the woman he did. Perhaps a bashful smile, a raising of her eyebrows. She sat in the front row.

"You?"

"Well," she said, "maybe." She had the straight blond hair and narrow features of an old New England family, wore a faded lacrosse shirt and Indian print skirt.

He walked over, leaned toward her, one of those people who held his face close to another, stared unblinking as a cat. He regarded this woman, so interested. "Really," he said. "Tell me."

"I might want to be an actress." She enunciated her words clearly, each of the consonants as exactly and effortlessly hit as a tennis ball. She politely declined her head, the way a golden retriever graciously wags its tail for a dachshund, good manners and not the slightest feeling of threat. "I've been in three college productions, once as Ms. Fellows in *Night of the Iguana*. That's pretty much a starring role. But since my grandfather, every child in my family has been a doctor. My uncle patented one of the kidney dialysis machines, the Sarvin 5000." She looked up at him, smiling easily, her teeth very small and white, perfectly straight. "I've tried to tell my parents this might not be for me."

Egren took his hands one at a time out of his pockets, spreading the fingers wide on his knees. He moved deliberately as in some complex procedure where adherence to the rules is critical. He inhaled slow and methodical, then paused. His words up to this point had been excited but spoken quietly. In comparison his next words sounded even louder than they were, the way the rhythmic ticking of a clock can lull you into greater shock at the alarm's inevitable blare.

"YOU LAZY SHIT!" he bellowed down onto her upheld face.

Some of the spittle from his lips hit her and she slapped

back in her chair away from him, and his noise and his spit, the chair knocking back on its legs and almost over.

Egren moved to the front of the classroom in a single stride and screamed his words at all of them. "You fucking whiners. Don't want a real profession? Don't want to work? Want to live off Daddy's money?" His neck was abruptly a brilliant red. None of his gestures exaggerated. He moved now narrow, direct, just to get there. A vein curved across his forehead, purple and swollen. Everyone in the class froze, like watching an automobile wreck on a sunny afternoon. One boy in the back began to giggle, high and silly.

Egren hit the desk with the flat of his hand. The desk barked. The students jumped. The boy shut up. "Last year's class was the same. Exactly the same. Didn't want to learn. Didn't want to study. But we changed them. They learned everything we asked. They're good students now. You will be too. You'll work harder than you ever have before. *And . . . You . . . Will . . . Succeed.*" Even in the midst of his yelling, his eyes continued to roam around the classroom, looking hard at each person. Monitoring their reactions, cataloging their expressions, noting it all.

He stopped then. The vein on his forehead beat. He licked his lips, looked out the window to that smooth British lawn. His voice became suddenly quiet again, smoothly modulated, unnatural in a way after all that noise. He leaned forward, smiled just as wide as before, his lips still wet. He spoke cheerful again, excited. He had every student's attention. "If you work hard, we teachers here will do everything we can to help you, all our resources, tutors, practice tests, lists of mnemonics, whatever. We will help you at three in the morning if that's when you're studying. We are good at this, we're experts. With your cooperation we will make you into doctors. With your cooperation we offer you four very tough years in exchange for a lifetime of an honored profession, money, the respect of your friends, your parents." He held his hands palm upward to the class. To offer help? To show they held no weapons?

He closed his hands, returned them to his sides, his voice colder. "Do not think of calling home to Mommy. She and Daddy sent you here. They know what is going on. They think it should happen. They paid a lot of money to make sure it would happen." He rubbed slowly at the sides of his mouth. "Do not think of complaining to the U.S. Board of Education, to the American Medical Association. We are no longer in the U.S. We do not follow their rules."

He dropped his hands to his sides.

"If you're not going to work, just quit now. Leave the island. There's no other way to get away from us. We will make your lives hell.

"Isn't that true, Keefer?"

Keefer jerked his head up, eyes wide. He didn't look at anyone but Egren, like they were all alone in the room. "Yes, s-s-s." He closed his eyes to get out the word, gritted his teeth. "Sir." He opened his eyes slowly.

Egren smiled, looked out the windows, over the students' heads. His eyes followed some movement off to the right. A bird, Jane wondered, a monkey? There was such a silence that if she closed her eyes she would never have believed there were thirty-six other people sitting in the same room, each of them alone. She noticed Keefer was still watching Egren, head lowered, eyes unwavering. Without Egren looking at him, his face no longer held just fear.

"Homework," Egren said, quite calm now, almost happy again. His eyes turned from one to the other of them, friendly, interested, watching them all. "First chapter of the *Intro Physio* textbook. Next class I will test you."

"Until the end of the hour," he said, "sit here and study."

He left the room and the stillness continued. Everyone faced forward, their mouths open, as though he were still standing there.

After one long moment a short woman snorted and stood up, began to pack her books.

Later, Jane learned this was the critical time. Those students who got up now, at this first yelling, at this first class, were the ones who actually left the school, took the plane back. While everyone else—the ones who stayed seated, telling themselves they would just see how bad it got, see how the others reacted, see what their own grades were—those were the ones who mostly ended up staying seated no matter what. They were the ones who firmly believed there was nothing else in life for them but here.

The woman finished picking up her books. One man wearing a loud Hawaiian shirt stood up also, grabbed his bag. Later Jane wished she'd looked at these two more than this, wished she could remember more about their faces or posture, their expressions or attitude. The woman, Jane remembered, had short hair that showed the nape of her neck. She said, "Yeah, fuck *that*," while she pushed open the doors, the man following. Everyone else remained sitting.

The doors swung shut behind them. Egren began to yell at them in the hall, his voice receding as he followed them toward the exit.

"Leave this building now, you are out of this school. Leave this building now, you'll never get into any other med school. You'll never become a doctor."

Their responses and his words faded with the distance, so all that was left was the general volume, his fury. Jane looked around, at the class that remained, thirty-three other first-year students and Keefer. They were eyeing the door nervously. She could smell the class now in the breeze from the fan: fresh sweat.

No one talked. The silence was loud. One woman belatedly, fumblingly reached into her bag, pulled out her textbook, opened it up. Most of the other students gratefully followed, including Jane. They rustled papers noisily. It seemed much easier to look at the book than at each other.

Jane bent her head over the first page. She had been warned the school was tough. She inhaled slow, uncapped her highlighter and bent down to read. There was nowhere else to go. From the corners of her eyes she noticed a lot of the other students just leaned over their books, weren't actually reading, eyes focused far beyond the page. She glanced over at the blond woman Egren had yelled at. The woman sat hunched at her desk with her hands over her face. Her uneven exhales were the only sound.

Once, Jane and her mother had been in a car accident. Jane was about eight. Driving back from an amateur dance performance, they rounded the curve on a country road to see the dark outline of a twelve-point buck in the center of the headlights, its unblinking disbelief. Her mother swerved, fought for control, the car skidding. Jane remembered noting with surprise the telephone pole, understanding they would hit.

Jane's skull cracked against the dashboard, a sound louder to her than any sound had ever been, closer to her even than her own ears, like two wood blocks clapped together inside her very brain. She pulled herself wobbling up and, before she touched her own forehead, she touched the dashboard, as though to check for injury there. She took some considerable comfort in the undented plastic. The dashboard lights and headlights had died. It was dark. The car around them gave one long exhale.

"Right," said her mother. "We should get to a phone."

By the light of the moon Jane turned her listing vision to her mother and saw she had become a black woman. It was a moment before Jane understood her mother's face was covered in dark blood, from the forehead to the chin, blood tracing its lazy curlicues down her narrow neck. Her eyes the only normal feature, although they blinked a lot.

Her mother pushed open her door. Jane ended up also having to slide out the driver's side because the passenger door was jammed shut. She trotted to catch up, one hand holding up her head. Her mother was silent, walking smoothly ahead, moving quickly but not running. Jane stayed three feet back, too scared to reach for her hand. The only aberration in her mother's walk was the way she kept raising her hand to wipe her eyes. In that two-hundred-foot-long walk to the nearest house, following the dark-faced stranger, Jane learned about the extremes of her mother's silence, all of its strength. The machinelike click click of her mother's heels was stronger than Jane would ever be; that sound alone could crush her under its weight.

At the hospital, once Jane had stopped shivering from shock, she was left with only a headache and a purple walnut-sized bump on her forehead. Her mother needed twelve stitches, wore face bandages and hand-painted head scarves for three weeks, extending the length of time the bandages had to be on in order to get the nose job she'd been thinking about. Afterward, with the bandages off, she'd appeared only more competently beautiful, confidently going about her life, driving her new BMW without hesitation. Jane realized, looking at her graceful mother in the bright light of day, that her parents could use any experience they went through to make themselves stronger.

Jane was the last person to leave that first class and she stood outside, blinking in the bright sunlight until Keefer drove by.

"Get on," he said, tapping the moped seat behind him. "I'll introduce you to Jonah. Explain things."

Obediently she clambered on behind him and held on with one hand while trying to keep the press of her belly away from him. He drove fast, through the school gates into the jungle. The shadow of the trees ran heavy over her face, a weight pushing down on her skin. At the first turn, after half-sliding off the seat, she gave up on maintaining any distance, pulled herself in against him, held on with fear. He was skinny like Marlene, but with a completely different type of energy, a shivering sense of movement about to happen. Under her hand she felt his heart shifting in its beat like some small creature she'd trapped, a hamster or a mouse. She thought he probably slept curled up on his side, twitching paws tight by his face, waking abrupt and dazed, dark eyes blinking.

Although later on Marlene would maintain, that whole first month, that Jane had a crush on Keefer, Jane denied it. She'd known from the moment she saw him he would never be interested in the likes of her. She was used to assuming most men were like that, especially the ones she found attractive. She searched the man's eyes for that first glance over her shoulder to a woman nearby. She worked at making it easy for the man, her posture hunched, conversation intellectual, no gaze that lingered. At the first awkward shuffle of his feet or clearing of his throat into silence, she excused herself to get another appetizer, to greet someone she knew. Left him to talk to whom he'd prefer.

Keeping a hand on Keefer's bony chest, pressing her body against his back was not as difficult as she would have thought. On this island touch seemed different. Bodies were so exposed in small shirts and shorts; chests, bellies, legs and arms, all so public and commonplace. Skin felt changed in this heat, not dry and clean and proper, but moist and soft, closer to the skin of a fish. It surprised her time and time again, moved her thoughts away from worries of propriety. Her parents and Connecticut seemed so far away. She held on to Keefer, knowing if she let go for even a moment she would fall off.

He parked in front of his bungalow, led her out back to a U-sided dock built so the ends of the U lay against the shore. At the far corner was a small shed. Their feet slapped along the boards of the dock, echoing against the water. She was glad Keefer walked in front. She listened to her feet for any echo of her limp. When he stopped walking and turned around, she stopped too. The water glimmered, ten or twelve feet deep. Jane had a momentary desire to just dive in, as deep as she could. Her head hurt from the sun.

Keefer sat down near the shed, took off his sandals and dabbled his feet about in the water. She gladly followed suit, the water cool against her toes. She half-watched the house for anyone who might appear called Jonah. After a while she looked down through the waves inside the U of the dock to see the smooth back of a boulder below.

"Look," said Keefer, "you gotta understand. All the teachers are like that. They'll motivate us however they c-c-c. Can. They get paid per student who successfully completes each year, a bonus for each student that passes the med boards. They'll do whatever they have to to motivate you."

Jane dipped one hand into the sea, ran her fingers over her forehead and neck. Her skin began to dry instantly in the heat, her fingers left sticky with salt. Listening to him, she had the sudden perception their parents were probably very similar. She wondered why she had never begun to stutter. Probably, she thought, she hadn't spoken enough around them. "But I already want to pass," she said.

He kicked his feet about in the water in frustration or emphasis. Looked around at the sea. "Everyone *wants* to pass. That's not the p-p-p-p. Point. Wanting hasn't helped any of us before. The point is whether you *will* pass. The teachers know how to make you. How to push you, further than you've ever gone before. It's going to get intense. Fast. To get by you have to step out of school occasionally. You have to have other things."

Jane knew there wasn't a single thing she wanted outside of the school's brick fence. She looked down at the ridge of rock, reached down to touch the water again. The rock was so smooth, so shaped by the ocean, the worn fluidity of sea glass. The waves floated over it, breaking her vision of it up and re-forming it. Creation and destruction. Subtle stripes ran down one side.

He got up and opened the shed, pulled out a drawing pad and heavy plastic bucket.

Jane looked back down and the rock was rising, was halfway to her feet, its mouth open, its ragged teeth shining.

She flipped backward fast, almost off the far side of the dock, clutching her hand to her chest. She'd never screamed in her adult life, not even practiced. The scream came out a little too airy and low, like a cow saying, "Ahgh."

"Hey," said Keefer, "Oh God, I'm sorry. I should of t-t-t-t. Told you. This is Jonah. It's perfectly fine. I forget. We're all so used to it."

Jonah's blunt nose broke the water first, the body perhaps seven or eight feet long, swollen as a drowned man. It twisted smoothly onto its side, to watch them more directly from its right eye. Jane stared, unable to look away from its slow revolution, its revelation, the long muscled heft of it, the slit mouth, its pale underside. Its teeth rolled into view, rows of them, more teeth than she could imagine, more than seemed necessary for any action she could think of.

Its eye was a perfect circle, no visible eyelids or tear duct. The pupil lost in the dark retina, no whites, like a horse's eye. It was looking right at her. Unlike a horse's eye, she had no idea what it thought, no feeling of trust or gentle scheming. No smell of oats and sweat or the sounds of a bit clanking between teeth, no hooves shifting their heavy weight about. Instead, there was the scent of the sea and an absolute silence, not even the whisper of its breath, only the willingness to wait.

She stared back, trapped into its gaze. Keefer pulled a fish out of the bucket and the shark looked over at that, its eye rolling smooth as a ball in its face. He reached over the dock with the fish. There was the sucking sound of the shark's mouth opening. Like a snake's jaws they unhooked, the whole skull changed shape, pulling the tip of the nose in and shoving both top and bottom jaws out and so apart,

the sudden almost-square cavern of pink gullet. Keefer slid
the fish right into its mouth. Its jaws retracted, closed with
a wet clap. Keefer took his hand back, whole and untouched. Jane exhaled. The shark chomped heavily, lazily,
water sloshing in and out of its mouth. Red shreds exhaled
out into the sea like steam. A chunk of the fish fell, spinning down toward the sand. The shark leaned its shoulder
after the meat, the smooth island of its side rolled through
the surface, then its tail swept through the water behind.

Jonah sank beneath the dock. Jane couldn't see it anymore. She jerked around to scan the water behind her,
eased herself more toward the center of the boards. She
kept her knees and hands close in to her body, looked over
the side. She would have sprinted down the dock back to
shore but she did not trust her legs right now, imagined
one knee collapsing, her body falling flailing arms first into
the water. Under the length of the dock she noticed a net
hung, creating a pen for the shark against the beach. Below
her, Jonah slid huge and weightless into view, sucked in
the fish's head as it went by. It continued to circle, gliding,
mouth open.

"Keefer." She found she was whispering. She tried to talk
louder. "Why . . . Why . . ." She didn't even know how to
frame the question.

Keefer picked up the drawing pad, started sketching
Jonah, fast shallow lines with charcoal. He dropped his feet
into the water, dabbled them gently about. "Got Jonah a
year ago. Always been fascinated by sharks. Always. The
guy who sold it to me had his hand all bundled up in some
cloth. Said Jonah b-b-bit him. Tried to up the price that
way. Jonah was only four feet long then. I brought it back
on my moped with its face in a bucket of water, tail flapping. Didn't die even then. Don't think it ever will d-d. Die.
Named it after my father. Has his smile."

The sketch built up from darkness, the curves of the
shark, the shadows of the water. It didn't show the shark

the way Jane was used to seeing sharks portrayed in draw-
ings: clear and up-close underwater, smiling for the viewer.
As though someone would take the time to sketch while
the shark was a few feet away, as though the shark would
stay still, posing. As though anyone could draw underwater.
She realized now the only way to make a painting like that,
in one position and anatomically accurate, was to prop the
body up in your studio, sketch fast before it began to smell,
paint the ocean backdrop in afterward.

Keefer's picture showed the shark alive through the surface of the waves, the way a swimmer would see one from
the level of the water, the way most humans see sharks.
Its smooth fin driving forward without effort, beneath the
water the half-seen mass.

"I've never called my f-father by his first name." Keefer
stopped, snorted in irritation. He pulled the drawing off and
ripped it in half, called down into the water. "Isn't that
right, Jonah, Joe? Joey-poo?" Starting a different sketch, his
feet beat at the water more quickly now. "That's the one
good thing about this place, that I can have Jonah, watch
him, that I can draw. My folks never liked that, the drawing.
I come from a family of businessmen. Successful businessmen. They told me to s-s-s-s. Stop. They told me the drawing was what made me upset."

He looked at her straight, charcoal still against the paper.
"They sent me to seven different therapists. I counted. One
of them was called Doctor Wise. 'Hello,' he answered the
phone, 'Wise speaking.' " Keefer turned back to the paper.
"When I'm h-h-h. Home, in the States, I cry a lot. At school,
on the street, in front of my parents' friends. After one
particularly bad crying jag—during a dinner party—my parents, the therapists and I had a long chat. We all agreed I
needed something to use my energies on. Something con-
structive. Medicine was our compromise. I was sent here."

"Are you happy here?" Jane asked.

Keefer snorted. "I haven't left 'cause my parents would

throw a fit. I haven't left because it's about as bad here as it is at home. I haven't left because of Jonah."

Jane spotted the shark rising smooth toward the surface, toward Keefer's kicking feet. Its blunt head slid through the water. She inhaled fast. Keefer glanced down, moved his feet out of the way, leaned over and ran his fingers over the shark's flank as it went by. Jonah, like a snake, did not respond, but continued to swing forward through the water. Dappled wet stripes ran down its sides, more distinct past the central fin. The tip of its tail stuck partly out of the water. From this close up she noticed the very edge of its tail was mildly transparent, the veins visible, like light through a rabbit's ear. So delicate. She leaned a bit forward in surprise, not much, a half an inch forward, an inch. Then pulled back, remembering.

"Hey, don't worry," said Keefer, taking another fish from the bucket. "It wouldn't hurt us 'cause it's got no idea m-m-m-m. Mammals are food. Never tasted them. Wouldn't hurt anyone because it would have to be sort of big to do that." The shark turned at the far side of the corral, sank slowly. The top of its fin dimpled the water from just beneath, no larger than the dimple a carp might make, cutting back toward them. Then the rock of its face rose in front of them, silent.

"Keefer, it's plenty huge," said Jane. "Look at it."

Keefer looked down at it, assessing, still holding the fish out. The shark's blunt snout pointed up like a waiting dog, head widening into a tunnel chest. Its mouth sucked open again, so impossibly wide and deep, like Jane might be able to see into its intestines if she leaned over, the body revealed for the eating tube it was. An eight-year-old girl, Jane thought, could slip without harm between its heavy jaws if she tucked in her head, wriggled once to get her shoulders through. Below the water, the shark's refracted body grew and shrank with the surface of the waves, like a magic act. Jonah's head rose higher in the water. Jane didn't see its tail move at all, its whole body just rose. She thought with its eyes on either side of its head it couldn't possibly see above it to where the fish was, where the fish ended and Keefer's hand began. The slashes of its nostrils twitched. In the hot sun even Jane could smell the dead fish.

"I guess," Keefer admitted, "I guess it has grown some."

"Well," he added, "Jonah wouldn't hurt anything because it's fed so well." He dropped the fish in. Its heavy jaws clapped shut, a sound like a belly flop. It threw its head side to side as though the fish struggled, as though it needed to break the spine. Water sloshed.

"Anyhow," he added, "what I was saying is, to survive at Queen's you got to have other things. You got to get outside of school."

"How?" she asked, distracted for a moment from Jonah. She glanced at Keefer, then to the jungle behind her. She could see a single tiled spire of the school rising above the treetops, nothing else in sight. "What else is there?"

"Oh." He smiled, looking down at the water. The shark sank, swung off slowly, tracing the confines of the pen. "You got to be i-i-i. Imaginative."

That afternoon Jane studied hard. She made flash cards, she highlighted, she took notes on the reading using correct Roman numeral outline form. She reread the chapter four times and highlighted a little more of it with each reading so in the end more than half the text was yellow for concept or pink for vocab. And each time she highlighted a pertinent term, while her pen squeaked in a straight line across the page, she looked outside to the sun glinting off the sea. Each time she flipped over a flashcard, her mouth moving silently round the unfamiliar word, she glanced around to the corner of the ceiling where she'd spotted a small green lizard who stared at her with pop eyes, sometimes running upside down to a new location, forearms flying, a completely soundless patter.

Jane wasn't here because she was an unmotivated student. She didn't ever flunk classes; she ensured that. She worked. She studied dutifully, arduously, ineffectually. Her fingers clutched the highlighter, panicked, turned the page. She also had extracurricular activities: swimming for a year, that semester singing in the glee club, the bridge club before it was discontinued from lack of interest. Lukewarm recommendations stressed her diligence. G.P.A. 2.7. It wasn't a great G.P.A. surely, not even really a decent one, but probably enough to get her into some med school somewhere with her father's reputation, with her parents' money.

That was not the point though. The point was, with those grades she certainly would not make it into Harvard, her father's alma mater. Each semester when she left her report card on the mail table for her father, it remained there for weeks, her father always saying he would look at it tomorrow. The flat white rectangle of the envelope lying there in the silence of the hall, unmoving.

And all year round whenever her father mentioned his day's work at dinner, he explained it in simple nonmedical terms, in short words like "breathing," "unconscious," and "brain." Glanced at Jane then, as if she might not have understood.

So at the end of the fall semester last year, her senior year, halfway through the organic chemistry final—trying hard to ensure at least a shot at Harvard—for the first and only time in her life, she unfolded her hand to read her cramped notes on the chemical compounds of lipids penned onto her sweaty palm.

Over her shoulder she felt the inhalation of someone's surprise.

And in that moment, before she'd turned to see the teacher's shocked expression, she continued to stare at her guilty palm, seeing the silence in her parents' house for the rest of her life on this subject also.

Eight

That night Jane woke several times, her jet-lagged body thinking each time it must be morning. She opened her eyes to darkness.

Each time she woke she tried to understand this as her bed on Potsdamn Road. She tried to find the hum of the air conditioner, feel its chilly exhale across her body, see the glow from her plastic seashell night-light. She tried to find Greenwich in the surf crashing and the dogs howling and the monkeys hooting and the heat plastering her nightgown to her body, in the darkness lit only by the moon glinting off the sea outside her window.

After she realized where she was, she lay there, blinking out at the sea, amazed, until she fell asleep again. She dreamed of the classroom, the shark floating slow as smoke in through a window, the teacher lecturing on, the students frozen. The shark curving around them, rubbing close as a cat, its tail thumping off the blackboard and walls.

At some point, in the darkest part of the night after the moon set, she woke to a ringing, a repeated jangling sound. She heard her mother vacuuming the jungle, cleaning up all that dirt and cluttered vibrancy. The jangling was each of the trunks of the trees being sucked up the vacuum's metal pipe.

Shaking her head, she sat up in the darkness, understood belatedly the sound of the phone. Not at all the electronic bee-da-beep of the cordless at home, this was a primitive sound; a sound that made one imagine the metal bell inside, the clapper furiously slamming. She assumed without thought it must be an emergency for someone to call this late at night. Smacking her rubber lips, she tried to climb out of bed. Pushed her face right into the scratchy mosquito net. She jerked her head back, heart racing, flapped her one good hand at the material. No idea where it started or ended, what it was. She heard Marlene stalk into the living room, lift the receiver only far enough to slam it back down.

"Fucker," Marlene said to herself and stumbled back across the floor to her room.

Hand now holding the netting, Jane realized gradually where she was. She patted the netting in recognition, stayed sitting up, gradually more and more awake. She began to worry, who might have been calling and why. She thought up scenarios bad enough for her parents to phone during what they would know was the middle of her night. They missed her, had to talk to her, wanted her back. She saw her father in the hospital, from behind, not as a doctor but as a patient. The dome of his skull glowed pink with his struggle, the spiderweb of tubes dripping down into him.

She waited tensely for the phone to ring again. She did not call home, even though there it would be the middle of the afternoon, because she could already hear the pause in their voices while they calculated the time for her, the pause before they asked why she'd called.

Unable to sleep, she decided to study, turned on the bedside lamp. Its faded light made the room seem somehow darker. None of the lamps in the bungalow worked well, cast any real light. If she turned on two at a time, both got weaker. In the distance, when the wind was blowing right, she could hear the wheezing rattle of the school's generator.

She listened to the jungle outside. The dark seemed scarier with one light on, with her lit up and onstage. The mosquito netting made crosshatched shadows on her books. She couldn't see even the corners of her room clearly. Something small rustled by the door, then another thing under her bed. A bug? A mouse, the lizard? Something buzzed low outside the netting, twapped its wings against the material again and again.

Later she woke into the motionless light of dawn, folded over her books, mouth slack against the paper, waking to the sound of water running through the pipes, gurgling and clanking, then Marlene lowering herself into the bath. Jane felt happy to hear the sounds of another human. She pulled the books up and began to study again, thinking of the classes coming up, of school getting intense, fast.

Nine

Jane followed the rest of the class, the very last student so no one could watch her limp. They descended slow down the marble underground stairs, through each of the refrigerator-style doors designed to keep in the cold of the earth. The marble muffled their voices and exaggerated the clicks of their sandals, their coughs, making it sound like many more than thirty-four people tromped down here. They all wore hospital-green coveralls, baggy and wide, making it look like more people also. She did not know how far down they went beneath the surface, twenty feet, maybe thirty. Stepping through each of the four sets of doors, she felt the temperature descend another ten degrees. Following Dr. Egren's orders, she had taken her arm out of the sling this morning but she still held it against her body in approximately the same position as before, gently rubbed her shoulder occasionally. She used her other arm to keep the danger of the doors away from that side of her.

After the last door she inhaled the cold deeply, as though hoping to smell the scent of fall leaves and crisp winds.

Instead she sucked in the sweet fixative of formalin in an unaired basement.

For a confused second she thought of the stench of brimstone along the cool marble hallways of hell. But then, she remembered, hell would be hot.

Just ahead of her Marlene exhaled, *"Phewie!"*

The students around her laughed sharp with nervousness and the echo. Several of them covered their mouths while they laughed, as though that might cut down on the stink.

Ahead, between the shoulders of her classmates, Jane saw the harshly halogen-lit autopsy room. The white walls, the rows of steel tables covered by green sheets; beneath the sheets lay lumpy outlines. Occupied tables.

Like the rest of the students, Jane stared. This class, she believed, would be the dividing line between her being just a normal person and her taking on the actions of a doctor. She was surprised by the number of mops and industrial sinks in the room.

Cutting into human flesh. She thought this was an honor. Her stomach felt a little upset, but she blamed any leftover jet lag. Her classmates jostled about like cows trying to get the tables closest to the exit, as though part of the successful completion of an autopsy would be a race out the door. The room, although bright and cavernous, made Jane feel claustrophobic. It was the stale air and the sensed weight of the earth above, the narrow aisles between the lumpy tables. The students threaded their way down the exact center of the aisles, maintaining the greatest distance possible, on both sides, from the tables. Several people joked feebly and the laughs hissed out fast between their teeth.

Jane wandered hesitantly down an aisle, staring at the outlines beneath the sheets. They all seemed to hint at huge rib cages. She wondered if they might have died of some epidemic, some tropical chest-swelling disease, if the school had gotten them for a discount. She didn't know of any such disease. She wondered if maybe the class was starting with something other than humans: a type of gorilla or wide-shouldered deer.

Over each body there were two sheets, one covering the top, the other the bottom, folded over each other in the area of the waist. For easy access, she realized, to the middle, to the organs, without having to expose the whole body, the human extremes of slack face or bony feet.

Because Jane was the last student in the door, she ended up with a body in the far corner of the room. The smell was thicker here. In spite of all the formalin, she could also smell something rotting, the sweetness of an open garbage bag in the summer. She opened her mouth, breathed through her teeth to lessen the smell, tried not to imagine the stray molecules floating through the air and down her throat, tried not to imagine swallowing rotting skin. On the side of the table hung a plastic bucket, a spray bottle filled with a clear liquid and several stainless steel instruments, including two saws and what looked like wire cutters and pliers.

"Now this is just grodie," muttered Marlene from two tables away, staring down at the covered body. She abruptly reached out and placed her bare hand flat on the sheet. Approximately on the belly, Jane thought.

"Huh," Marlene said. She took her hand back, looked at her palm and shook it. Glancing around, she saw Jane, smiled a little in embarrassment.

Scared, Jane realized, even she's scared.

The outline of Jane's cadaver seemed a little smaller than the average. She felt relief, thinking each cut she had to do was decreased. Combine all the cuts together and she might have a yard less overall to slice through. She stared at the outline of the chest, imagined pulling back the sheet from an alien form, a frog-type thing, huge chest, small head, mouth agape. She wished she had at least one lab partner to work on this body with, as they did at other schools,

someone to look to for clues about how to take this, someone for whom to keep her face formal.

A door opened between her and Marlene. Professor Burnett stooped out of it, his four tutors following. He wore a
white lab jacket, long pants and an old mottled scarf around
his neck. Through the door he straightened up slow. The
size of him and the fact of the scarf made all the students
stand still for a moment. After only a few days here in this
humidity it was already hard to conceive of scarves anymore, of mittens, creases and central heating. The lab jacket
looked like it might have an insulated lining.

He stood—the kind of man so big all around that when
Jane glanced behind him to his tutors, they appeared somehow inadequate, half-made. His hands hung down, wide as
separate beings, ridged and scrubbed pale. His face pulled
long, eyes slow as a bear's The only color in his face was
in his lips which seemed quite red, almost inflamed, tho
edges of a wound. You might at first want to smile if you
saw Professor Egren staring wide-eyed and bushy-browed at
a classroom, but you wouldn't want to if you saw Burnett.
You'd want to step back like he might need more space
than most people to breathe, you'd want to step back out
of the possible circle of his arm.

"Burn-out" was what the upper classes called him. Jane
had heard ten years ago he'd been a big name in orthopedic
surgery in the States, all the best hospitals, big money, es-
teem. Now he taught here, at Queen's. On the brochures
for the school they listed him and his credentials, the prizes
and publications, showed a picture of him from back then,
his wide confident smile, scrubbed hands held up in benediction, walking into the operating room, the nurses clustered small behind, following him anywhere.

Burnett ran his eyes slowly over the room, his mouth
shut, his hands slack by his hips, looking over the cadavers,
the instruments, the students. The tutors stood behind Burnett, three steps back. The class waited silent. Just before

he finished his inspection, his heavy head jerked to the side like someone had yanked fast on his hair. His expression did not change. He did not look embarrassed. He didn't look surprised. He pulled his head back up with deliberate patience, the way an adult acts round a child when he's losing his temper.

"Latin name for kneecap," he said, his voice very deep, echoing off the stone walls, his lips so slow and thick they seemed almost to trail behind the words.

There was a pause. The students waited. Most of them thought he would continue the sentence.

"Patella," Michael called from the middle of the room.

"Yes," Burnett said, "yes." He lowered his chin down slow, then back up, a glacier's nod. His red lips parted. "Correct."

All of them looked over in envy. Michael nodded quiet, agreeing with his right to be correct. It angered every one of his classmates. He glanced over at Jane, innocent even of pride. The last two nights some of them had studied more than they ever had before, out of determination, out of fury, out of fear. After a moment Jane smiled back at Michael, hungry. She wanted to be inside his skin.

"A simple question," said Burnett, "but one which every one of you should be able to answer. And you will. Learn every bone in the feet and legs by tomorrow. I will start testing. This lab will be your hardest class this year. You will learn over eight thousand new words of vocabulary. About the same number of words as if you were becoming fluent in a foreign language."

His head jerked fast to the side again. Jane realized it jerked into the position people held their heads in while they thought, pursing their lips.

He didn't speak until he'd pulled his head back up straight. "The most effective way we have found to teach about the human body here at Queen's is to go through it all three times. Each of you gets one new cadaver per semester. Each time we go through it in greater detail. The information is then reinforced after a significant interval, one of the best techniques for successful recall."

"You will have this cadaver for four months. It must remain in a recognizable state. Specimens deteriorate pretty quickly in this climate, even with formalin. Keep every exposed piece moist using the formalin bottle at your table. Spray every inch of it before you leave at the end of each class. If you don't do this, you will be trying to learn anatomy from something that looks like undifferentiated leather. Also, mold can grow." As he spoke he stood quite still. Jane kept waiting for him to make a gesture or expression to go with his words, but he stood with his face and hands settled as if he were waiting for a bus all by himself, like he was reading a speech into a phone.

"I will not abide practical jokes. One of the major lessons each of you should take away from this class is respect for the human body. I catch anyone taking some structure out of the room or throwing it at another student, I will flunk them. No warning. No forgiveness."

Structure, Jane thought.

"When searching for the correct location to cut in on, always find the nearby bony landmarks. Orient yourself. Change scalpel blades regularly, they get dull and can rip rather than cut. This lab room will be open twenty-four hours a day for studying. I encourage you to spend time here outside of class. Plan your studying well. This is not a course you can cram for.

"You will now pull on your examination gloves, open up a fresh scalpel and start with a ventral incision down the center line from the suprasternal notch to xiphoid process. In other words, this." He pressed one blunt fingernail to the scarf at the base of his neck, trailed it down to the middle of his chest. Held it there for a moment, watching them. "Continue to follow the instructions in exercise one of your lab book. My tutors and I will be around to help you. If you think you're going to faint, put the scalpel down before you do so. Don't fall on it."

There was a pause, then the students began to move, the busy crunkle of plastic being opened, gloves snapped on. The sheets were folded back with a slower rustle.

With the clear gloves on Jane barely recognized her own hands. They were like a stocking mask pulled over the face, distorting features and colors, her fingers gleaming dully plastic. She thought this was how she would change as a doctor, becoming hard and confident, unrecognizable, hairless like her father. She flexed her hands twice in front of herself, felt a little relief that the mannequin hands responded. She reached out to the body, paused even before she touched the sheet. The chill apparent, like the cold breath of the freezer.

She could remember seeing death up close once a long time ago, as a child, the actual process of death. She hadn't recognized it at the time. She'd found a baby bird on its side at the base of a maple tree in the backyard. It was a small bird, a chickadee or perhaps starling. Its beak was open, panting, its bright black eyes jerking all around. She carried it into the house and cupped it loosely in her hands until its eyes stopped moving and its body got stiff as feather-covered wire. When her mother told her this meant it had died, she didn't believe her, for she thought it must take a lot of energy to hold oneself rigid like that. The bird was playing a game like Statue, hoping she'd put it down discouraged, then it could flutter away, hide. It took her mother an hour of persuasion to get the body away from Jane's sweaty child hands and she only succeeded by promising to leave the bird where it could fly away if it woke up. She went upstairs with it and Jane sat downstairs for a long time, wondering if her mother was putting it on the window ledge or even higher, up on the roof so its mother could spot it easily. Jane heard the toilet flush and wondered where her mother had left the bird while she sat down upon the seat.

Jane inhaled, firmly grasped the bottom sheet and pulled it back. The color surprised her, the color of a body with the blood all drained out, the color of a body preserved in formalin. Dingy, like a body molded from congealed bacon fat, overlaid with the lightest hue of yellow.

So motionless. More motionless than in being asleep, or even being unconscious. No "being" in it at all, no verbs. It was a rubbery rock, a log, an inert thing. Even the skin was without the slightest variation in color or tone, no hairs standing up or muscles tense, slack. It looked fake, like plastic vomit. It wouldn't fool anyone.

Her hands continued to pull the sheet down as far as the thighs. A washcloth lay over the genitals, the lumps beneath male. Looking down at the cadaver's ribs, Jane unconsciously held her breath, waiting for it to exhale. Only when her lungs began to hurt did she realize what she had been doing.

She shook herself then, pulled back the upper sheet, uncovering the body as far as the chin. The arms folded over the rib cage had created the appearance of a bulging chest. Black plastic bags were tied over the hands and its head was wrapped in bandages like a mummy, exposing only the generic meat of rib cage, haunch and legs, similar to so many other animals. Aside from these coverings, the body lay limp and lewd as a plucked chicken. Although it was hard to tell with it lying down, it seemed short, five foot one or two. Each of the ribs was outlined with what had been hunger. She could have hefted the whole thing up in her arms.

Looking around with a sudden thought, Jane saw every revealed cadaver in the room was just as skinny, as skinny as the men in town. There was no way to tell race from the cadavers' greasy lack of color, not from the hidden facial features. This was how, she realized, the school got three separate cadavers for each student in class. If your children are hungry enough, how much could a dead relative cost? Three months worth of wages, half a year? Certainly less than two hundred American. The body of your husband, the body of your mother. She took her hands slow away from the sheet, rubbed them against her sides.

The other students had already begun, she noticed, cutting open, peeling back. There was the low murmur of the lab tutors pointing things out, directing. They smiled with encouragement. Burnett stood back, against the wall, his slow eyes watching it all.

"Great," she heard the tutors say, "yes." They spoke happy, their voices rising with enthusiasm. Her father would see nothing wrong with where the bodies came from. The students needed bodies, the Indonesians needed money. The autopsies had to be done on someone. At least this way the Indonesians benefitted too.

She forced herself to stand up straighter, exhaled, took her scalpel out of its foil wrapping. This was medicine, a tough field. The scalpel balanced heavy in her hand, mostly steel handle, a half-inch-long blade at the end. Curious, she tried its edge against her lab book. It cut so cleanly into the black cover she couldn't see the line afterward. She looked around one more time at the other bodies.

Placing a preparatory hand against the naked chest, she felt through her glove a rubbery cold, like touching a wet suit in the shape of a human body. She wondered how much of what she had until then thought of as the feel of the human body was simply the sensation of heat.

Directly beneath the skin stretched the hull of ribs, no extra weight here at all. She felt strange about the intimacy of the touch, like a lover, the nipple peeking out between her fingers. She would never touch a stranger like this if he were alive, wearing just a washcloth. She pointed the scalpel down toward the collarbone, now in the position of threat, a robber. She noted the point of her blade vibrated above the skin, light and constant as the needle on a lie detector test.

Her image of herself as a doctor had always been of her healing, not cutting. She'd imagined herself from behind, winding clean bandages around a patient's arm, covering up the ugliness of a wound with white smooth linen. Her head bent down in concentration, her shoulders slumped low with exhaustion. She saw herself spooning soup into another's needy lips, the thin tongue rolling out, trembling and weak. She'd never minded the thought of long hours, of waiting on others, of working with bodily excretions. She'd thought before she had arrived on this island her problem would be giving injections, sliding that long pin in through the dimpled point of skin.

In fifth grade she'd once tried removing a splinter from a classmate's hand. The girl had gotten it from running her hand along the bottom of her chair; she'd turned to Jane because she was closest. It was lodged in the meat of the palm. Jane had tried, no one could say she hadn't, but each time she managed to grasp the end between her nails and started to pull, the girl had winced and Jane found herself letting go. The area got redder and redder from her fingering. By the time the teacher had been called over, he'd had to use a needle to tease open the swollen flesh and pull out the wood. The girl had cried so hard, her head bent, snot drooping down from her nose with each exhale, that the teacher announced in frustration it was all Jane's fault for not pulling the piece out immediately.

Jane didn't think she had waited that long, her scalpel against the chest. She thought she just stood there for a moment, suitably solemn, pausing before starting her chosen craft.

Several times she pictured her father and her blade pushed close enough to touch the skin.

Burnett stepped in beside her, looking down at her unstained gloves. Her head fluttered up. All around her she saw the open chest plates, the white yaw of ribs. She heard the handsaw rasping, the crack of bones.

"Commence cutting," he said. She looked up to his face a full head above her own. His red lips parted, waiting.

She clenched her hand tighter on the scalpel, pushed the blade down anew, up to the boundary of skin. Paused there, her fingers trembled, the point of a dowser, sensing something below.

"Cut," he clipped out.

She looked up at him helpless.

"Okay," he said, more gently now, and picked up her hand. At first she thought it was to offer consolation, to give her strength. She didn't struggle. His hands were so big they could afford to give her strength. They enfolded her fist completely, the scalpel in the center.

He moved her hand toward the body.

She realized his intent. Now she struggled. Her feet slid about on the wet floor, she made a huh-huh noise. She could not even slow their descent.

Together their hands slapped into the chest, punctured the skin, ripped down and across. A rasp like a zipper. She closed her eyes for the spurting blood. It didn't come. They slashed again, the belly. The skin's dry lips parted in exhaustion. Two mouths gaping open, then three.

He stopped. Keeping her hand in his, the clasp of a friend. His red lips slightly open, breathing. She saw in his expression the barrier of skin meant nothing to him, dead or alive. His eyes turned to her calmly. He could cut into this body all day long. He could slice into her just as easy. Twisting her hand back in against her gut or face. His expression would stay the same. She felt that as distinctly as the flat pressure of his overgrown fingers. She took one step back along the leash of her arm. She was so surprised by all this.

"Got it?" he asked and let go of her. The scalpel fell from

her hand to clatter on the tiles. She could not turn her eyes from him. His head twitched to the side.

"Doctors," he said, "cut flesh."

He walked on to another student.

Almost immediately her face began to knuckle in, shuddering. She looked around, astounded, at the white walls, the opened bodies, the pale faces of staring classmates. She slid right down behind her table, pushed her face into her hands, trying to hide. Expecting her own fingers, her mouth touched the wet plastic of her gloves. She rubbed her lips off fast on her shoulder, bit her arm to keep quiet. The rest of the students bent their heads back down, worked on, silently. No one came over to help her. No one spoke to her. Her breath rasped harsh through her nose. All around her she heard regular snipping and watched pieces fall to the ground. She covered even her head, bit her knee until her mouth rubbed as dry against her coveralls as more fabric.

He walked by. She saw his shoes, unmistakable, huge. Leather businessman's shoes even on this isle. They clicked forward, heel then toe, heel then toe, the weight of power, the leather of confidence. The circle of the shark. Her head turned to follow them.

"Cut," she heard him whisper above her. And he paced away.

She pushed up immediately, stood swaying, flooded with fear. Her hands shook. Her shoulders still jerked. The body lay gray and slashed. She saw one cut ran through its neck, the dry severed straw of its jugular, the yellow globs of fat, the white strings of tendons. She scanned about for him. He'd stopped in the aisle four tables away, his oversized face turning slow toward her. Her breath came out in a pant. She grabbed the scalpel, clutched it like a dagger and stuck it as fast as she could into the dip of the neck. A moment of tension, then through.

So easy, so smooth. She stared down at the knife. Like finding a pocket made especially for the blade.

She blinked down at the instructions on the lab handout. One hand held the scalpel upright inside the neck. She began to cut quickly, trying not to think, not to see, not to smell, just hurry before he came back. She wiped her tears off as she went on the shoulder of her coverall, staring down at her alien hands.

Afterward it was lunchtime. She scrubbed her hands for five straight minutes. The smell of formalin still lingered, as though it had seeped down into her flesh, the way it had seeped into the cadaver. From the washing, her fingers were wrinkled and pale.

The lunch was creamed corn shipped to the island in cans, sliced beef under a congealing sauce, a slop of rehydrated potatoes. Few first-year students even tried eating, most silent, drinking soda, some giddy with jokes. Jane sat down, uncomfortable, in the seat next to Marlene. Marlene didn't talk, leaned low on an elbow to stir the food round and round on her plate into one uniform glop, nothing distinguishable. Then she shovelled the food in fast, determined.

Near the end of the lunch hour, Jane tentatively levered a bite off the meat. It looked gray. She placed it flaccid in her mouth. As she pulled the fork away she smelled formalin. She spat the meat out fast into her napkin, dry-heaving beside the table for a moment, kept her face turned from the others.

Drank water instead.

Ten

~~

Of the thirty-four students remaining in Jane's class, four left—James Dow, Christina Taut, Sandy Steinwitz and Charles Benning—on the school plane on Sunday evening at the end of the third week. No one went down to the landing strip to see them off. Once they'd announced the decision to go, people ignored them as though they had never existed, including Dana, James's girlfriend of the last two weeks. Still, they all knew when the plane left. Every student heard the plane leave, the whir of its engines as it strained to rise. The vibration became toylike with distance as it circled once. Then the silence settled in.

The remaining first-year students didn't even pull their heads up from their books. They continued to study as they had been studying now for almost three weeks, day and night, between classes. They had already fallen into the schedule the fourth-year students had maintained for years. During the day they studied in their bungalows or at The Bar, near a fan or in the breeze from the sea. At night, after sunset, they moved to the library. The school had only one generator. The main one had broken. The library and autopsy lab were the only places with decent lighting. Lights elsewhere on campus glowed weak as dying flashlights. If a student tried to read near one, a headache rose, flooding out slow from the eyes. The school apologized for the inconvenience. It had applied for another generator to be imported; the Indonesian government was considering.

Meanwhile each night the students studied together, at their desks, in the library, in sight of each other. The library's study area was in the shape of an amphitheater, no interior walls, the desks on wide ascending levels round a central stage where announcements were made, demonstrations sometimes given. Every student was assigned a desk, the first-year students at the bottom, then each class going up, alphabetical order, so Jane sat on the lowest row, only five people below her in the alphabet, feeling, on the back of her head, the eyes of all the rows above her, feeling them watch her scribble notes or turn the page back and then forward. Above her were the noises of paper riffling and highlighters squeaking, cards flipping and questions whispered.

Above the central stage, a ten-foot-wide plastic cross section of the large intestine turned in the breeze of the fans, along with a mobile of chemical compounds. A human skeleton swayed high above Jane's head. From this angle she could see most clearly the separate wired bones of the skeleton's feet, above them the hollows of the eye sockets, dark and unblinking. The teachers said the library had been designed to increase camaraderie, the sharing of support and knowledge, the communal experience.

Studying with concentration and jittery movements, the students guzzled iced coffee and caffeinated sodas, scrubbed their brows, turned the pages. Even with the twenty-foot-tall windows open to the breeze, even with the ceiling fans constantly turning, the place still smelled rank, like a high-school locker room. The slow steps of the tutors worked their way down the rows visiting one student after another.

The tutors had all graduated from good medical schools in the States, Stanford and Cornell; they'd taken this year off before their residency in order to tutor here. They got paid a base salary plus extra money for each assigned student who passed a class. There were no boarding expenses. These tutors still had four to seven years of low-paid residency and internship stretching out before them. They weren't from wealthy families. At Queen's they got paid well.

The tutors were kind, encouraging, in their middle twenties, both male and female. Cheerleaders. They offered different ways of remembering the information, smiled wide each time a student got the answer right, declared the student to be quite smart. If, as the hours passed, the student didn't seem motivated enough, the tutor mentioned the name of a teacher casually, Burnett or Egren. The student worked, renewed.

Every few hours a teacher made an appearance at the library, walking down between the desks, scanning the rows of bent heads for someone to quiz. It didn't matter what time of day or night, seven in the evening, sometimes two in the morning.

That night after the four students left, Egren dropped by the library, about eleven-thirty. The students stiffened one by one as they caught sight of his slow patrol, his loose smile. Some stared back openmouthed and trapped, others crouched over their books, avoiding eye contact. Neither response seemed to work in deflecting Egren. He paused before a desk chosen for a reason no one could ever understand. Good student, bad student, it didn't matter. Everyone listened to Egren's first question above the hum of the fans. Some turned back to their books, others watched over the edges of their desks. Either way, they listened. The chosen student sitting up straight, the heat rising slow up the neck, the student prefacing each answer with "Sir." They had learned their manners.

The teachers were all male, in their fifties: Burnett, Egren, Krakow, and Messen. They had been educated during a time when authority was all, when medicine was unquestioned.

If the chosen student answered a few of Egren's questions correctly, Egren nodded, pleased. "Very good," he would say, his voice loud enough for them all. He always had his favorites. All the teachers did. "Impressive. Keep this up, you might just transfer out of here." The rest of the students looked over. "Back to the States. Land of air conditioners and MTV." He made the gesture of clicking an invisible switch, hummed low in his throat the rising vibration of an air conditioner, held his face close to it, smiled and shook out his hair.

That Sunday night, Egren stopped in front of Keefer. He'd been picking on Keefer the whole time Jane had been here. Each time Egren asked harder and harder questions, leaning in closer, until Keefer couldn't answer one, either through ignorance or an inability to get the words out through his stutter. Just at the sight of Egren walking down a path or checking his mail, Keefer's Adam's apple started jumping in his thin throat.

That Sunday the students remaining on the island were a little quieter in the hours after the plane, a little more still. They sat in front of their books heavy, leafing pages back and forth. Into that silence, at Egren's second question, Keefer began to yell back.

"Hey, fuck you," he yelled, his voice tight. Jane looked up from three rows down. She had been pretending to study, she had been trying to study. Keefer threw his skinny hands out in gestures that looked a little like sideways punches. "How am I supposed to st-st-st. Study when you're always asking me these questions?"

Jane thought she saw a smile flicker across Egren's lips. He inhaled slow and full, and then yelled back. He yelled back much louder than Keefer.

"First off, Mister Keefer Christiane, don't swear at your professors. Do not say Fuck or Shit or Asshole to any of us or within our hearing again. No matter who your daddy is." Egren's voice boomed out, loud and full, his neck already red with the volume.

Keefer yelled back. "Well, if you started acting like a professor maybe I wouldn't s-s-s . . ." Keefer's voice was shrill, tight in the throat.

Egren kicked Keefer's desk, a sort of soccer kick, powerful, one leg back, arms up for balance, the bark of wood, the lid of the desk jumped up. Keefer jerked to the side like he was the one kicked. "Secondly, Keefer," screamed Egren, taking two fast steps around the desk so he stood with his face directly over Keefer's. Keefer jerked his chin into his neck, his eyes skipping side to side. "I'm not taking up that much time. I'd say not more than ten minutes a day. What do you say, Christiane?"

"You're h-h-h . . ." Through the spasming of his lips, Keefer exhaled hard. Jane thought this could be the start of him crying. She looked down at her books, away from his bare face, away from his open mouth. It was too painful to watch. She listened for another exhale. It wasn't that she wished she could take his place—she was much too scared of Egren for that—but this was unfair. A lot of the others were worse students than Keefer. With many of the answers he gave to Egren, she hadn't even learned the vocabulary yet. She believed Egren preferred to argue with Keefer because of his stutter, because he thought him weak.

"Christiane, ten minutes? Fifteen? What would you guess? Keefer?" All the teachers had this habit of using the students' names again and again, repeating them in the spaces between their words. Jabbing at the name like a button.

"How about you nod, Keefer, you just nod when I say the number you think. Fifteen minutes, twenty?"

Jane heard Egren inhale then, a wet close sound. "I'll take that as a yes. Fine, if you are awake sixteen hours a day, twenty minutes is what? Less than one fortieth of your day, Keefer. Probably less time than you use in the bathroom. More than enough time remains for you to learn how your mitochondria produces all that energy you so blithely waste. The Krebs cycle, Christiane. Name the two types of hydrogen carriers."

Jane glanced from the edges of her eyes at Egren. Every muscle and blood vessel in Egren's face was bloated with purpose, his mouth pursed.

There was a long pause.

"N.A.D. and . . ." Keefer's voice began, quieter than before. Jane clenched her hands. "N.A D. and . . ." His voice was muffled a bit, like his head might be tilted down, facing the desk. Jane still didn't look at him. ". . . G.D.P."

"Wrong," Egren bellowed out. "Wrong."

"Calder," Egren called, clear and strong. Sarah Calder was the would-be actress he'd yelled at during the first class. She sat four desks away from Jane. She jumped at her name, sat still then, breathing fast out her mouth. "Sarah, what's the answer?"

There was a pause. Sarah looked around at the desks near her, at the people's faces. "N.A.D. and F.A.D., sir?" she replied uncertainly.

"Yes," whispered Egren into the silence after her voice. "Yes." His voice abruptly quiet, hoarse with pleasure.

Sarah blinked twice.

"You are turning out to be so good at this," whispered Egren to her, clear enough for them all.

Sarah smiled hesitant up at his face.

Egren looked around now at all of them. They were all watching, no longer pretending otherwise. They knew it wouldn't end here. Egren smiled. His lips wet. "Calder, does Christiane know what he is doing? Does he?" He inhaled again. Jane thought she never heard him exhale while he was yelling at a student. He just inhaled over and over again, the air moving wet in through his teeth. He must get bigger and bigger. He must gain in height. "Would you say he is a good student?"

Sarah's smile faded, her eyes flickered, to the left, to the right. Jane got the feeling her eyes were not really focused on anyone, on anything. Glossy with panic, her eyes were focused instead on the air about two feet in front of her, blind to everything outside her head. The whole school watched, their heads leaning forward over their desks like they were driving by a twisted car.

"Maybe," she tried out, tentative.

"What?" yelled Egren.

"No?" she said more quietly.

"Can't hear you," called Egren. "Need the complete sentence, the full name. Nice and loud." He paused. "Make it loud."

"Please," she whispered, "please."

"Calder," Egren warned.

She tightened her jaw. "No," she bellowed, her voice ragged at first, then gaining in strength, with frustration, with anger. "Keefer Christiane is not a good student."

After that there was silence. Keefer said nothing; out of the corner of her eye Jane didn't see him even move. Sarah shut her mouth slowly. Neither of them looked at each other. The teachers tried to foster competition. After a quiz they sometimes read off the students' names and ranks, reminded everyone the bottom four or five students would probably flunk the boards. The teachers pointed out the sixth student, asked the person to stand up, said this was their competition.

Egren nodded. Looking around slow at each one of them to make sure his work was done. He strolled down the aisle to the exit, his breathing evening out. His face losing its redness. He pulled a candy bar out of his pocket just before he opened the door, surveyed them all one last time, the silence, their faces. His slack smile. He ripped the wrapping open and backed out with his shoulders. The door swung closed behind him.

No one looked at each other. They all bent their heads back down over their books. A lot of the first-year students flipped to the section on the Krebs cycle and studied.

Jane watched these displays hard, noted each moment of fear, noted the sweat and shivering eyes, the trembling. She took comfort in the students' terror. Still, once the teachers were gone, the others calmed down quickly.

Keefer got up, left out a door on the opposite side of the library from the one Egren had exited through. Three of the older students cracked a few jokes, laughed harder than necessary. Others put their heads down for a moment, dozed, mouths open and slack against their papers. When Keefer came back fifteen minutes later, his skin had lost its mottled heat, his Adam's apple stilled. He sat back down in front of his books, sighed, scrubbed his head and turned the page, his hand shaking only a little, his thin back hunched in its determination.

Jane sat up straight in her chair, never talked to another unless they talked to her first—which they didn't do all that much for she looked so serious while studying. She thought everyone was disgusted with her because of what had happened during the first autopsy class. She thought somehow she had shamed herself more than Sarah Calder, more than Keefer or any of the others. She sweated constantly, even when the teachers were away, even when they weren't yelling. Sweating from the armpits, along the creases of her belly, sweat dripped slow down her back under the weight of her hair. In the humidity it stayed on her skin. She smelled, sharp and rancid, different than she'd ever smelled before. Even when she first sat up in bed, she could smell it insidious and revealing. She took two showers a day, three. Her skin was always damp from a shower or perspiration, her hair always wet. Fear like a constant itch across her body.

Everyone else seemed able to eat. They lined up jostling for the cafeteria food. The food had not changed at all for being on the other side of the world, in another culture. If anything the meals were more processed and bland, having had to travel all the way here: tuna melts, canned peaches, peas cooked to the color of granite, hot dogs, french fries, limp salad bars. The students ate hungry and fast, drank lots of water. Some people ate a fourth meal later, at The Bar, eating mechanically, almost without hunger, looking sullenly over their books. At the cafeteria Jane lined up for food dutifully, at the table examined the offerings with confusion, nudged them around her plate in hopes of spotting something appetizing. She put small chunks in her mouth when her classmates were watching, smiled wide around at the table, hoped she might remember hunger. The food felt like paste in her mouth, lumpy and thick. She chewed. She chewed so long she never actually had to swallow. She drank lots of water and fruit juice.

And at night she could only assume everyone else was sleeping.

Each evening in the library, across the dish of the amphitheater, Jane watched the students visit one another, the bodies leaning in, everyone's relationships there for all to see. Perhaps only the fourth-year students had a complete view, but everyone had a good view. Becks Ripling, a third-year student, visited Randy Nally, a first-yearer, at least three times each evening. Jane guessed Chris Martell started sleeping with Ned Trufow sometime during the first week. The two of them sat quite close, studying anatomy, knees touching. Ned picked up a lock of Chris's hair for her attention. Jane's eyes followed the movement of Ned's hand, up to Chris's hair, touching, moving back. Jane's mouth rolled silently round the syllables of the pelvic bones. Ilium, Ischium, Pubis, moved her lips, repeating the words.

Marlene was also on the very bottom row. Several male students visited her each evening for advice, to settle a medical question or to test her with flip cards. She yawned and stretched, her body pushing tight against her clothes. She talked with whoever it was, leaning back in her chair, tracing the V of her shirt with her fingertips. The man leaned forward, watching her with the same intensity Jane thought a hunter would use when he swung the gun up to his eye. Marlene snorted, amused, ran her knuckles up the hair on his calf, tugged on the end of his shorts.

Jane knew, while her mother's flirting was a bluff, this was real. Marlene watched the man, her eyes lingering and lidded. She had been born a New York City Jew but she was the color of the sands of the Middle East, blond-brown in her eyes and skin and hair. There were subtle gradations of color and sheen that changed in the light and then the shade. A few times, when Marlene was tired, she looked just like any other thin woman, her skin flat brown as clay, but most times the gold in her eyes or hair flickered and Jane had to stare. It helped Jane forgive Marlene her rudeness. It made the men crave her rudeness, to have it turned on them, her eyes regarding them alone.

The only times Jane had seen Marlene faded were down at the bungalow. Three times so far, in the morning Marlene had walked out of her room, head-down to the bathroom, breathing heavy and slow through her nose. Jane had stopped trying to say anything cheerful to Marlene at these points. Marlene had never bothered to respond to these comments, and Jane herself was tired now, having a harder time remembering that lighthearted inflection. Instead while Marlene was in the bathroom Jane sliced some fresh fruit into a bowl: kiwis, an orange, maybe part of a pineapple. She tried to eat a bite herself, holding a piece wet and pulpy in her mouth, swallowing with big gulps of water.

Left the rest for Marlene. Although Marlene never thanked Jane for the fruit, she also didn't make fun of Jane for it. And Jane noticed when she returned in the afternoon, most of the fruit was gone.

At the library Trent visited Marlene the most of all the men. He was the man Jane had seen the first day in The Bar pushing his way in next to Marlene. He stood tall and angular, walked with a certain choppy grace, the way a young Doberman walks, big-boned and swinging, like his body was built for another speed than walking, like his bones might pop out of his skin. He had black hair brushed back from his face, falling thick and curly to the base of his shoulder blades. He never seemed to blink, had the habit of tilting his head to the side to look at you, his eyes wide open as the stare from a bird, as from an alien intelligence. He watched you, just watching, not understanding at some point he was supposed to turn away.

When Trent talked to Marlene he whispered, his voice so low it wasn't even a voice, merely air drifting through lips moving as though they spoke. Marlene acted differently with him, leaned close to catch his words, not sitting back and observing. He lounged on her desk, sprawled across it, whispered something, laughing, the cartilage in his neck silently jerking. She laughed too, not a quiet giggle, but an exuberant haw-haw, slapped her hand down on his bare thigh. Didn't care that her laugh broke through the library's muted silence.

"Fuck," Jane heard her harsh whisper. "Holy shit." Jane glanced around the library, up the bowl of desks, every face in the building turned down toward Marlene.

As regular as a tide, once a night at the library, Michael visited Jane. "Would you mind quizzing me?" he asked, handing her a diagram of membrane transport at the cellular level. He got every one of the questions right. He tested her in turn. When she got one wrong (which she did invariably), he thought up a simple way to remember the information, or a visual way to explain it to her. Then he tested her again. She worked hard not to disappoint him. In his world, wrong answers were a cloud rolling across the straightforward sunshine of hard work. His confident smile faded in confusion.

When he finished testing her she thanked him repeatedly. She knew from the way she acted around him, her parents would appreciate him. With him, she smiled exactly the same as she did with her parents.

"I've also learned," he added, filled with the love of his own knowledge, "of a mnemonic for the bones of the hand."

"Yes," she said and, "really."

"Silly Lucky Tim Peels TNT," he started, speaking seriously, waiting for her to repeat after him before continuing. He pointed out the location of each bone on his own hand, tracing the outlines on his fingers, his palm, making slow repetitive motions to show each bone's range. She watched his hands. Compared to all his precise height, they seemed small, the plump milky fingers of a child. The kind of hands, she thought, that had never explored their own limits. She wanted those hands, to carry them around with her in her book bag, to fall asleep with each night soft against her face, the dusty skin of marshmallows. She listened to him talk, her mouth slightly open. She found here her mouth frequently hung open. Each time she noticed, she shut it. She thought it might be the lack of sleep, or the heat making her mouth open in a dog's pant.

When a teacher asked Michael a question in the library or in class, Michael thought it through slowly, answered correctly, nodded afterward, not even cocky. Just certain. She thought if he were in a burning skyscraper he would step smoothly down the stairs, following the ordained exit route, obediently holding on to the banister. She could not imagine why he was here at this school.

Michael quizzed her on the bones of the hands, the

makeup of a cell's cytoskeleton, the action potential of neu-
rons. Midterms, he said, were only twenty-six days away.
He told her the count every day. She imagined once it got
down to a week he would switch to hours. She stared down
at his legs, hairless and smooth, curving with muscles he'd
never used to any extreme. He'd grown up in Kansas, relative of the family that owned Singer Sewing Machines.

"Jane," he asked again, "did you hear me? What makes
up a myelin sheath?"

Startled, she looked up at him. His hair was smooth as a
mathematical formula. It was the kind of straight hair that
would not change in any way going from the humid heat
of this island to the dry Arctic. The pale line of the part
was drawn straight as morality down the center, the hair
lying neat on either side.

"A Schwann cell," she answered. He nodded. Sitting at
the desk in the library, near him, she answered many of
his questions correctly. It seemed easier to do so in his aura
of certainty. But if one of the teachers went by, she found
herself watching, the slide of her eyes following the slow
prowl, her mouth open. The answer to Michael's question
gone from her mind.

She didn't think Michael was romantically interested in
her. This was not the animal leaning of Marlene and Trent.
She thought he must just think she was a serious student
because of the steady tilt of her head over her books. Or
maybe he felt sorry for her from the episode in Burnett's
class, was trying to protect her from the same thing happening again. Maybe such extreme embarrassment, even another person's, really bothered him. The abasement of
another's soul.

She liked his questions. She liked being around him. He
was a good student. He didn't get in trouble, was not angry
or cynical. He never swore. She wanted so to be him. Her
parents would be proud. She was hungry to be associated
with him in any way.

*   *   *

Time passed differently here, on this island. At the library some nights she found herself scanning row after row of bent heads. Already she knew every name, most gestures and speech patterns, the clothing commonly worn by each of the one hundred other students. With the students in her class she also knew the individual smells of their sweat, what they tended to eat and how quickly, mouths left open or not.

When Jane thought about it, it felt more like she had been here for three months than three weeks. Her class was together so much of the time, in the classroom, in the lab, in the library. Everything was so intense. It was like being in camp as a kid, telling ghost stories late at night to the same people you jostled around with on horses during the day, the same ones you brushed your teeth with in the morning. Three weeks felt like forever, your cabin mates becoming every one of your friends, acquaintances, your whole family. Your counselors becoming every authority figure. You could remember no other life.

Every night the whole school studied together at the library, by the light of just that one generator. Keefer told her the teachers wanted it that way, planned it that way, to keep the students all together. To allow them to work on the students even at night.

Jane walked over sometimes to Keefer's house in the afternoon, when she could not study anymore, when she found herself in her bedroom staring out at the sea for twenty minutes at a time, the open book in front of her. She walked over then to Keefer's for the exercise, to wake up and sit beside him on the dock. To watch Jonah circle smooth and certain as the planet's spin.

Jane noticed how quickly she got more used to the shark, to seeing it, to watching it get fed. It was like learning to drive, learning to watch the road slide by at seventy miles per hour, learning to hold on to her life with just one slack hand. Now she sometimes sat on the edge of the dock as Keefer did, cross-legged, the ends of her bent knees hanging out, above water. She needed to feel awake, to think clearly. Her heart beat faster, her breath came uneven. Jonah circled, gliding closer, its black eyes ranging over her, her knees, the sky above. When it was still three or four feet away she jerked her knees back. She jerked her whole body back, abrupt and scared, breathing fast, watching Jonah sway toward her.

Halfway through the third week, she stayed still while it swam by. She hadn't meant to. She simply hadn't remembered to be scared, hadn't remembered she existed. Her mouth open, her head heavy, the sun pressing on her shoulders. The names of the segmental bronchi scrolled through her head like across the screen of a computer. *Apical, Anterior, Medial Basal.* The words were in a small font, she noticed, written out in cursive. Jonah came closer. Her face turned toward it. She heard the slight burble of water round its fin, a lackluster drinking fountain. She smelled the salt from its skin. *Posterior Basal, Lateral.* She could feel her heart beating faster in her chest, a distant unreal throb. Such an unlikely structure, this restless noisy machine in her warm and silent chest. Staring down at the shark, she watched it pass within eight inches of her knees, within easy reach of her hand.

Keefer said the generator had been broken for as long as he'd been here.

Eleven

"Today we will start by working on the female mammary glands," announced Burnett, looking around the classroom. He examined the stretched-out cadavers just as much as the standing students. When his eyes reached Jane, he watched her for a while. His slow eyes fixed on her face, his red mouth moving round his words. She stared back, unable to look away. Her head hurt.

"If you don't have a female cadaver," Burnett continued, "pair up with another student who does. You will return the favor when it comes to the male anatomy. Both students make sure they palpate and cut equally. Start."

As soon as he said, "Start," Jane shook her head, looked around with alarm, the students pairing up with their friends.

"Psst," Jane heard behind her. "Hey. Doris. Come on over."

Jane turned around to see Marlene gesturing her over with her scalpel.

When Jane stepped hesitantly over, Marlene added, "I'm not watching no man palpate nothing but my own breasts in front of me." She brushed her hair back with her gloved hand. "Let's get to it," she said. "I want to catch a swim before Histology." Marlene pulled back the sheet from the stomach to the shoulder.

Marlene's cadaver was of a woman older than Jane's corpse, its thin flesh sagged in over its ribs and stomach leaving the bones even more obvious. The outline of the jutting hip bones beneath a sheet seemed strangely sexual. The left breast had already been removed. It lay in a plastic bag by the feet. In the hole where the breast had been, the front of the ribs was missing, as well as the lung and heart. Inside, just the smooth back of ribs curved like the hull of a canoe. Marlene squirted the body and the hole with the formalin bottle until everything glistened.

Jane closed her eyes against the smell, against the spray, breathed through her mouth, imagined her tongue and throat pickled, rubbery as the cadaver's. Formalin wasn't like other smells. She couldn't seem to get used to it, couldn't get it to fade into the background. Instead it seemed to get stronger each day, until by now she could almost see it when she walked into the lab, a yellow haze shimmering under the bright lights, like heat or a chemical smog. Inside the body she could almost feel it, the greasy yellow fat. Everything in the room was marked by it, finger smears on steel surfaces, the tables, the instruments, the sinks. She couldn't get the smell off her skin, none of them could. They had all tried washing until their hands were raw, tried showering, using perfume and different soaps. The smell still seemed to ooze from their pores.

A week ago Burpie Loomer had discovered rubbing his hands with mint-scented shaving cream worked, if not to completely erase the formalin, at least to disguise it. Within two days of the discovery the school store had sold out of shaving cream, even the kinds without the minty smell. The school ordered more. Meanwhile the male students used soap and hot water to shave. They appeared in school with stubble and facial cuts. Each cut they cleaned with alcohol as soon as it happened. The tropics were not like temperate climes. Here, a simple grazing of the skin could become infected, could lead to gangrene, to sepsis. Every student knew about Carrington Rault, a fourth-year student who had lost her middle finger last year to chewing on her cuticle. Jane had seen for herself the airy gap in Carrington's hand when she reached for the lunch tray.

On the right side of Marlene's cadaver a skinny dug hung, still affixed in the normal way to the rest of the chest. For the first few classes a lot of the male students had seemed amazed by the breasts, glanced up from the stretched-out cadavers to the outline of the female students' chests. They hadn't realized what women's breasts *could* look like, drained of blood and cold as gristle, drooping flat as socks. It surprised the women too. Lately, each time Jane unhooked her bra for the shower, she found herself looking down her front a little from the side, a little hesitant. At the sight of her own breasts, she always stared for a moment at the pinkness of her nipples, a color that had begun to seem unnatural to her.

By now, though, for most of them, the cadavers bothered them a lot less. Marlene reached for the cadaver's breast. Matter-of-factly, she pushed the breast up from hanging off the side to more over the ribs. She began palpating the nipple, then the ducts underneath.

"Feels like rubber over some meat," she said. "Some bumps in there." She unconsciously moved the tips of her fingers in circles like she was doing a breast exam, checking for cancer in a cadaver. She looked directly down at the breast while she probed. "Huh." When she finished, she cupped her own breast for a second through the coverall, rolled its flesh between her fingers. "Huh," she said.

Jane turned away in embarrassment, found herself staring right into the eyes of Trent, three tables away. His tilted head, hair falling to his shoulders, his bared clean teeth. He

watched her, unblinking. She turned away, forced herself
not to check back to see if he was still watching.

It was Jane's turn. She touched the woman's breast.
There was a spot near the nipple that had dried out to the
texture of cardboard, there was the sensation of cold. She
looked up, in the general direction of the ceiling, as she did
during gynecological exams to give the doctor more privacy
between her legs.

After a moment she heard the slow pace of Burnett's
heels approaching, along the wall behind her. Like a dog,
she could recognize his step by now, the exact click-clack
of his toes. She began to breathe out her mouth, shallow
and rapid. She didn't know any longer what was between
her fingers. Her only thought was to keep her hand moving
so he might not pay attention to her.

Burnett stepped in close behind her. She could see only
part of his leg and the bulge of his wide hand within his
pants pocket.

"Why don't you start the incisions?" He spoke from just
above her head. "Acromion to the xiphisternal junction. Go
around the nipple. Reflect the skin flap up."

She did not look at him. Reached for the scalpel and made
the cut fast. She began to peel the skin off the breast by
running the end of the scalpel's handle back and forth beneath the skin, breaking the connective tissue and tugging
the skin up a little further each time. He still stood behind
her, did not move away. She could hear him breathe down
on her. She did not change her speed, did not look up, slid
the handle back and forth beneath the skin. Back and forth.
She tried to hide her fear.

"Sometimes," he said from so very close, his breath warm
against the back of her ear, "sometimes fingers are the best
instrument. More flexible. Less liable to puncture."

Involuntarily Jane looked up, only as far as his red lips,
then back down. She put the scalpel down quickly. She slid
her finger under the skin instead, feeling the fibers break-

ing, feeling the wet surfaces separating. She breathed shallow out her mouth. Head down, watching the outline of her finger move back and forth under the skin of this woman's breast.

After a long moment she saw his leg step back, heard the click-clack of his shoes walking away.

She exhaled.

Marlene touched her once on the elbow. Just a slight touch, with a finger and a thumb. Jane noticed then she was pulling so hard on the skin, the whole breast was stretched up toward her, the skin to the point of ripping. She forced her fingers to let go. She had an image of Burnett holding a scalpel bright in his hand.

She looked up for him, to check his location, the direction of his attention, his back a wide door walking away.

"It's okay, honey," whispered Marlene, "it's okay."

DAY TWENTY-NINE

Jane lay down on her bed at midnight, hot and rumpled across the sheets. She scooped her hair away from her, laying it like a separate being across the pillow above her. Stretched out below it, she tried not to touch it or her own skin, spreading even her fingers away from each other, kicking the sheet down to the base of the bed, hiking her nightgown up diaperlike between her legs. Even with the knowledge that the bedroom door was closed, she wasn't able to sleep nude and spread out on the bed. She kept feeling someone was watching her, from the window or the silently opened door. She would wake repeatedly, have to sit up and look all around. In her cotton nightgown, she sweated slow and thorough.

All evening at the library her eyes had hurt from lack of sleep, her head drooping, her mouth slack as she studied. Now, in bed, she was abruptly wide-awake. Irritated, she ran one hand under her hair and scratched her head. Beneath her hair, her scalp felt moist and hot as in a body cavity. On this island there were no reflections in her hair's smooth surface anymore. In this humidity it curled wide and turbulent, rising high above her shoulders. She had to cup her curls back to peer out, the opposite of how she'd acted in Connecticut.

She ran one hand over her collarbone, under the edge of her nightgown to her sticky breast. She lay there with her hand against her flesh so she could feel her soft unmarred skin, its heat, the ribs' continued rise and fall. Reassuring.

Waiting for sleep, she tried to remember feeling cold during the winter at home, curled up tight under many blankets, the clean sheets against her cheek. She remembered as a child tugging the weight of her snowsuit on one leg at a time, waddling outside into the snow, clumsy as an astronaut in all her layers of clothing. The red bracelet of skin between her mittens and sleeves. She remembered breaking off icicles and sliding their surprising chill into the heat of her mouth.

She flopped back in the snow, seeing her breath rise cloudlike and regular above her. Swiped her scratchy nylon limbs back and forth to make a snow angel. Lying there still afterward. Such silence. Not even the wind moved. Her eyes closed. Feeling darkness come to her lids one flake at a time.

A mosquito landed on her face.

She slapped at it, could not tell if she got it, wiped at her sticky skin. She waited impatient for sleep again, listening for the mosquito's buzz. Here the noises as well as the heat bothered her. A lot of the noises she could identify, the waves, the birds, the monkeys, but behind them something else shrilled, rhythmic as the throb of a wound, sometimes rising up in volume until it whirred bright as a dentist's drill.

Jane never figured out what made this noise: insect, bird

or frog. Whatever it was, there had to be a lot of them, they had to be everywhere. At dusk once, driving to the library, she'd parked her moped and hesitantly walked into the undergrowth, toward the loudest swelling of sound, hoping to find the culprits sitting out brazenly on leaves, throats swollen with noise, but wherever she stepped, cautiously watching for snakes and spiders, a circle ten feet wide of silence moved with her like a gracious dance partner, while behind her the noise started up again. The jungle leaned in over her shoulder, watching. In the distance something hooted. She looked back over her shoulder after twenty steps and the road had disappeared in the underbrush. Only jungle surrounded her as far as she could see. She beat her way back to the path hurriedly, sweating more.

For a little while she slept, dreaming she stood back at home in Connecticut on the wide marble terrace by the front door. She could smell the sweet pine of the shrubs, hear the TV. She stepped closer to see the shadow of someone moving away down the carpeted hall, but when she reached for her key, she found her pocket strangely hot. She reached in further. The heat became painful. Struggling for the key, her hand began to melt. The key slippery now with grease, the nubs of her fingers awkward.

She woke, her head jerking, her breath startled. A pack of dogs snarled nearby. The dogs fought and howled every night, the wind bringing distant cries to her from other parts of the island. This time it sounded like they were just beneath the patio, fighting in the sand by the house. Sound was very misleading here. The sea wind pushed noises so close sometimes she could hear Susan Newcombe, on the porch of the next bungalow seventy-five feet away, whispering with Jenny Custule, hear the whispers to the slight hiss of Susan's s's. Then the next moment the wind shifted and Jane couldn't even hear the bangs of their shutter, although she could see it rapping the side of the house.

The dogs seemed almost in her room now, the snarling

all around her. Jane lifted her head, looked around the
floor, then out her window. She could see nothing but
empty sand and the sea glittering in the setting moon.

A body bumped against the stilts under the house. Jane
started, clenching her hands tight by her sides. Fur rasped
against wood. The snarling got louder, more intense. She
lay on her bed listening. If she went out there to stop it,
they might attack her. She remembered the white teeth of
the dog in The Bar, the click they made next to her fingers,
the sound sharp as metal. She wondered if the door to the
bungalow was locked, how strong the screens were. More
and more dogs joined in, barking now. Not barking long
and cheerful like pets in the U.S., not confident cries of
alarm to their owners. These dogs barked clipped, almost
involuntary, coughs like jungle cats. Ten dogs, fifteen? How
could she tell? Bodies thumped against the stilts, the rasp
of claws or teeth. Hair rustled against the wood of the
house. She listened for any sound from Marlene in her
room. She wasn't sure Marlene had come home last night.
She listened for sounds of any dog in the house, the click
of its nails on the floor.

Then below the house, one dog began to yelp, to scream
high and fast. Until the silence came.

Jane lay awake for a long while afterward, waiting, hoping that the dog would make another sound. She was sure
she would recognize its voice. She heard only some scuf-
fling, some breathing; gradually these sounds also faded.
She did not unclench her hands.

There was at least an hour before dawn but already she
could feel the heavier heat of day begin to gather in the
dew and the dark. The first roosters in town began to crow.

The phone rang.

She slipped quickly out of the mosquito netting and ran
for the phone in case Marlene had returned last night. Jane
picked the phone up, smacked her lips once and placed it
gingerly to her ear.

The man at the other end of the line was already talking full speed, crying it sounded like. "Fuck you," he sobbed through static. "Fuck you, ya whore. You're a lying son of a bitch. You're a tramp. You're a . . ." Here he paused.

"Excuse me," Jane attempted, her tongue a little slow from sleep. "But who would you like to speak to?"

"Honey?" he asked of her.

A slow moment passed. He hung up.

Jane stood there, holding the humming receiver against her ear, replaying the voice in her mind. She couldn't imagine Bertie ever yelling like that at her. She didn't inspire such passions. She remembered the diamond ring that had been on Marlene's left hand. She turned on the light. The clock beside the phone hummed and clicked. One digit rolled over, 4:27 A.M.

Since her arrival on the island each of the three or four times the phone had rung in the bungalow, Jane had run for it. She wanted to talk to her parents without looking as though she needed to talk to her parents, without having to call them. She wanted to talk to Bertie, to her neighbors or even the cashier who worked at the local Friendly's. She wanted to hear voices that had known her back in the States, voices which still continued there, without change.

Without seeming rushed, Marlene got to the phone first, every time. "Howdy," she answered and laughed at the response, settling down in the chair for a long chat. Jane stepped back, her breath still fast from her rush. She touched one hand to her stomach, watching. Cradling the receiver in against her shoulder, Marlene gave Jane a cold look until she left.

So at 4:27 in the morning, left with the phone in her hand, Jane slowly dialed the number of her parents. For the past few days she'd been trying on and off to call them. After more than three weeks had passed here, she figured they couldn't consider her needy for calling them. They couldn't think of her as wasteful of money. Every time so far Jane had dialed what she believed to be the correct international exchange followed by their number, she heard a rapid buzz/stop/buzz/stop. She didn't know if this was the Indonesian busy signal or if it meant she had dialed the number wrong. It couldn't be her parents' phone was busy each time for they just didn't use the phone that much. She listened to ten or fifteen cycles of the buzz/stop each time just in case it was some type of ringing. No one ever answered.

This time, after dialing the final number she heard a rapid series of clicks, tones far away and mechanical. She waited. A phone rang so distant and dusty it must be a crossed line. Her head hummed and her tongue felt heavy. She thought she should probably drink more water soon. She listened for the buzz/stop sound. Instead, a click. A very faint woman's voice said, "Hello?" A pause. Jane realized the ringing had stopped, that this was her mother's voice.

"Hello?" repeated her mother. For a long moment Jane couldn't picture her mother's face. She could see only the neon yellow splatter pattern on her mother's favorite Lycra bodysuit.

"Hello?" said Jane slowly. "Mom?"

"Hello, hello?" said her mother. "Is anyone . . . What? What?"

"Mother," called Jane considerably louder. She hoped Marlene wasn't home and trying to sleep. "Mom, it's me, Jane." She found she was smiling widely, pressing her ear closer to the receiver. She specified her own name as though her mother had many children, many who could address her as Mom.

There was a pause, then her mother said, "Oh, Janey. That you?"

Jane stilled, listening hard. The connection was so faded she couldn't tell what emotion was in those words.

Before Jane could answer, her mother said, "Hold on," and put down the phone. It clunked against a hard surface.

Jane waited. She saw a gecko climbing up the table leg, heading for the light. She looked around at the bamboo furniture and hand-trowelled walls, turned the light off quick. She did not want to see this bungalow right now.

After a moment her father got on the line also.

"Janey," his faint voice whispered hearty. "So good of you to call on my early afternoon."

Jane thought about it for a while before realizing it was Thursday afternoon for them instead of Friday predawn, that her father came home early from work on Thursdays. "Hi, Dad . . ." she started.

"It's been such a busy . . ." her mother said. "What?"

"Nothing," said Jane. For a moment no one spoke, each waiting for the others.

"Well," commented her father, "I have to drive your mother to the gym soon."

"We can talk for a moment, darling," her mother said warm and confidential. Jane wondered for the first time how well they were getting on without her. Her voice got louder to talk to Jane. "Is it exciting over there? Down there? Whatever."

"Well . . ." Jane started to say.

"Oh," said her father. "It must be. A foreign country, tropical—What, Janey?"

"Nothing." Jane understood there was a pause both ways in the transmission, because of the distance. Each time she talked, her parents continued to talk over her; then paused a moment later for her voice. Of course they could talk smoothly to each other from the kitchen extension to the living room.

Her father paused for a moment before continuing. "Tropical island. Med— What was that? Nothing what?"

Jane didn't even respond this time.

"Hmm, ahh. Tropical island, medical school," finished her father.

"You must be learning so much," said her mother. "Are you studying?"

"Of course," answered her father. "Of course she is."

"She's our Janey," added her mother. A phrase, Jane remembered now, they used quite frequently, 'our' emphasized as much as 'Janey.' "You must be studying constantly. You taking time off? You meeting new people?"

"Of course she is. All those students," said her father. "And the teachers. Lots of new people to meet."

They continued, talking loudly, with great cheer, as though reciting lines for others to overhear. The conversation they must perform at every social occasion, chuckling indulgently over their daughter off in Asia learning to be a doctor, such an adventure. Jane stood still, her ear pressed against the receiver. She didn't speak at all. Her smile gone.

Then her father asked if she'd thought about what specialty she might choose. For the first time both her parents waited for her response, waited so patiently she shook her head back and forth to wake up, looking around at the dark.

"Radiology?" prompted her father after a moment. "I know it's too early for you to choose, but we're just wondering. You thinking of Pediatrics?"

She straightened her back as though they could see her, nervously scooped a little hair forward over her shoulder.

"Umm. My specialty," she said. "I haven't really . . ." She heard the echo of her uncertain voice down the silent line, the voice of a child. A monkey coughed nearby. She listened to her voice change. "I've been meaning to talk to you, talk to you both. Things aren't what I . . . aren't what I thought they would be."

The silence on the line continued for three full seconds. She hadn't planned this. She hadn't planned this at all. She could hear her father exhale out his nose. She closed her eyes slow, heard it coming. Pressed the tips of her fingers against her eyelids.

"Eighty-three thousand dollars," said her father. "Eighty-three thousand."

"You said you wanted this," said her mother. "You said you—"

"I'll take care of this," said her father.

"I'm not . . ." Jane said, her voice louder, "I'm not . . ." Her face felt hot. She shrugged her hair back.

"How I got so successful," interrupted her father, his voice so loud, overwhelming, "how I got so successful was standing by my decisions. Even when others thought I was wrong, I wouldn't back down. You're not a complainer. You've never been a complainer."

She kept her fingers pressed into her eyelids. She could not move at all. She could see his pink scalp shifting over the bulges and divots of his words, over the tectonic plates of his mind.

"Stick it out," said her mother, reasonably, so much more quietly than her husband. "Janey, it's just four years." Jane knew in all likelihood three of her mother's fingertips ran bone by bone down the sternum checking unconsciously for fat.

"Med school is hard," said her father. "It's supposed to be. You're not a complainer."

There was one long silence. A waiting, determined silence.

"Mmm," Jane managed, a vaguely positive sound. Her parents' breathing began to relax.

"You'll see," said her mother, "we're right."

"It's not supposed to be fun," said her father.

"Need more money or something?" added her mother. "For decorating or something, to go out on the town? Janey?"

Her parents paused, patient.

"No," Jane replied. "No, I don't need anything." She added after a moment, "Thanks."

Her mother mentioned how glad she was they'd had a chance to talk. She said she'd missed her. She said she loved her.

Jane glanced at the clock, 4:31. She said good-bye. She timed it right. It slipped clean into the conversation.

"Study hard," her mother said.

"Make us proud," added her father. Both their receivers clattered into their cradles. The line went dead.

She held on to the receiver for a while, warm in her hand as flesh. She heard a bird hoot outside in the jungle, the waves hiss on the beach. She put the receiver down, walked back slow to bed.

Twice more before dawn she woke fast, out of a sound sleep, her heart beating wildly like someone had just shaken her. And nothing was happening. Each time she woke, it took her a long time to fall back asleep.

Twelve

With a little over two weeks to go until midterms, Jane limped slowly down the stairs to the anatomy lab around ten-thirty at night to review the parts of the heart. This was the first time she had come down to the lab at night; she'd been stalling. A lot of the other first-year students were spending two or three evenings out of the week down here. Only the light in their part of the lab was turned on while they worked. The rest of the room hung behind them dark and so close to cold, shadows under the sheet-covered tables. The metallic plink of water, the rustle of each movement against the tiles. Each rip of skin echoed, crack of bone, the thud of flesh into the plastic bucket at their side.

Even Marlene came back spooked from here. She said it wasn't standing alone among all those cadavers that bothered her. It was that she didn't trust the lights on the island, the high-pitched whine of the generator. She kept imagining what would happen if there was a power outage. She would be on the far side of a room filled with bodies, thirty feet below the ground.

When Jane pushed open the door some of the lights were

already on. Claren, Keefer's girlfriend, sat at one of the empty dissection tables, her legs crossed, books spread in front of her, pen in hand. Her red hair shimmered in the light. She glanced up over the edges of her glasses at Jane, her straightforward stare. Like a politician, Jane thought, like a mannequin, not a hint of her feeling self-conscious. This was the first time Jane had seen Claren when she wasn't blotchy from the heat. She glimpsed how Claren would be pretty back in the States.

"Umm, hey," said Jane. She turned on the light for her area of the room. In this large room, empty of students, her voice echoed. She walked to her cadaver listening to the creak of her leather sandals, the rustle of her coveralls.

"Hey there, shark lady," answered Claren. She turned back to her books, scribbled something in the margins and capped her pen. "You've discovered the best place to study. Quieter than the library, bright and so cool." She stood up to walk over to Jane's cadaver. "I'm glad you're here. I want to learn more about you. You're a cipher." Claren was the type to ask a lot of personal questions. She liked to lean in, eyes unblinking, asking question after question. Jane had seen her do it to many of the first-year students. Afterwards she acted as though the answers entitled her to a special friendship with that person. Jane watched her approach.

If Jane had ever tried describing the couple of Keefer and Claren to another person, to someone who had never been on this island, she probably wouldn't try to describe Keefer physically at all, not his skinny capable hands or the nervous way he had of holding those hands to his lips, of pausing there, head tilted, eyes motionless, looking off, looking in. She wouldn't describe his hair, crew-cut tight round the curve of his skull, baring the narrow tendons at the back of his neck like the tendons behind a young boy's knees.

Instead she would describe his stuttering, his lips twitching, his whole face knotted, struggling as though with another's will for his own mouth. She would describe

Claren's expression while she waited, the tightening of her lips, so perfectly hers, a settling of her chin, her glance away. Jane might imitate the way Claren spoke then, so easy, so smooth, a spilling of the very words he was trying so hard to jerk out. Jane would show afterward his mouth closing slow.

Claren leaned over Jane's cadaver with interest, pressed one bare finger into the spongy lobe of a lung, the way a person might check on the ripeness of a fruit. "I got a really good grade last year on this stuff. Want any help?"

"No, that's OK. I'm just trying to get the parts of the heart straight." Jane pulled the heart out of its plastic bag and returned it temporarily to the chest cavity.

"That's easy," said Claren, reaching forward to twist the heart around. "This is its original orientation, see? With the hollow for the oblique pericardial sinus fitting snug in against the lung. This way you can easily spot the superior vena cava above, with the inferior below. And to the side the pulmonary veins." Claren pointed so quickly to each item Jane leaned closer, trying to follow along. "In figuring out the coronary arteries, it's best to start with the left one." She continued to lecture.

Claren's parents both worked in real estate, selling office parks in California. She was the eldest child. She talked easily, ate efficiently, head down to her task. She seemed to like alcohol a lot, some of the more traditionally female drinks that still had some kick to them: strawberry daiquiris, sombreros. She got more physically affectionate when drunk, pulling Keefer in close to her, inviting others to touch the velvety nap of his crew cut. She tended to wear short skirts, but when she stood up the backs of her pale thighs were marked with a perfect contour map of the seat, the blood visibly pooled, reminding Jane uncomfortably of some of the less well prepared cadavers.

Sometimes when Claren announced the words she believed Keefer was trying to stutter out, Jane thought she was wrong, that Keefer had been trying for different words, trying to make a different point. Jane watched Keefer blink and look down. If Claren was ever wrong, he never said so.

Sometimes at a joke, Jane and he would bark out laughter at the exact same moment, the rest of the room chiming in afterward or not at all.

"You seem," Claren mentioned, "like the type of person— and tell me if I'm wrong here—who would have lots of brothers."

Jane looked up at her. They were leaning in over the cadaver, pushing the blood vessels of the heart apart enough with their fingers to trace the nerves. Their heads just a few inches above the chest cavity. Turning her eyes back down, Jane realized while she had attempted to follow Claren's information, a curl of her hair had fallen onto the chest, draped against the remaining lung. She let go of the heart, straightened up, scooped her hair back with her gloves and wound it into a knot on the back of her neck. She knew later her hair would swing against her back heavy with the smell of formalin even after two or three shampoos.

"Am I right?" asked Claren.

The hands of the cadaver appeared so small in their black plastic bags, so round. They must be clenched tight, Jane understood for the first time. Inside the bags, they must be still holding on.

"Yes," Jane found herself replying. She'd almost forgotten the question. She realized Claren was waiting for her to elaborate. Jane listened to her own voice like to a stranger. "Yes, brothers. How did you know?" She clenched her own hands experimentally, felt the snug fit, her fingers nestled tight into the pads of her palm, her fists round as rocks, unbreakable. "I have three brothers. My mother wanted more children after them but the doctor told her it was a bad idea. She had me anyway because she wanted a girl so much."

Jane thought soon she would laugh out loud, explain the joke, but instead, under the halogen lights she looked into Claren's pale stare and added, "I'm the baby of the family. The favorite."

DAY THIRTY-TWO

"Come on, bookhead," Marlene said. "It's Saturday night. Take an hour off and come to The Bar."

Surprised, Jane glanced up from the books she was packing for the library. Marlene jingled her moped keys. Jane could see this invitation was just an impulse, Marlene wasn't going to wait long. Jane still hadn't memorized the parts of the intestines, the function of each part. She had to make flash cards for the anatomy of contractile cells. Her whole face hurt from sleepiness.

"OK," she said.

Jane knew some of the other students had been going to The Bar at night for the last few weeks, but was not prepared for how many students were there. At least a quarter of the school. She had assumed if a student wasn't at school, she or he was probably sleeping. She was surprised by how loud The Bar was, all that slack laughter, bellowed voices, the tables being slapped, someone yelling for attention. At school everyone moved so quiet, desperately studying or hunched down, hoping the teacher wouldn't call on them. Here, the students moved wide and exuberant as though they could stretch their limbs out of the school's influence, as though at The Bar they could actually get away, off this island for an hour, maybe two. The room looked the same as the first day Jane had walked in here with Marlene, only now the first-year students merged in perfectly with the rest.

Marlene was popular. Jane had known that from watching her at school, but here at The Bar it was even more obvious. When Marlene sat down at an empty table with Jane, Ned Trufow, Claudio Ferregi, Nina Sheiffer and Walker Rice got up from other tables to join them. Other people turned around to watch Marlene from the tables nearby, expectant. She ordered a hamburger, just yelled it out. The waiters did not nod at her request, did not register it in any visible way, but no one aside from Jane even looked at them. The waiters kept their heads down, preparing things behind the bar counter, walking out among the tables only to serve food and beer.

When Marlene's hamburger was served someone yelled, "Your first patient, Doctor Diemer."

Marlene looked down at the hamburger. "Homus burgus," she identified.

Jane looked sort of sideways at the burger, the glistening meat. It was strange to see something dead that was still red, that had not been bled out and preserved. She hadn't been able to eat meat since the first autopsy.

Marlene checked under the bun, pressed one finger into the flesh. "The patient presents with a sizzling high temperature, complete paralysis from the bun down, no apparent pulse or respiratory functions and a bit of onion halitosis." She looked around at the crowd. "I.e., fucking dead. An autopsy is called for." Picking up her knife, she sliced into the burger with the heel of her hand resting down on the bun to stabilize her fingers, proper surgical technique. She put the slice of burger in her mouth, chewed a little exaggerated. She knew she was onstage.

"What'd it die of, Doc?" called out Claudio.

"Hmm," she said, turning the food over in her mouth for better sampling. "The subject appears to have been exsanguinated, lacerated into a patty of undifferentiated material, then given a first-degree heat burn." She nodded. "The subject died of trauma." She ticked her head to the side in imitation of Burnett, waiting until she pulled her head back up before she spoke again. "Definitely trauma." She cut off another bite of the burger. "Time of death—probably before the condiments were added."

She traced the lettuce distally out to the sesame-seed bun, discussing the extreme crenellations of the lettuce, the strange polyplike crustaceans on top of the bun. Her audience spurred her on, asking questions, laughing. Marlene's voice got louder, her gestures more theatrical. She never laughed herself.

After several minutes of this, Jane wasn't sure Marlene was enjoying her performance all that much. It reminded Jane of watching comedians on TV, the ones who spat out joke after joke, no laughter on their own faces, just the quick-eyed watch for boredom in their audience. The two sides of Marlene's face seemed almost to be splitting, one side stretched up so far, the other side still and heavy. Jane imagined the two sides pulling away from each other like bubbles, like cells during meiosis.

After the hamburger Marlene chain-smoked, lighting each cigarette off the end of the last, sucking them in with long hard drags. Her breathing audible between her words.

On the last drag of a cigarette, partway down the filter, she coughed, harsh and hacking. She stubbed out what was left of the cigarette, held up her hand in a gesture that said she would continue talking in a moment. She coughed so hard her eyes watered and her head went down, her mouth gaping open and wet. The others at the table waited for the next joke. No one stirred.

Jane hesitantly looked around at the others' faces. She touched Marlene's hand, leaned closer. "You OK?" She noticed for the first time the yellow stains of nicotine on the insides of Marlene's bony fingers.

Surprised, Marlene pulled her head up and looked at her. Their faces quite close. Jane could see the tears in Marlene's eyes, red blotches on her neck. Both sides of her face were still as clay. Her head was stooped like that of any other thin woman. Her eyes stretched wide open like she hadn't ever noticed Jane there before, sitting right beside her. As though this was the first time she'd ever really looked at Jane, her housemate.

Strangely enough, this was the first point Jane understood this island really got to other people also.

"Want some water?" asked Jane, worried.

Marlene looked down at Jane's hand touching her own, shook her head, not as though she were saying no, but more as though she were trying to wake up. She scrubbed the sockets of her eyes with the heels of her hands. A little mascara was rubbed onto her underlids. She blinked down at the burger sitting on the table half-eaten, cold, the bun soaked through to the bottom with grease. The others still waited, watching, for the next joke. She turned again to look at Jane.

"Come on," Marlene said. "Time to go." She got up quite quickly and left The Bar without even checking that Jane would follow, as though it was assumed. Started her moped just ahead of Jane. At home she walked straight into the bathroom, locked the door and ran a bath, didn't come out until long after Jane was in bed.

But, after that night, sometimes in the afternoon, Marlene stayed with Jane in the bungalow, studying, turning pages and smoking. On some of these days, looking down at her books, she swore lazy and continuous under her breath; other times the simple pace of silence lay between them.

DAY THIRTY-SIX

In Burnett's class Jane had less and less of a problem cutting, her hands learning to move smooth and controlled. She watched them, surprised at their grace, at their knowledge and confidence. They folded back the peritoneum, slid in, cupping up a loop of intestines. Her scalpel traced a shallow line across the attached soft fan of the mesentery;

the fingers peeled the protective membrane as smoothly as though it had only recently and wrongly been laid over the organ, like she was just fixing it.

She felt such a distance from her hands when they touched the body like that. It was like watching the movies Burnett showed of real surgeries, of live patients, a sternum cracked away to expose the beating heart scared and squirming in the chest, or the eyelids pinned back to show the shocking white heft of the eyeball. The surgeons themselves were hardly ever shown, just their gloved hands, the antiseptic green gowns, so interchangeable. It could have been the same operating room and table, the same knives, the same person cutting in all the movies, all generic parts of some giant machine.

While Jane cut she sometimes found herself blinking down at her hands, at their delicacy and competence, at their plastic unrecognizable shimmer.

That day after anatomy class Michael waited for her, until everyone else had left. It sometimes took her a while to clean her tools, to wet and cover the body. Sometimes she found her fingers would start to shake at the end, after Burnett had left, her fingers shivering hard. She struggled to grasp the zipper of the instrument bag, missed, tried again, tugged it closed in awkward jerks.

From the door in the back of the room came two islanders dressed in coveralls. They glanced over without interest at Jane and Michael. One began to slowly swab the floor, mopping any pieces of flesh over toward the central drain. The other went to the nearest dissection table, jerked the sheets completely off the body and sponged the table down around the limbs. He spritzed formalin in everywhere, tugged on the skin flaps like a mother checking clothing on her child, and shook out a crunkling plastic sheet that he tucked in carefully on all sides of the body. She saw the sheet settle down on the skin of the shoulders and legs, sticking to the liquid, magnifying everything, like fingertips pressed against glass. He threw the green cloth sheet on over that. She searched the islander's expression while he moved from table to table, tucking bodies in for the night. She watched the other man scrub hard with the mop at one spot. There was no emotion she could see in the two men, no censure or disgust. They could have been mopping up and making beds in a hotel. She wondered what their own burial practices were. She thought, from the way these men moved around the bodies, these cadavers must have come from other islands.

She finished cleaning up, her head so tired it seemed to be listing slightly to the side. Michael nodded at her, paced with her down the aisle to the door. He didn't appear to notice her shaking fingers, her listing head. He hadn't glanced at the islanders more than once.

Michael walked such clean lines. He strode down the aisle between the cadavers as though he were walking down a wide sunny street on his way home.

And when he held the first of the insulated doors open for her, he asked, "Want to go out on a date sometime?"

She looked at his face. Behind her she heard the rustle of plastic, the grunt of the islander shifting a body.

She got a little fascinated by that phrase, "out on a date." The words were so foreign to this island, so old-fashioned. Like any type of date was possible on this island, the two of them going out alone. The only places to go to were the cafeteria or The Bar. It seemed in character that even on this island Michael would ask her out in such a way.

Jane realized she hadn't answered yet.

Michael was still looking down on her, his expression beginning to change.

"Oh," she said. "Why, sure."

He smiled, then nodded, almost the way he did when he got an answer correct in class. He was confident again; nothing remained from his expression a moment ago. "I'll pick you up at your place at seven on Monday. I take Monday evening off from studying. It keeps me fresh."

Today was Wednesday. He'd given her five days notice, as though there was a danger here her calendar might fill up. She nodded, trying to nod like him, fast, confident. Her chin ticked down, then up, a light switch, a radio signal. He led the way back up the stairs.

That afternoon she took a break from studying to go on a walk. Her head hurt, her body ached with fatigue. She thought if she exercised she might sleep better at night. She thought if she sat all day studying for all four years here, her heart might pause one day from sheer boredom.

She headed up to town. She hadn't walked through town since she bought a moped up at school on the third day here. Each day driving to and from school, coming around the corner into town she heard the harsh echo off the houses of her moped's engine. The chickens scattered in front, flapping their wings for extra speed, the islanders sitting in doorways or in the shadows of trees, staring at her, slow heads turning. In the early evening as the sun set, when she drove back up to study at the library, the women were lighting incense in front of each house, setting pieces by each carved god. The smoke curled out in sleepy ropes from the shrines. She could smell the incense, thick and purple, drifting through the trees even halfway up the hill to school.

Sometimes, driving into town, she pretended she didn't see the islanders staring, she focused doggedly ahead. Other times she flashed tight smiles over at them. Mostly each day she stared back silently, at the people, at the town, like at a TV set, understanding even if she stopped, even if she got off her bike, walked right up and touched a person, on the shoulder, on the face—a woman, a man, a child—she would still be half a world away from a connection.

She'd learned by now no student ever stopped in town,

not even to buy fresh vegetables or fruits. No student talked to the islanders, no one exchanged hellos. It was as though the students' island was only superimposed on the islanders' island, like when a person walked through the lit square of a projected slide, for a brief moment striding across a sandy beach heading for the sailboats. The things the students needed to continue to imitate their old American lives were available up at the school. Everything in town was foreign. The closest the students got to the islanders was accepting a food tray in the cafeteria from an islander's hand. Only the men worked on campus or at The Bar. The women didn't seem to leave town, constantly working in their clean bright sarongs and shirts, one woman with a baby on her hip feeding chickens, another squatting grinding something in a bowl, a third swaying slow down the street with ten large paving stones balanced on a towel on her head.

At the cafeteria, Jane glanced down sometimes when she reached for her tray, saw delicate toffee-colored fingers, pale long nails. Looked up surprised into the man's face, wide cheekbones, delicate nose, dark eyes. The man stared, no expression, mouth closed, hand holding out the tray. She wondered what he saw. Taking the tray, she nodded her thanks, looking away, embarrassed for what she assumed was hate.

That afternoon she headed toward town on foot, to take a look at it. At first she tried for what she used to think of as exercise, jogging up the empty road, rising each time high on her left ankle, but she worried one of the other students would come round the corner, see her limp fully stretched out and bobbing. Also jogging was not made for this climate. Her face heated up tight as a balloon, she heard the slow rise of a nonexistent wind in her ears, her vision narrowed. She slowed down, pacing nervous by herself through the jungle, head lowered, mouth gasping. Listening to the sounds of things moving in the underbrush all around.

Her parents expected her to marry Bertie, her boyfriend back home, the one she'd slept with. Going out with him was the only thing she'd ever done that she was sure had pleased them. He was the son of a senator, from one of the few families in the state richer than hers. Each time she went out with Bertie or he gave her a gift, her mother casually reported it to her bridge club. From the kitchen or the study, Jane would hear Bertie's name mentioned, sandwiched between reports on the new material for the living-room curtains and the schedule of their upcoming Aspen vacation. Jane sometimes thought if her mother knew about each time she and Bertie slept together, she would report that also, in the same offhand victorious voice.

He was a polite man, a quiet one, so skinny he had a tendency to tuck his butt in under him when he stood so no one could be sure of the exact perimeters of its lack. She admired the strength of purpose it would take to eat food as he did only in order to stay alive, especially in the midst of such plenty. He seemed in many ways to be a good person. He gave Jane presents, made her soup if she had a cold. He always told her she had beautiful hair.

Mostly, though, their relationship reminded her of the buddy system in first grade, where you are allowed to wander further from the rest so long as you have your buddy's hand clasped tightly in your own. His parents had known he would be a lawyer in the family law office since before he was born. His father had been giving him stock in the company, the maximum untaxed limit every year since he was one year old, so inheritance taxes wouldn't hurt him as badly. And Bertie was expected to attend every one of the board meetings along with his brothers, expected to learn his moral boundaries from his father's business dealings. He never complained, but he never talked of enjoying it either, and sometimes under the auspices of a date he and Jane would drive away from their homes for hours on the highway, a hundred, two hundred miles across Connecticut, Rhode Island, Massachusetts, up to the wilds of New Hampshire in the purring silence of the Lincoln Continental his father had given him for his eighteenth birthday. Both Jane and Bertie perched in the darkness on the far sides of that huge leather seat, each looking out opposite ends of the windshield into the lit tunnel of the headlights, not talking, the only sounds the static of the air conditioner and Bertie's occasional shifts about on the seat from one bony shank to another. Both of them watching the miles accumulate behind them, the knowledge nestled deep in their twin brains that their parents were happy with their progress and they were far away.

In some ways Jane thought those times in the car, driving, were their closest. Certainly closer than they were during sex when they tried hard to make the right sounds and faces, but were pressed so much tighter together than either of them thought was polite.

She remembered the first time he asked her out, his hands clasped hard around his books, his head down, staring at a spot on the ground with such concentration she looked down to find out what was upsetting him. His tension was so great she felt relief that his question was just about her Friday night. He was the other shy person in her English class. She remembered thinking he was the only one she would have wanted to go out with, although out of embarrassment, she would probably have said yes to whoever asked her.

The whole of Bertie and Jane's courtship was given such importance by everyone, their parents setting out to meet each other immediately, returning dinner invites, sizing each other up. She knew something between her and Bertie had been changed with all that attention, that parental eagerness; something became different for both of them. The first movie Bertie and she went to, her mother saw her out the front door down to Bertie's car, waved good-bye from the steps as though Jane was starting a much larger trip than the one just into town. Jane remembered the deadly seriousness with which Bertie and she clasped hands the whole way through the feature, not even shifting their sweaty grasp, the sense of responsibility. The first time they had sex was as carefully considered and scheduled as the signing of a mortgage.

Jane knew her parents imagined their own life for herself and Bertie in another ten years: married, living in Greenwich, three or maybe four miles away, a large house, a rolling driveway. The only differences being that Jane and Bertie wouldn't be as good-looking, not as successful, their acreage a little less.

Bertie seemed very distant now. She tried to summon memories of him, the way his upper lip still gaped forward to make room for the childhood overbite that braces had long since erased, how he pinched the tip of his tongue between thumb and index finger to wet them just before he turned a page. How Jane and he held hands under the table during each of their family dinners, their parents taking for a sign of love what was more a silent promise that this dinner would end.

His mouth on her mouth, his hand searching awkwardly under her shirt for her breast, rolling the nipple between his fingers. She saw herself lying back, lying still, mouth opening.

She smelled formalin.

She shook her head, took a left turn that did not head directly into town, shy now about appearing in public, the islanders staring at her when she had such thoughts. This was only a footpath, so narrow ferns and bushes *thwapped* against her legs on both sides. She walked for a few minutes, feeling brave for moving through the jungle on her own, thinking she could learn to live here, she could adjust to the heat, she could feel at home here on this island.

She found herself abruptly in a clearing, nude island men bathing twenty feet away in a flat black river, laughing, flicking sheets of water at each other. One ran, legs pumping in exaggerated motion through the water. Two stood waist deep, hand in hand like young girls. Their fast speech was so foreign the sounds fell apart in Jane's ear like birdcalls. Their actions appeared so different from the silent waiting she had seen them do in school and in town.

One boy downstream squatted over a bowel movement, his face concentrated and hunched. He finished, straightened up, his reflection below him wavering as it imitated his motions. Both boys watched her. His intent stillness slowly spilled out to the other men. They turned, finding her pale silhouette against the jungle, the silence of the clearing settling between them, the water continuing around. None of the men covered any portion of his anatomy, no one turned away. Brown skin, thin bodies almost hairless. Genitals as dark as bruises, drooping velvet flowers. The men were so thin it was as though they were more than bare of clothes, as though they were bare of skin. She could see each of their bones and muscles, the joints and articulations, the thin layer holding in their guts. The lip of the rib cage and the spine of the hips pressing forward through the skin; the concave bowl between was beating with blood, the shaft of the thigh muscle leading down. They were vividly alive.

It was time for her to go. She realized this was a dangerous situation, this waiting was not peace. She stepped slowly away, not turning her back to them. No way for her to know what they thought, not even if they called it out in their language, not even if they waved their feelings openly in their alien hand gestures: Fuck you, Go away, Come and join us. We mean you no harm.

On the way back to her bungalow, walking fast, arms swinging, face red, she smelled incense drifting slow and sweet from town.

Thirteen

The class she liked best—or at least the only one she did not dread—was Krakow's. He was the newest teacher here, only arrived this year. He still blinked a lot in surprise at it all, the same as she did. His body was short and wide, not fat, but more like a hedgehog was thick, a different type of animal entirely from Egren's lanky cadaver frame. He stood half-bald and bristly, slightly hunched into his weight like he was cold, like he was warming himself against his own flesh. Except that he was sweating, a damp mound of heat, with his own clothes sticking to him under his arms and round his belly and in a triangle down his back. He smelled damp and close as an unaired basement.

His heat rash grew each day, raised blotches hot and in-flamed across his cheeks and forehead, down his chin and neck, around the blinking surprise of his green eyes. Jane thought the rash must itch terribly. She watched sometimes when he raised the edge of one pinky to tap tentatively on a welt in a tender area, around the lips or in the crease of his nose. His eyes blinked as his finger touched the skin.

The way he acted in front of the class reminded her the

most of the professors she had known in the past, of what she used to think of when she heard the word "teacher." He loved histology, the study of tissues. It showed in the way he threw his short arm out, pointing, so excited, at cellular structures projected on the screen, tracing small grains and squiggles in what looked like crosssections of purple foam. Krakow spoke fast, his breath sucked in wet between the words. He knocked the projection screen back a bit sometimes with his exuberant jabs, so the slide waved and bellied around, structures fuzzying and enlarging. He enjoyed the very words, rolling them off his tongue like the names of wines. Chromatids, kinetochore, glycogen.

When he finished describing a slide and looked back at the class he seemed disappointed every time. Jane turned to look at the class also, to see what he saw. Slack mouths, eyes held too wide to be absorbing anything. A few faces turned to the window watching a seagull stalk across the lawn.

Krakow generally didn't call on anyone in class, seeming to believe the students would willingly volunteer to answer the question he'd called out. Michael answered a lot of the time, but sometimes Krakow asked if anyone else wanted to make a guess. Krakow was so endlessly hopeful. Rather than answering the question immediately for the class, he asked a question he considered more leading, obvious. He held out his hand as though reaching for the students to drop the answer in his hand. It was that close. His gesture never worked. The students looked around at each other, pursed their lips as though thinking. Used to the motivation techniques of the other teachers, few even tried for Krakow, not unless he asked one of them specifically, not unless he put them on the spot. He asked simpler and simpler questions while the class stared out the windows or fell asleep with their foreheads propped up in their hands. They all knew their scholastic records—in some ways they took pride in them. Jane never answered herself—especially not a very obvious question—for fear of getting it wrong.

This stalemate would continue each time until he either answered a question himself or got genuinely out-of-control angry. His face heated up, glistening with sweat, jaw protruding, his eyes no longer focused on any of them. His anger wasn't like the other teachers' here, not calculated and timed. It was real. He punched the chalkboard, the table, the students' desks. He grabbed the slide off the projector and made slashing gestures through the air as he yelled. Each time he stepped, his foot kicked the ground hard like a little kid having a tantrum. The times he stepped close to Jane she saw his eyes were more than half closed. She thought he could easily hit any of them, he could crack the glass slide onto a student's head, kick the projector over. At this point all the students sat up straight, feet flat on the floor, eyes riveted to him. Now they tried hard to answer the question. He had their attention at last.

Still, she admired him, for loving the material, for caring about learning on its own, for assuming each of them would try as hard as they could simply because they should. She admired him for being continually surprised at their lack of knowledge and effort. She thought he and she were a lot alike.

She sometimes smiled at him when he first began to get mad, while he still held his hand out to the class for the answer to the question, waiting. She smiled in sympathy and respect and if he noticed her smile at all he blinked over at her for a moment, his face tightening in confusion, his heat rash turning redder from embarrassment.

One day all this changed. One day when she smiled at him he suddenly snapped. "You, you with the smirk," he yelled, jabbing his finger at her. "Jane Guy." His face was dark red, his neck blotchy. "What type of cell do hemidesmosomes and desmosomes anchor?"

She turned her head slow around the classroom, everyone

watching her. The grin pasted on her face. Her tongue was slow, her hearing hummed. Not even English appeared in her head. *Bonjour*, she heard in the voice of her ninth-grade French teacher. *Comment allez-vous?* The silence spread. She looked up at the ceiling. Krakow saw the blankness on her face. He put his hands on his hips, tasting his victory already.

"Basal cells of keratinizing squamous epithelium," her mouth uttered abruptly. She turned back to him, felt the start of her astonished smile.

He jerked his head in, his double chin folded out underneath, red and inflamed with the rash. He looked up fast at the ceiling, then around the classroom where she had looked.

Turning back to her, his eyes narrowed, crafty. He whispered into the silence low and hissing. "You're cheating. I don't know how, but you're cheating. Just like you did in college."

She gaped at him. Felt every face in the classroom swivel to stare at her. Never had she thought the teachers had access to her records. She started to look around, knew her face was slack with guilt. The first person she saw was Marlene, Marlene's eyes open wide, Michael just behind her. Dropping her head onto the desk, Jane covered her ears with her arms, covered the back of her head with her hands. Still she could hear the whispering in the back of the class.

After class she didn't go to the cafeteria for lunch. Instead she walked down to Keefer's dock, hid out there until it was time for Physiology. For the rest of that day's classes she took a seat in the back of each room, as far as she could get from everyone, kept her head down writing notes. Not even her parents had ever spoken those words to her.

On this island, there was nowhere to get away from all those who knew about her or would know soon.

Next time she walked into class Krakow told her where to sit, in a corner away from all others. Excited by her embarrassed obedience, he told anyone who tried to sit within two seats of her to move elsewhere. She sat alone and self-conscious, head bowed. He watched her throughout class, proud as a new bully. During class he asked her another question. He made a large display of following her gaze around the classroom, waiting for her method or compatriot to be revealed. She found, with him watching like that, with the class going silent, the answer rose panicked to her lips after only a few choked moments. She smiled hesitant, so proud after the correct answer, thinking he must believe in her now.

Instead he narrowed his eyes, asked her another question, watched closer, seemed to believe he just had to figure out how she was doing it.

DAY THIRTY-EIGHT

She spent the afternoon with Keefer on his dock. He was not in the same year as her at school, only sharing that one class with Egren, so there was still the possibility he didn't know yet. He didn't say anything about it or act in any way different.

Keefer dropped his feet off the dock, splashed them about in the water like a child. She sat down heavy beside him, her gaze sliding through the water to the shark's lazy kick off the bottom. Jonah began to coast a slow circle round the pen. Her eyes drifted toward the creature like they would have turned toward movement on TV. She swung her eyes ahead of its arc to Keefer's feet.

Metasophalangeal joint, came the words lazy as another's thought to her mind. Intermediate cuneiform bone. His lanky brown toes.

"Don't you know," she said, "that's one of the signals for a shark to attack? The irregular movements of a dying fish."

If anything Keefer kicked his feet about harder. "Then,"

he said, "it is the p-p-p. Perfect p-p. Proof that Jonah isn't dangerous." He was stuttering more these days. Egren inter-rogated him at least twice a day. Sometimes in the library, just sitting still by himself, Jane had watched Keefer break out in a sweat, soaking slow through his shirt, in a triangle down to the back of his shorts, his eyes flicking back and forth over the pages. He didn't try to speak much anymore, not even in The Bar. When she saw him sitting there, all hunched down into his silence, into his fast eyes moving over all of them, his Adam's apple pumping in his neck, she felt his pain as her own. She wanted to protect him somehow, anyhow, with her own body, pull him so tight into her arms that no teacher could get at him, no parents could reach him. Sitting there he looked so small she thought she could almost fold him over a few times and push him warm under her shirt. Hide him away.

Claren yelled out at them from one of the windows of her and Keefer's bungalow forty feet back from the beach. "Did I tell you guys I ran over a chicken today?"

Keefer's head jerked, but he didn't look up. His feet kicked harder against the water. The shark glided just un-derneath, eyes ahead. Jane glanced up to the bungalow po-litely, saw Claren wasn't looking at them, wasn't even visible. Claren appeared briefly in the living-room window, moving toward the bathroom.

"I was driving through town," she yelled. "And this bird started running down the road right in front of me. I tried to go around it but the thing kept swerving back in front of me every time I turned away. I would swerve left, it would swerve left. I went right. It went right. It must have been trying to commit little-chicken suicide. It went under my wheel and the whole bike bumped up, like over a jump. I was going to stop afterward—it's not like I wasn't—but half the town started yelling real angry, running after me, so I gunned it instead. Christ, it was just a scrawny rooster."

The bungalow walls were so thin Claren didn't even need

to yell. In some way the empty spaces inside the clay walls seemed to amplify the sound. She could speak loudly in their direction, through the wall, and if the wind blew the right way, they would hear her words as though she stood beside them.

The wind changed direction. Jane could see Claren's face and some of her red hair now through the bathroom window, her mouth moving wide round her lost words. Claren held a washcloth in her hand, glanced up. Jane looked down.

The shark passed by again, six inches out from Keefer's kicking feet. It didn't look at either of them. Watched the water ahead as hypnotized as a driver watching the highway, continuing in its seamless circle.

Keefer sighed. "I like you, Jane. You're very p-p-p-p. Peaceful. I feel good around you." He picked up her hand, held it in his. Where their skin touched, the sweat rolled out immediately. The skin of her cadaver in autopsy lab felt cold and hard as rubber. Living skin surprised her more and more.

She glanced at Keefer, his cheekbones, his gray eyes. He watched the shark. She was glad she knew he was easy with touching, with smiles and hugs, that he lived with Claren, that he held her hand simply as a friend. She was glad she knew he touched her easily because she was fat and not that pretty.

After a moment he pressed the back of her hand down onto the middle of his thigh, held it there, just where his shorts ended. She realized her body would block Claren's view of this. She thought that accidental on Keefer's part. She thought Claren would not care so much about why Jane was touching Keefer's thigh. Claren would not care about the friends part. Claren would just yell and stomp.

Jane could feel the muscles in Keefer's thigh clench and slacken as he kicked his feet through the water. From the motion she got a better idea of the feel of his legs, the bristly male hair, the flat muscle. She wished she could take her hand back from this knowledge, but thought Keefer would think that rude, would think she didn't like him. He wouldn't understand that three times so far, at night when she couldn't control her expectations, she had dreamed of the full weight of his bones rocking tight on top of her. She did not like this. She was changing in this heat and jungle.

During the day, on this island, she found herself watching the way the men at school walked, shoulders swaying, bare legs, so frequently bare-chested. A lot of these men were already going out with someone. None of them would be interested in her. She found herself noting chest hair, muscle tone and the outline of bones, staring at their flat male nipples, such a variety of living shades from tender pink to flushed purple. She thought this interest in men's bodies must be from working on her cadaver so much, a simple interest in the way the male body she studied for many hours a day had functioned when alive. She knew the students' nipples would be sticky from sweat.

After each dream of Keefer she shook herself awake, got up to get a glass of water, rubbed her face. Walked up and down until the tight feeling left, blamed this sweltering and half-nude island.

The shark rolled by again, closer this time, smooth and slick and shadowed by the water. Jane forced her eyes down to it instead of at Keefer's flat jogging thigh. Its black eye pointed up at her, the tiny fisted brain behind planning or not. Its mass slid through the water with all the weight and inevitability of a rock. Its eye rolled over to Keefer just as its fin brushed his left foot. Jane saw that. She saw it about to happen, saw it happening. Its fin rubbing along Keefer's foot, the grinning head so close. For a moment all three of them joined by touch: fin to foot, thigh to hand.

The shark didn't reach for Keefer. It swam on. Jane stared after it, her mouth open.

So cool, she thought, forgetting for a moment her hand

clasped in Keefer's, forgetting her fingers pressed tight against his leg. So cool in the water, so fluid in its motions. Never hot or stressed or scared.

She watched it, noticing the faded stripes along its back, pointing to a start or end she could not conceive of.

Fourteen

〜

Marlene was in a rush to get to The Bar. She stood outside kicking at the base of the screen door while Jane worked inside.

"Come on, girl," said Marlene, pressing her face in against the screen so her nose went all fat and white. "I ain't got all day. Let's move."

"I'm not going." Jane kept her head down, hoping Marlene would leave soon. She wasn't ever going to The Bar again. She assumed even the upper classes knew by now about her cheating. In a few hours she would have to walk into the library. She pictured them all turning to look at her, the new knowledge written there on their faces.

"Why?" Marlene asked slow and sly. "You working on a new cheating system?" She laughed and rolled her face away again to watch something move through the underbrush on the other side of the road. "Come on. I'm hungry."

Jane found herself breathing heavy out her nose, glancing fast from one side of the desk to the other as though looking for something that had just been there. Her voice when it came was harsh. "Don't you ever mention that again."

"What?" asked Marlene, jerking her face back to stare inside, genuinely startled.

There was a moment of complete silence.

Marlene repeated more insistently, "What?"

Jane found her voice again. "What what?"

"What am I not supposed to mention again?"

"That," Jane grunted, closed her eyes, "the cheating thing."

"The cheating thing?" Marlene stepped back from the door a bit, into the sunlight. Her eyes narrowed. "Girl, where do you think you are? Who do you think makes up the student body?" She ran the back of her knuckles across her mouth, snorted. "Me, senior year I hot-wired my dean's car. You know, for fun, a practical joke. Also, I hated him. I was going to drive it down to the transvestite prostitute area, leave it parked there, maybe some condoms on the front seat. I got caught still on campus. My parents got the felony charges dropped, but I wasn't exactly the prime med-school candidate after that."

Marlene stepped close again. "Don't you know your stock went way up with most everyone from Krakow blowing the whistle? Shit, people think of you as human now. Claudio wants to know if you're cheating here, wants to know how. He can't figure it out. He thinks you're a fucking genius."

She slapped the door with the flat of her hand so the spring twanged, then strode off to her moped. She called back over her shoulder, "Sometimes you can be a real perspectiveless shit."

Within half an hour, Jane found herself walking slow down to her moped to join Marlene at The Bar.

Jane found people more tense than they had been last time she was here, the noise greater, the gestures larger. She stood for a moment by the door looking around for Marlene.

"Look, I'm not fucking with you," Randy Nally told Sarah Calder at the table closest to Jane. "Egren told me not only are midterm grades thirty percent of the total, but the teachers use them as indicators of future performance. In other words, they're going to dump bad on whoever does worst." He held up two fingers side by side. "Scouts' honor."

Sarah had a glass of beer halfway up to her mouth. She studied it in front of her, then put it back down without drinking any.

Jane stepped around them to Marlene, sat down beside her.

When Marlene saw her, she snorted once in surprise, touched her on the arm and without consultation ordered her a Long Island iced tea. Claudio came over.

"Your hair is very beautiful," he said and touched it. She could tell he'd already had a few drinks, for he'd reverted to an ape's style of using the backs of his knuckles to touch things. He leaned his face in close enough for her to tell his last drink had contained rum.

Jane looked down at her drink, swirled it around nervously, leaned a bit away from him, a little closer to Marlene. Like a lot of the men here, Claudio had taken his T-shirt off and stuck it in his back pocket. He pulled it out now to run it across his forehead and neck.

"How you can take care of your hair—make it so, ahh"— he held out his hands with the T-shirt, rolled them round a few times loosely—"big—and get all those answers correct in class, I just don't know."

To look busy Jane took a sip out of the iced tea. She felt it go as directly to her head as if it were injected into her bloodstream. She wasn't eating much these days, she'd never really drank. She nodded or shrugged at all of Claudio's questions, glanced occasionally down at the perfect V of his chest hair like it was a third face at the conversation. The more she denied any method for cheating, the more secretive she sounded. The drink made her entire body relax, so even her scalp felt like it was loosening up. Before she'd finished the glass she began to grin, at the humor in it all. She found herself beaming loosely around at the bar, at her classmates, at her position.

DAY FORTY-ONE

"Sixty-one hours until the first midterm," Michael proclaimed, looking at his watch.

Her date with Michael was as quiet as her studying. They sat at a separate table from the others at The Bar, sipped herbal teas. The Bar was noisy, full of exhausted slap-happy fear. Few people had slept more than five hours a night for the last few days. The night before, Dana Bork and Sarah Calder had both started crying within half an hour of each other in the library, just putting their foreheads down on their books and sobbing. Dana didn't even have the energy to cover her mouth to muffle the sounds. While one or two students moved to comfort them, the rest continued to methodically squeak highlighters over vocab words. Even the tutors didn't seem as benevolent and even-tempered as they used to.

Tonight, as always, Marlene's table was crowded. She looked over at Jane and Michael frequently, her neck red. She was drinking hard.

"Coffee bothers me," said Michael. "If I drink coffee any time after noon I wake up at three in the morning and watch the ceiling for movement." He snorted at his joke, exhaling smooth out his nose. This was the first time Jane could remember seeing Michael down at The Bar in the evening. Jane didn't even think of suggesting beer. She watched the way he so carefully spooned the tea bag out, wrapped the string twice around the spoon to squeeze the bag thoroughly dry. Unwrapped the bag and left it, wide end down, on the edge of his plate. Because of Krakow's announcement of her past cheating, she had been half-expecting Michael not to turn up for the date.

Marlene glanced over again at Michael and her; a few others followed her glance. Jane saw in their eyes the two of them become one. She was not unhappy with this. She knew Keefer would hear about her date before the end of the night. She thought this way he would know she understood he didn't care for her. She thought he would be relieved she knew they were just friends.

Michael did most of the talking. He told her how to organize her time. "Morning is the best time to study," he announced. "Five o'clock to seven-thirty." He looked at Jane, eyes as confident as if he'd just told her the liver produced bile. "No interruptions that early and the rising sun makes your mind rise."

Jane nodded. He was the expert on scheduled effort. He did everything with the minimum of energy. He walked so effortlessly around campus, so confidently, his feet following his thought, that hazy child's smile on his lips. He believed in the eventual triumph of efficiency, his ideology. The concept of entropy must personally offend him.

"Reading is best in midmorning when comprehension is clearest." He spoke most sentences with such clear emphasis, Jane thought he should have some type of gesture to punctuate his statements with. He should slap the back of one hand into the palm of the other on the word "comprehension"; he should hold up fingers, counting off his major points. Yet he never made any gestures. He talked with his arms down by his sides all the time as though in the final round of "$10,000 Pyramid" where moving your hands would cost you the show.

"The afternoon is when one should make notes, write reports, arrange information and schedules." He nodded. "The evening, just before one sleeps, is the time to memorize. Memory-retention studies have proved this. Knowing the best kind of work to do at each time of day, I schedule my time a week in advance. How many pages, how much vocab."

From what he said, Jane thought he should be a tense person, rigid and angry, but he wasn't. Like a young boy deeply involved in his own game, he was certain of his own rules. So certain of its rewards, he was generous with his knowledge, his understanding of the world. She liked sitting in The Bar with him. She wished she could be as confident as he.

"I hope you do not doubt," he said quite suddenly, looking hard into her eyes, "that I believe Krakow to be mistaken about you."

Jane jerked her chin forward, her face slack, then wondered if the openness of her reaction showed any of the truth. She froze her face, pulled it back into what she hoped was a more confident expression, suggesting an innocent soul, similar thought patterns, a clean conscience. Michael was already looking back down at his tea.

"The last afternoon of each week," Michael continued, "an hour is set aside for the time it will take to schedule the next week."

The way he had brought up the subject of her cheating was just the way her parents would, never actually saying the word "cheating" and moving quickly back to the previous conversation. She felt a moment of real warmth for him. With time, though, she began to feel the strain on her face muscles from the expression she assumed in his presence. With time she began to feel more and more shame for being who she was sitting near him. When The Bar got so noisy they could barely talk anymore, he suggested they leave. She quickly agreed.

Michael drove to his place. She parked her moped and walked after him into his bungalow slowly. She thought she should want this. She would be here for four years. It was possible, perhaps even probable, Bertie would dump her in that time, find someone his parents approved of more, write her a letter explaining kindly, cleanly, passionlessly why. Michael would please her parents just as much. His morals were as solid as theirs, his family must be rich for him to be here. He believed in her. She thought if she had a boyfriend here, if she were sleeping with someone here, maybe she would stop looking at all the men's chests.

When they walked into his bungalow he did not even turn on the light but reached out, took her in his arms and pressed her immediately to his body. She hadn't thought it would go like this. She was startled. After a moment she managed to make herself loosen, flatten in against him, her hand tentatively touching his shoulder, the side of her face flat against his chest. There was a hint of formalin from his hands, the smell muted by soap and cologne. Here, she heard his heart, his secret pumping slow and full onward. Calm as a river, reliable as a washing machine. His hands moved along her back, rubbed her shoulders like a parent would, traced each of her ribs like a doctor palpating her bones.

Gradually her breathing slowed. She pressed closer, listening to his heart. Waited for more, tilted her head a little up toward his to make things easier. In the darkness this was OK. He could be anyone.

Instead he pulled away, ran his fingertips tenderly over a curl near her ear, tucked his shirt in more carefully like it might have gotten mussed and walked back out the front door. She followed confused. He drove with her to her place, waited patiently on his moped while she walked up to the door, her limp a little worse than normal from the awkwardness of it all. He waited there until she'd gotten the door open, as if there were a lot of crime around here. He didn't offer to come in.

"Night, Jane," he called over the putter of his bike. "See you next Monday?" As though they wouldn't be seeing each other every day at school in the coming week, at every class.

She looked at him sitting so straight up on the moped seat, so confident and clear. She realized he was the only

one to call her by her real first name. Not Doris like the
other students, not Guy like the teachers, not Janey like
her parents. For the second time that night she felt warmth
for him.

Visible in the glow of his headlights, she smiled wide,
nodded. He drove away.

Inside she walked restless round the bungalow three
times, kitchen to bathroom to her bedroom, trailing her
hands over the walls, windows and doors, the uneven plaster rasping beneath her fingers. The last circle she made
she kept her eyes completely closed. She ended up in the
doorway of her bedroom, head down, one hand on either
side of the jamb. Her breath was audible. She opened her
eyes, shook her head, packed up her books for the library.

As she drove through the gates to school she noticed a
long lumpy shadow lay across the lawn in front of the library. At first she thought it must be a new series of bushes.
As she got closer she saw it was mopeds parked in a haphaz-
ard fashion all across the lawn rather than in the parking
lot, at least forty of them. Some of them had fallen over on
their sides. Behind them she saw the students. A dark mass
of backs. She parked her bike on the road and walked over,
curious. Everyone standing around drinking. Littered
around them were strange objects, some of which Jane
could make out from the outlines as tennis rackets or stacks
of books, lumps of perhaps clothing. The students were all
listening to someone yelling in the center of the group. Jane
wove her way in and before she even got there she realized
that of course the person yelling was Marlene.

". . . wrong with this school," Marlene yelled, breathing
in deep between each phrase. "I'll tell you. They . . ." Marlene spotted Jane, pulled her in close, hugged her.

"Hey, chickie, where ya been? We've been waiting for
you to start. You left your boyfriend back in bed?" Marlene's
voice was loose, slack with laughter. She didn't continue
with what she had been yelling earlier. Jane looked around,

saw all the pale moons of the people's faces, the only clear detail the darker shadows of their eyes. She ducked her head down. Marlene grabbed her hand with a bony and strong grip. Wiggling her fingers around a bit, Jane tried to relax Marlene's fingers. After a moment she just let her hand go slack. Marlene swung a bottle of vodka out to Jane so it hit her in the arm. Not a pint bottle, a gallon jug with a handle. There was no way to drink out of it but straight from the mouth. Jane shook her head. She'd never seen Marlene like this. Mostly it was the others who got drunk while listening to her.

"Right then," Marlene said. "Let's get down to business." She kicked her pink child-sized suitcase out on the ground in front of her, poured half the vodka gurgling over it. Some of the liquid splashed onto Jane's sandals. The cold surprised her and she stepped back as quickly as if it hurt. The alcohol evaporated off her skin, feeling almost like someone exhaling soft on her toes. The others drifted in a wide circle round the suitcase, watching Marlene, their mouths slightly open. Jane saw someone—she thought it might be Sarah Calder but in the darkness she couldn't tell for sure—stumble a little to the side simply trying to stand up straight. People seemed more drunk than normal, but perhaps Jane just hadn't watched the gradual transformation over the whole course of the evening.

Marlene tapped her pockets, pulled out the matches.

"With this," Marlene intoned in a fake British accent, "our fuhrst annual bohhn-fire, I hereby officially deee-clare and pronounce our mehdical careers beee-gun at this bloody institution." She lit the match with one hand, flicking the head of the match against the box with the ball of her thumb. The match hissed into life. Marlene held the matches high above her head. Jane worried that in pouring the bottle Marlene could have gotten some alcohol on her fingers.

"Cheer up, duckies. Remember, you're here at med

school, you're getting to know each other, studying hard. You're learning if you're a man or a boy, a woman or a girl. When you look back at this time in a decade or so, you'll realize these were the worst years of your life." She tossed the matches in.

The explosion barked a giant's cough. The flames were an almost chemical blue, so bright after the darkness. The flames flickered, hypnotic. Fire so powerful. The students all tilted their faces down toward it. Jane took a step forward. In such hot weather it seemed surprising to see a fire. It was surprising to see a fire not stacked neatly on andirons, not captured safely in a fireplace. To see a fire out in the open, shivering against grass. It looked much more dangerous out here, no longer something contained and comforting, no longer the center of a contented family scene. Not a single person spoke. The flames crackled.

The fire began to die down. The suitcase hadn't really caught yet, the fire just danced across its surfaces, ran along its edges. Marlene tilted the bottle over it to pour the rest in. At the first touch of the vodka the flames jumped up. For a single frozen instant Jane watched the fire slide *up* the spilling arc of vodka, drawing a hissing line of light against the darkness toward Marlene's hand. Jane's mouth opened. Marlene flicked the bottle in fast.

It exploded with a crack of glass. Bits of fire were caught on the flying shards, a shimmering momentary jigsaw. Jane felt something touch her hair and she reached up to find it. Nothing there. Miraculously no one seemed hurt, and the spectacle had been quite pretty. No one stepped back from the fire. The crowd applauded, hooted. If anything they pushed in closer. Jane didn't know why but she stepped in closer also. The fire flickered and jumped against the grass. The night was so dark and hot. Midterms were in two days. They studied all the time and it seemed such a long long time since anything different had happened.

People began to add things to the fire. All the students had brought something. Burpie Loomer added the framed photo of an older couple. Chris Martell tossed in her teddy bear and college yearbook. Every type of graduation present was lobbed in, thumping into the flames, sparks flying, the fire growing: leather desk organizers, many tennis rackets, a portable computer, a pearl necklace, an entire encyclopedia volume by volume. A field hockey set including shin guards. Fifteen or twenty sweaters and suede jackets packed by cautious parents. People threw in bottles of rum, cans of beer, watched the explosions. The tennis racket strings pinged back as they burned through, the pages of the encyclopedia rustled like someone flicking through them quite excited.

The fire quickly got bigger. They stepped back. The heavy smoke blew first one way and then the next, covering them in the cloying stench of burning wool and melting plastic. Only when the heat got too much would they step back a bit, standing with their legs far apart, moving with the cautious balance of the fairly drunk.

The fire stood as tall as a human, spat out sparks and glass, flames sometimes detaching themselves from the rest of the fire to rise majestic into the night, like hats thrown upward. The students passed bottles of rum and vodka around hand to hand. The first time a bottle went by, Marlene insisted Jane drink, held it to her lips tilting it higher and higher until the rum spilled down the side of Jane's face and she choked. It seemed the harsh burn of it went well with the heat on her face, and so once or twice after that, when the bottle went by, Jane drank. All around her the students watched the fire, their features jumping in the light; behind them their shadows stretched and shifted like dancers. People flattened to shifting silhouettes, to bright flashes of skin, an arm tossing in, a face turned away. It

was difficult to determine who did what. When these outlines threw something in they sometimes yelled out insults
about the teachers or their parents or this island. Sometimes
Jane recognized the voice, other times she didn't. Many
things seemed distorted and unfamiliar. Even Marlene's
face right next to her looked different, stretched tight and
hard, the eyes glittering. Jane thought in this light she must
also look different, like someone Marlene had never known,
someone with unknown possibilities.

Bit by bit the fire rose, a heavy mass of shimmering
light. The students stepped back, squinting up into its
height. It devoured the whole night, burned its way into
the eyes, so even when Jane looked away from it, the
etched outline of the flames flickered against the dark. It
seemed more powerful than anything she'd ever really
examined.

Looking at it, into its thick center of fury, hearing the
breath of its destruction, she wondered what it would be
like to be the fire, to be this brilliant hypnotizing creature.
She took half a step forward. For a brief moment she felt
this jolt of pure power roiling up inside, burning up everything she touched, changing it all into ashes and the light
steam of release. She felt herself letting go, affecting people,
destroying. She felt what it was like to be the fire, to burn
everything, to touch them all.

Something warm ran down the side of her face. She
thought it was the start of flames, her body melting into
them. But when she touched it her fingers came away dark.
Blood, from somewhere in under her hair. It ran down her
neck, the shoulder of her shirt sticking to her. She stared
at her hand. The head so highly vascularized, she remembered, pterygoid plexus vein, maxillary vein, retromandibu-
lar. After a moment she remembered to probe around a bit
under the hair. She found a flap that didn't seem attached
right. No pain, no sensation there at all. No one else seemed
to notice the blood. She looked behind her into the dark

night, the black lawn and shimmering trees. She didn't want to leave Marlene's side, to let go of her hand, walk away from the bright safe cluster of people. It seemed like away from Marlene, anything could happen on a night like tonight. Jane pressed the fingers of her other hand against the wound.

When a vodka bottle came by, Jane let go of her head rather than Marlene's hand, took a gulp, passed it on. Her fingerprints bloomed dark and wide on its white label, bleeding slowly down, warping into a monster's grip. The next person to grab the bottle didn't notice.

They threw in furniture now, school desks and chairs; two men heaved in a couch Jane recognized from the library. One of them stumbled after it for two steps, hands outheld, as though about to dive in also. The bonfire spread, throwing its arms up high into the air, fifteen feet, twenty. It crackled and spat and rustled with power, a magical field, a gateway to another place. At least five feet separated it from the nearest bush when the wind changed, the flames tilted. The bush's leaves shivered, first with wind, then with something else. From the bush the fire quickly scuttled to the tree above, swarmed up its branches as agile as a bright monkey, leaves wilting at its touch. Smoke hung in the air. The bonfire lit up the crowd's faces. The flames stood taller than the tree, leaping and dancing, jumping higher and higher from the crown, up into the night. Landed on a potting shed with a thatch roof. Grew to cover that also like hair. The fire shivered and strained now fifteen feet from the chemistry building.

Jane stared, standing with the rest of the motionless students in the flickering light, mesmerized by destruction. She didn't try to stop the fire. She didn't run for help. She watched, entranced, her mouth open, hand holding tight to Marlene's.

A fire alarm went off, a shattering vindictive howl.

Krakow stood yelling in the door of the library. The students shook their heads heavy, sleepers waking up. They looked around with slack faces, ran for their mopeds. Leaving nothing more certain in their wake than their clumsy shadowy rush away.

Fifteen

In the morning Jane looked at the damage with Michael.
The hole in the lawn, the blackened skeletons of chairs and
computers and unidentified things. She wondered what she
could have been thinking. Michael couldn't even look for
long. He walked only near enough to get a sense of the
destruction and then, grimacing, turned his eyes away,
stood there waiting for Jane to be finished surveying the
scene. He didn't bother to ask her if she'd been there the
night before, just assumed she hadn't. If it were a traffic
accident, she guessed he would glance only long enough to
make sure the correct help had been summoned, not curious at all about how badly people had been hurt or what
they looked like. He'd drive past at a normal speed. She
thought she'd gape so hard, she'd forget about the accelera-
tor entirely until someone behind her honked to bring her
back to her own body.

She picked her way cautiously through the wreckage into
the center of where the fire had been, stood there looking
around, the ashes from the fire soft and fluttery beneath
her, the cinders squeaking. The tropical sun bright on the

damage as a spotlight. She tried to reconstruct the fire last night, how the crowd had looked, where she'd stood. How different everything had seemed in the night, in just the fire's light. She ran her fingers through her hair. The cut in her scalp had turned out so small she could find it only by the sore spot. Somehow she thought it should be larger. The shirt she'd worn the night before was as caked with blood as though someone had died in it.

Michael called her name. Jane started.

"Hey," he said, "you're going to get your sandals all dirty."

She looked at him, then down at her sandals, one hand still in her hair. She blinked, changed her expression and began obediently to walk toward him as he watched. Only later did she realize she hadn't been conscious of her limp at all.

Of course there was punishment. At ten-thirty that morning Dean Craigy, the dean who'd interviewed Jane back in Connecticut, convened the whole student body in the auditorium. In filing in, everyone was scared, most fought for the back seats, slouched low wherever they sat. No one looked Craigy in the eye.

"First off," Craigy announced, his voice shaking with anger, "I do not want you to think that last night's outrage, last night's wanton destruction of property, will go unpunished. Through reliable informants we have ascertained who the two ringleaders were." The auditorium stilled, became so perfectly quiet Jane could hear Craigy's belt buckle clank against the podium when he rocked closer. "These two will be expelled without ceremony or explanation. These two will be leaving on a plane this afternoon. Their parents will be informed of their crime." Craigy smiled, his forehead sliding back. It was an exact duplicate of the smile he had given Jane's parents in Connecticut, no change despite the different circumstances.

Marlene's shirt rustled as she exhaled beside Jane. Jane had stopped breathing at all.

"These two vandals," Craigy announced, "my informants tell me, are Gene Rowbothom and Rick Draper."

Marlene tensed beside her, starting to stand up before realizing he had not said her name. She relaxed, her knees went completely slack, her arms, her face. Around them there was instant noise. Laughing, booing, cheering, all at the same time. Jane breathed out slow, slid her hands in round her own waist, shaking. She tried to remember if she had even seen Gene or Rick at the fire.

"This," yelled Craigy, "is what will happen to you if you commit an act of vandalism. We are watching you. We will catch you."

Rick stood up first. Looking around at all of them, he hesitantly touched his cheek, like someone terrified of the injection until the moment after. He jerked into motion, sidled loose-legged down the row of people to the aisle and the exit. Gene stopped by the podium to argue with the dean before following Rick out of the auditorium, looking for his help, stumbling slightly on the threshold. Outside, Jane saw Rick on the lawn making a slow circle, looking up at the sky and the trees, his arms held out.

By now Marlene was smiling, grinning in fact. This morning before the dean's speech, many of the students had walked around and around the damage the fire had caused, even the ones who hadn't been there the night before. They stood there, staring, taking pictures. It looked so much bigger in the morning light, much more impressive. For the first time the students here had something to be proud of, had something to bind them together more than their past failures.

Craigy began to whisper theatrically to all the students about how much they'd been given by society, by their parents and the world; how the gift of that much education and material resources meant a bond, a trust; how last night they had broken that trust.

Jane tried to concentrate on his words, but she spotted Bob Feldington and Susan Newcombe starting to play Rock, Paper, Scissors low in their laps just off to her right. She noticed Keefer sketching, on top of his anatomy lab book, a caricature of Craigy yelling, sweat flying, eyes bulging. Jane kept her head down, certain if the dean looked at her once he would see the guilt in her.

Marlene leaned over and whispered, "What're your brothers' names anyway?"

Jane stared back blankly before she remembered, glanced over at Claren. Answered with the first names that came to her mind. "Sam," she whispered. "Sam, Craig and Keefer."

"Keefer?" asked Marlene.

"Yes," said Jane, trying to smile. "Strange coincidence, huh?"

"And for the rest of you," Craigy called, getting louder now over the rustling sounds of their inattention, "your punishment will be to replant the lawn you have destroyed, to scrub by hand the side of the chemistry building clean. To rebuild the potting shed you burned to the ground."

Craigy paused here to survey his audience. "Also, I will announce a change in our policy that has come about partly because of this episode. Your professors and I have been concerned for a while about the amount of alcohol consumed on campus. We believe last night's destruction of property would not have occurred without the consumption of this dangerous drug, one with so many medically adverse side effects.

"This leads me to declare that from now on there will be liquor restrictions. Each student can buy one book of thirty alcohol tickets per month from the school store. Each ticket will be good for one drink. These tickets will be the only currency The Bar and the school store will take for alcohol. Also, The Bar will close at midnight, from now on, instead of being open twenty-four hours." He paused, surveying the students' shock. "We hope this will eliminate the incidence of activities such as last night's."

There was a long startled silence from the students. Then they began to boo, slow and rising.

"Things," Dean Craigy called out, holding his worn face up to the crowd, "will be different here." Someone to the right of Jane stamped hard and rhythmic on the wood floor. Within three beats the entire student body had picked it up, a hollow quickening thump of feet against wood that drowned out every other sound. Jane could see the dean's mouth still moving. The booms of the floor surged through them all, made her chest feel like a drum.

"Things," Craigy bellowed, "*will* change here." But Jane could no longer hear his words. After the speech, Michael—who had sat fairly close to the front—told her what Craigy had said. Other students heard different versions, including "Kings will chain beer." Which they assumed referred to a newly hired security man locking up the beer at night.

The dean was the first one to leave the auditorium. Frustrated, he stalked slowly off the stage. As he left Jane risked glancing up at him, caught his eye. He looked right at her and his expression did not change at all. He did not see her guilt.

Cleaning up the damage from the bonfire took the students the afternoon, turned into a party. Claudio and Burpie brought five-pound bags of potato chips and pretzel sticks they'd nabbed from the cafeteria. Several people brought beer they'd bought before the ticket rule went into effect. It hadn't been refrigerated, so it was hot in its aluminum cans sitting in the sun. People drank it anyway, tilting the cans back high and gulping against the hot metal, hoping someone from the administration building was looking out the windows, watching. Some students did the work, others stood around, told of college pranks, sang songs that had been Top 40 when they left. Nina Sheiffer and Megan Quigly worked out dance routines involving spinning hands and clicking heels, shuffling about in the ashes. Midterms were the day after tomorrow. Not one person mentioned them. Rick and Gene had already been escorted to the plane.

About halfway through the afternoon the plane puttered over the trees, already pretty high in the sky. Jane noticed no one else looked up. The group quieted down for a moment at the first sounds of the plane, then got louder, loud enough they almost drowned out the engine. After a moment Jane turned carefully away also. Standing still, facing away from the plane, potato chips held forgotten in her hand, Jane found she wasn't able to pinpoint when exactly the sound disappeared.

With almost one hundred students, the work went fast. The last thing to be done was to rebuild the potting shed, and when the timbers of the shed rose slow in the air, creaking and twisting, Claudio began to bellow a sort of extended Tarzan call. Some students joined in, not any words, just raw sound. They yelled loud, got louder, ululating. Jane stood next to Keefer, looking up at the beams swaying into place. Keefer put his hand on her shoulder, threw back his head and bellowed. Jane could feel the narrow weight of his fingers, his chest filling wide beside her with sound. She knew if she moved her hand out just an inch or two she would touch his bony hip. Claren stood on the other side of him.

And Jane opened her mouth to bellow so hard she could feel the pressure behind her eyes, so she shut them as she screamed. With her eyes closed like that she heard clearly, her voice, their voices, all of them together. For one long moment the students screamed louder than the jungle.

And after that day, when the students passed in the hall, they looked each other in the eye more, not scanning their notes last minute or looking down at the ground muttering vocab under their breath. When they looked at each other they didn't necessarily say anything, just looked, a silence between them, an agreement, a communication.

And after that—although during the day Jane maintained to herself that she was ashamed of her part in the bonfire—in the darkness sometimes on her moped she remembered that brief moment of being the flames. Of feeling the heat pour down her face.

Sixteen

⌒

Two days later everything was different.

Her first midterm was with Krakow. He sat her in the far corner, in a chair he turned elaborately around to face away from the rest. When Jane sat in the seat and looked straight ahead, her face was three feet away from the corner of the room where one brick wall met the other. She could examine in great detail the thin lines of mortar. She stared at it for a moment or two, blinking. She'd gotten an hour and a half of sleep last night, two hours the night before. Her flesh seemed to hang as heavy as draperies on her bones.

Krakow passed out the test, handed it to her last. He stared at her as he placed it flat on her desk. She tasted acid in the back of her throat, looked down from him to the exam. Her eyes scanned the first question. He backed away slow. Her hand picked up the pencil, waiting to fill in the answer, waiting for her to decide. The clock ticked forward. Her lips moved around the words. Blearily she glanced over her shoulder to the front of the class. Krakow stood there, his mottled face shining straight at her, smiling. The heat hummed.

She turned back to the test, heard the slow crackle of her breath. She couldn't keep the whole of the first question in her mind, something about the progeny of pluripotent bone marrow. Over the last day and a half, the more she thought the information wasn't sinking in, the harder she'd studied. She'd begun to believe she'd never learned the information in the first place. She'd panicked.

Hazily she scanned down the test for a question on something she remembered. She thought if she could answer just one question, just start the test off, she could do the rest. After her eyes reached the bottom of the page they settled on her hand, her hand which just yesterday she'd watched cup six inches of her cadaver's excised intestine up around the mouth of a faucet, turn the water on to clean the membrane out. The shit running down into the sink, no smell remaining except that of formalin. The empty, almost translucent skin left in her hand, the water coursing down through it, filling it up, making it shiver as though alive. Sausage, she understood for the first time. She'd stared at the bright membrane rippling with water, at her hand holding the membrane, until Chris Martell, waiting for the sink, jabbed her in the side.

Looking down at her hand holding the pencil, she noticed the crisscross of the skin's texture, a mud field that had dried into separate tiny plates. She'd read the pages on bone marrow, she'd read all about its progeny. She'd highlighted the important phrases, made flash cards and spoken the words. She stared at the back of her hand, trying to remember a single word, a single concept.

Through the skin of her hand she could see the outline of a blue river winding its way over her bones. Tug back the skin, she knew, and there would be pink striated muscle, white tendons, a few yellow strings of fat. She listened to the stuttering progress of a hand-powered lawn mower outside, the scraping of pencils on paper. Time passed. A hum began high in her ears, a feeling of heat in her face.

Her vision gradually moved back. Strangely enough, she could see now not only her hand from above, but the back of her own head bent over the test, her thick blond hair, the stiffness of her shoulders hunched in. She noted her skin looked very pale from above, almost bloodless. One white bra strap visible and Marlene sitting behind, glancing over worried at Jane's clenched form. Jane's viewpoint continued to drift back, up. She could see the tops of the heads of all the students writing and rustling about, tugging on their lips and sighing. Claudio rubbed his nose with his wrist and there were faded spidery notes written in blue ink all down the inside of his arm. From close to the ceiling Jane noticed for the first time her right hand moving down the test, filling in each answer as firm as a machine.

She woke up afterward in the cafeteria with the same hand wrapped tight round a cup of hot coffee. The inside of her fingers, she realized, was burning. She could feel the blisters rising on her palm, the flesh cooking. She looked down at her hand, at its white knuckles and raised tendons clasping so hard, and for a moment she didn't even think of letting go.

The anatomy exam was that afternoon; six bodies lay on tables in a circle in the center of the lab. Burnett explained the rules. Three or four students would start at each table. When the buzzer rang, the sheets would be pulled off the bodies, revealing pins stuck upright into organs. Taped to the pins were numbers which matched up with questions on the test, questions like: name the enervation point, or where does this structure enter the venous system? All the students had ten minutes to answer the twenty questions on the body in front of them. When the buzzer rang again the students were to proceed clockwise to the next table. There would be no moving on to the next table before the bell rang, there would be no loitering after the bell. The study assistants and Burnett would enforce that.

The bell rang. The sheets were pulled back. Jane stared at the first body, at its yellow skin flaps pinned back from the smooth bowl of the rib cage where the heart lay all alone like a muscled bag someone had dropped. Numbered pins stuck out of the heart and between the peeled ribs. Her own heart began to beat fast, her ribs moved in and out. Her face got hot and the back of her head quite heavy.

She began to rise into the air again, looking down on the cadaver, peaceful as a balloon. This time not even surprise. The sounds got very distant, the rasp of pencils, the drip of water in a metal sink, a cleared throat echoing as though down a long tiled hall. She felt calm again, almost warm, and it was only then, from high above, she saw the similarities between the cadaver and her own body; the skeleton and hair, the toes and fingers, the tender skull and smelly meat of it all. The differences so subtle between lying down and standing up, between warm and cold, between breathing in and ribs open to the air, between clenched and rigid. The haze of formalin everywhere.

From far above she gazed down at the heart, all alone in its ribbed ditch, and it was like she could see the whole body as clearly as she could see into the chest. She could see how all the muscles fit together, where the nerves ended, how the bones connected. So far above, she wondered how she could make out this clearly where the pins were. She thought this must be how God saw, so far above, only a distant curiosity regarding the actions below.

The bell rang. She wondered distantly if she'd answered any of the questions. She watched her body walk to the next table, clutching the test in its blistered hand. She watched all of them dance on clockwise round their stationary partners in the center.

Afterward, as Jane stood by the exit for a moment with her cheek against the wall, Marlene walked up, placed her cold palm against Jane's forehead. Jane smelled cigarettes and formalin. She smelled perfume and sweat.

"Honey," said Marlene, "when's the last time you slept? When's the last time you ate?" For once her voice was quiet. Jane turned toward her, her head rotating slow as the moon. "You look worse than some of these cadavers. It's time for you to lie down."

Jane imagined herself pushing one of the bodies over and lying down on a steel table, the stillness settling deep into her bones. Imagining this, she stared at Marlene, her mouth still open, her eyes unblinking.

For a moment she saw confusion in Marlene's face, before Jane remembered to blink her dry eyes and twist her lips back in a smile.

Seventeen

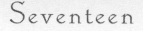

She dreamed of holding out her blistered hands and they exploded into flames, the flames running up her arms. In her dream she threw back her head and laughed.

She dreamed of Burnett and he was lecturing on how to remove skin, the dermis and epidermis, to remove it cleanly and without injuring the fascia just beneath, without damaging nerves or the delicate blood vessels. It was something he had lectured on forcefully several times in the course of the semester. People still cut too deep, tugged too hard, sliced and ripped things.

In the dream he told the students, skin could be thought of as tight clothing which needed to be removed carefully. Like peeling off a leather dress, he said, no need for hurry or brute strength.

In the dream he called a student up to the front of the class, Dana Bork, asked her to bend over for the demonstration. His shoe on her hair, the knife moved. Strangely, there was no blood. His gloved hand grasping for the first clean tug back from her narrow shoulders. Her face scrunched up and looking away.

Midterms were over. Jane had slept some, not enough, but some. Feeling had returned to her face. She smiled now occasionally, when she remembered to, when she concentrated, and Marlene seemed relieved, perhaps believing Jane's strangeness before to have been caused only by exhaustion.

Still, Jane couldn't remember the last time she'd eaten a real meal, and her problems with sleeping continued. She'd doze for a minute or two. The vivid shifting dreams, the images. Her snort into the night snapped her upright in her bed. Blinking around into the dark, thinking of failure. Lying back down slow. Out her window she watched the stars twirl above her through the sky. On the bed she restlessly followed their path, her body lumpy with itches and subtle pains. Not satisfied with remembering bad things she'd done in the last few weeks, she searched further back, remembering misunderstandings in high school, during adolescence and younger, the time she reached for her daddy's hand and touched his zipper instead.

The black market in alcohol took three days to develop, a week to perfect. The islanders shipped the liquor in on their boats. The students could buy it illegally at The Bar or after hours at what was called the Red Door, a house in town with an unpainted wood door where you could get drinks in any quantity. An illegal beer cost about ten American dollars. A bottle of vodka cost up to a hundred. None of them had anything else on which to spend the money their parents kept sending them.

The teachers tried to believe the students were getting drunk all the time on their legal thirty-drinks-a-month limit. Most people used up that limit within ten days. The students considered it almost patriotic to drink more; with each drink you were affirming your lack of belief in the teachers, your contempt for the school. Some of the students began to develop the habit of coming into class in the morning without brushing their teeth, stale beer on their clothes. Two students, Anne Shapiro and Coco Rialto, were expelled after being caught drinking Midori on the beach in front of The Bar, a drink which The Bar didn't serve. Marlene gargled with a teaspoon of scotch each morning, then went up to the teachers after class to ask questions, leaning close and smiling. She knew what she was risking. She leaned toward it, half-hypnotized. There were five more weeks until final exams, two more semesters this year, three years after this one. The pressure wouldn't let up.

DAY FIFTY

"Farmers," answered Jane, not even smiling at the thought. She could see the house now, two stories, only half-painted, panting dogs lolling about on the unmowed yard, a car partially disassembled in what had originally been a flower bed. "My family have been farmers now for three generations." Her lips felt slightly numb. She touched them with her fingertips to make sure they were actually moving.

"Connecticut?" asked Keefer, his voice a little high from surprise. These days Keefer jumped at loud noises. Last week he had shaved off the rest of his hair. To keep himself cooler, he said. If anything, the similarity of baldness emphasized the differences between him and her father. Her father gleamed pink and muscular with power, bloated with blood and health. Keefer looked like a refugee, wiry and miraculous. His emotions were bared from all angles now, his ears left exposed and deserted. She watched him run his fingers over the bared curve of his brain, touching it hesitantly like the edge of a wound. His Adam's apple twitching in his neck.

She loved him, she thought, like a brother.

Claren was fighting more often with Keefer, or maybe it was Keefer fighting with Claren. It was hard to even get clear what the fights were about. It certainly seemed neither would give up gracefully. The more upset Keefer was, the more he stuttered. The more he stuttered, the more Claren patiently filled in the words she believed he was trying to say and then added her objection to them, explaining the fallacies. Gradually she worked up to speaking whole sentences for him, gave examples. Their arguments sounding more and more like one person talking to herself, arguing both sides, with a kind of irregular clicking in the background, a clicking that gradually faded, until Claren reached the end of her debate and smiled, thinking she had won.

"Connecticut?" Jane said. "Oh yeah, with a roadside stand, a lot of herbs and organic produce. The organic stuff really brings in the bucks." Her farmer-parents appeared in her mind, slightly fleshy, smiling, the tendency to rock back and forth in their rubber boots, generally a dirt trail or two rubbed by mistake across their faces.

"You afford here?" Keefer asked, gesturing to the island with his chin. He spoke less these days, less often, each word weighted and measured, skipping articles and adjectives. Sometimes before he spoke, he moved his lips silently, testing out his speech. Like a mime, he talked more with his gestures, with his touches.

"Oh," she said, looking down at the water. She could sense Keefer's face turn in her direction. "My father's brother is an anesthesiologist, quite successful. Patented the Halodine Pump, perhaps you've heard of it. Sort of the black sheep of the family, for not going into farming. My dad tries to get along with him but Uncle Augie never has the time. Normally arrives about two days late for Christmas. Augie doesn't have any kids, never wanted any. Still, he liked the idea of another doctor in the family. Gave me the school as a gift. He can do that sort of thing. Has that sort of money."

The shark rolled by, its dead eyes staring straight ahead to the next turn it would make, the one it made hundreds of times each day. She bent a little forward from her waist, wondering what it would feel like to touch its skin, to run her hand along its wet side, to curve her fingers over the blunt ledge of its nose.

When she turned back to Keefer, he was still watching her, his brow tight.

When Jane went to The Bar with Marlene, Trent often sat down at Marlene's table too. He tended to slouch, to lean in ways limber and easy. Somehow he made the viewer conscious, more than most people, that underneath his clothes he was naked. Perhaps it was the loose way he carried his wide shoulders, his straight male hips, his ribs pressing their pattern out against his shirt when he slouched at the table. She thought that nude he would act no different. Like the islanders, he would be as confident and natural as when he was dressed.

His hair fell in lank curls, thick and uncombed. The curls rolled across his shoulders. His eyes brown and slow-moving. They watched what he wanted for the length of time he wanted and then they looked away. Sometimes she watched his eyes point for five or ten minutes straight, at the table, at Marlene, at the ceiling. His tilted wide stare, the circles of sleep under his eyes, the white sheen of his teeth. Jane sometimes thought he was almost asleep, almost in a trance, his eyes so unfocused. Then his eyes blinked, rolled, and he stared right back at Jane. She immediately turned away, flustered and heart beating. She could tell from the angle of his head out of the corner of her eye he continued to watch her for a while. He never felt a compulsion to be polite.

He had a habit of pausing when he walked into a room, even when it was a room he'd been in many times before, even when the same people were there as before. She'd noticed this in the first few weeks of school, began to watch for him to enter, searching for what was different about his entrance from other people's, trying to understand why he paused. His stopping there in the doorway with his head tilted, looking out from the side, not as though he were surprised at what he saw, but as though he were rethinking something, perhaps going to change his mind this time. He stood there, motionless, his slow eyes, the flat stretch of his body, his hollow belly, and she never was sure what it was he considered. She knew when he did move it would be fast, sloppy and strong, the desperate swing of his limbs, his loose hips rolling. She waited. She did not know for what.

He seemed always on the edge of things, of tiredness and hunger, of hatred and laughter. Each time he stood there in a doorway, thinking, the image came to her mind of a dog blinking in surprise at the soft snick of the chain coming off. Each time he stood like that, large and impulsive, she thought his next move could be anything, anything at all.

In The Bar, Trent sat beside Marlene. People had to move aside for him. Marlene made them do it.

"Hey," she said, "Buggaloo, move your big butt on over for my lover boy." As Trent sat down Marlene stared at him. He looked down at the table, then back at her, sudden and clear. She ran her hand up to his thigh. Jane tried not to look at where Marlene's hand stopped. They began to whisper, so quiet even Jane sitting on the other side couldn't hear them, Marlene's harsh laughter bleating out, Trent's white teeth opening in a smile, his laugh abrupt as a bird's. The nights Marlene didn't leave with Jane, she went home with Trent.

DAY FIFTY-FIVE

Her third date with Michael. He laid her down on his bed, pressed against her as politely as a dance partner, no clothing removed, no hands rubbing anywhere but along her back, her arms.

She became conscious of her breath, tried to quiet it down, still it sounded loud in her ears, rasping and needy. She touched his hips gently, hesitantly, suggestively. He shifted away. He sat up and turned on the light. Asked if she wanted any tea.

Walking toward the kitchen to get the tea, he looked so hurt. Lonely as a child. Afterward she hated herself.

One of the cadavers from anatomy class disappeared, the one that had been Sarah Calder's. Sarah said she didn't know where it had gone. She said she came into class in the morning, the same as everyone else, and it was just gone. The sheet fallen rumpled to the ground like the body had sat up abruptly, remembering an old appointment. Every part of it taken, even down to the pieces in the plastic bags.

Burnett was in a rage. He said no one, *no one* had ever taken a body from his class. This school was bad in general, but this class was the worst he had ever seen, first the bonfire, now this. He got more and more furious, standing in front of Sarah, no one to focus his anger at but her. He abruptly said that she was expelled from school. She didn't argue, couldn't seem to speak, but stood there, frozen, with her mouth open. Burnett stepped toward her. Jane thought he would hit Sarah if she stayed there in front of him silent for another moment, he would slap the flat of his big hand hard across her slack face. Sarah stepped back instead, fast, hands fumbling, searching behind her so she wouldn't trip. She left the room. She left that afternoon on the plane.

There were only twenty-five students left in the first-year class now.

Marlene came home late that night, driving up fast.

Jane sat up startled at the noise, straight out of what could perhaps have been called sleep. She realized she really had to pee.

Marlene just dropped her moped over on its side rather than pushing it up on its kickstand. There was the clank of metal. She took the steps up to the door two at a time. She'd been out with Trent.

It had rained recently, torrentially, as it rained only in the tropics, harsh and complete as applause. The jungle was quiet now, dazed, thinking it through, things dripping.

Jane heard Marlene push open the screen door, the pull and slap of it behind her, her fast steps into the bungalow. Her breathing came a little rough, maybe through her mouth. Jane waited. After she didn't hear anything for a few minutes, she wrapped the sheet around her (she'd forgotten one night to wear a nightgown during midterms and had not worn one since) and tiptoed cautiously for the bathroom.

From the door of her room, she spotted Marlene standing framed in the living room window, nude, looking out at the beach, picking at the dry skin of her lower lip with an abstracted intensity. Her wet clothes lay by her feet in a heap. At first Jane was stopped by the unconscious grace of Marlene's body, the long line of it. By the perfect silence of the moment. Her body gleamed white in the light, the buttocks being the only softness. Beyond her the sea rolled, upset by the rain, fracturing the moonlight. Jane thought, if Marlene weren't picking at her lip, this would be one of those scenes painters put on black velvet.

Jane had already started backing up into her room, silent, when she noticed four, maybe five, marks along Marlene's back and butt, roundish dark blotches, discolorations on the smooth skin.

It wasn't until she was back by her bed that she understood they were bruises, quite large ones, in different stages of healing.

The next morning Jane noticed Marlene was wearing less revealing clothing these days. She moved sometimes more cautiously, sitting down slow. Jane realized she had been doing so for a while. Trent, on the other hand, frequently wore no shirt, his skin smooth and untouched.

DAY FIFTY-SEVEN

The humidity made everything damp here, walls felt sweaty, paper got moist, ripped slow and easy in the hands. The midterms when she got them back were curled at the edges; each test had a sweat smear in the lower right-hand corner where the teacher's hand had rested while grading. The ink was already blurred, bleeding gradually out into the paper. She wondered if after enough time the ink would erase itself completely, the white paper dyed evenly a light blue.

Her grades on the tests were all in the low nineties, A-, A. The class average was seventy-two. She tried to feel happiness, could muster only disbelief. She knew her parents would be sent her grades. She tried to picture her parents' satisfaction, their victorious smiles as they scanned the school's letter. They'd always told her she would finally learn how to take tests well. They'd always told her she would have to.

After a while of trying to picture her parents holding the letter, perhaps standing by the mail table, perhaps seated in the dining room, she realized she could not picture them anymore except as they stood in front of the Porsche, in the photo she had of them tacked up on the wall. She could not picture her father with his arms in any way but hanging slack at his sides, nor her mother with her hands anywhere but holding each other decorously in front of her pleated blue hips. She could not remember the backs of their bodies, the sides of their faces, how their faces moved while they talked. She could not picture them other than politely smiling straight ahead into the camera.

That afternoon she stood in front of the photo trying to remember how her mother sat, how her father buttered his bread. She tried sitting like them, gesturing like them; nothing specific came to mind. Even the system her father used in folding up *The New York Times* to read had become blurred and disordered in her mind. She noticed for the first time her parents' photo was curling up at the edges, around the tacks. She took it off the wall to flatten it out, centered it between the pages of her heavy histology textbook, closed the book.

The next morning when she opened it again, the front of the picture had glued itself firmly to the page. Jane pried at its edges to pull it off, slowly and carefully. No matter how gently she did it, the rim of the photo just stretched out further and further. In desperation she tried one fast jerk. The image ripped with a soggy sound. She looked down at the photo, at the pieces in her hand and on the page. What remained on the book she scraped off with the back of a knife. The colors of her father's face had bled ghostly and backward onto Fig. 16.9—the schematic illustration of sensory hairs in the inner ear. Her mother's torso had become just a blue mush of paper, shaped now short and wide. The only piece of the picture that remained affixed to the photo's back was a pale patch of skin near one edge. It could have been her father's scalp or her mother's knee. After a while of wondering what she should do with the picture now, she realized she couldn't throw it away. She hung the remaining piece of skin back up on the wall.

DAY FIFTY-NINE

Krakow was furious about Jane's good grade on his mid-term. In the whole class only Michael and Claudio received better grades.

During lunch hour Krakow marched up to Jane in the cafeteria. At the time Jane had been looking at her tray, an empty hot dog bun sitting on its side next to a bowl of canned and syrupy fruit salad, the pulpy grapes almost translucent. If asked, she would not have been able to say what she was thinking about. Her eyes were just moving over the tray, over the fruit salad, over the bun, moving over them round and round. It was a state perhaps close to sleep. Suddenly Krakow was standing there, rapping his knuckles on the table beside her tray like one would knock on a door. She jumped her head up, focused fast on his red face. Her eyes hurt.

"The difference between fibroblasts and fibrocytes," he barked, triumphantly smiling all around at the students, thinking he was finally about to catch her unprepared here in the cafeteria, without her standard method of cheating. The students at the nearby tables stared. The unwritten rule being that the cafeteria and The Bar were sacred, the only two places where teachers couldn't bother them.

Jane licked her lips, her tongue dry. She let her gaze float slowly down his face to the rash on his neck, seeing the way each red inflammation must swell up over days, then heal. She thought that on a time-lapse film the skin on his neck and face would bubble like a swamp.

She realized time had passed. He was waiting. She could feel the exact press and release of her heart, looked down at where her hands had been blistered. Recalled the question with effort.

"Absence of collagen secretion," she heard her mouth articulate into the silence.

Krakow snorted out, almost as loud as a sneeze, became

smaller with that one exhale. He looked around again at all the other students watching him; he had such a different look this time. She saw now he *had* to prove her cheating.

After this day Jane began to get jumpy outside of class also. Even in her bungalow, even in The Bar.

There were only six weeks until finals. She had to do well. She had to be able to transfer out of here at the end of second year. She needed to leave this place.

Eighteen

Marlene was the first one to say anything.

"Doris," she asked, "you losing all the weight for Michael?"

It took Jane a moment before she even thought of looking down at her body. It was the first time she had done so in a while. Her shorts appeared baggier than she remembered, her T-shirt hung loose. It looked a little like she'd been shrunk, not only skinnier, but shorter also, like in a science fiction film where the protagonist ends up so small that family pets and common household appliances become threats.

In the last two months she realized she hadn't really examined her body routinely like she used to, not hefted its parts in her hands and sighed, not tried on her tightest pair of pants once a week, lying down on the floor to tug the zipper closed. She hadn't had time, hadn't had the energy. At night she undressed in the dark, not wanting to look, not even to touch her lank humid limbs. Her flesh appeared so magnified and slack with sweat. Rolling out of bed in the morning, she focused on her fear, tugging on another pair of elastic-waistband jogging shorts, another oversized T-shirt, stepping fast over to her books.

Now, with Marlene watching, she hesitantly smoothed the folds of her T-shirt against her body. She could feel the curve of her ribs much more easily than she remembered, the column of her stomach muscles. Everything bared, somewhat smaller and more fragile than she would have guessed it would have looked like. Ten pounds lighter, she wondered, fifteen? She was surprised she could lose track of her body like this, lose control.

She pulled up her T-shirt to touch her belly gently, traced the outline of her new navel with confusion, ran her hand over it again. Something about it seemed familiar.

Looked up to see Marlene staring. Jane's hands froze on her body. She tried to remember the question.

"For Michael?" she asked.

DAY SIXTY-THREE

The tongue from Sarah's cadaver reappeared stapled onto the mouth of the portrait that hung in the library's lobby, the portrait of Queen's first dean, Ranulph Bleek. It was the whole tongue, not just the part you can see easily in someone's open mouth. The tongue all the way down to its root in the throat. It sagged long, muscular and vaguely obscene from the dean's lower face, his tight smile obscured. By the time Jane heard and went to see, there were a lot of students already there, watching two islanders getting up on ladders to pry the tongue off. Dean Craigy paced back and forth at the base of the ladders overseeing the work, while the students clustered back, fifteen or twenty feet away, on the stairs and at the edges of the hall, watching it all, watching the dean. He had gotten increasingly bad-tempered since the bonfire, muttering to himself and swinging his leathery face back and forth with suspicion as he walked down the halls. Now he shot his narrow eyes all about, to the students and then back up to the work. His neck mottled.

Although the men worked carefully, the painting ripped a little in two separate places from the staples. The paint beneath was shown to be bleached from the formalin, in an outline of the event.

When the shorter islander stepped off the ladder with the tongue held out awkwardly between his finger and thumb, the dean cuffed him hard on the back of the head.

DAY SIXTY-FIVE

Jane was watching her hands cut up the detached penis, slicing it in cross section to look at the corona of glans and erectile materials. Marlene was supposed to be helping. She was supposed to be doing part of the cutting. Instead, she stood back, her arms wrapped tight around her ribs, watching. Watching the penis, watching Jane. Occasionally Jane glanced up at her worried.

Marlene asked abruptly, "How can you do that?"

"What?" asked Jane.

"Cut that up like that."

Jane almost laughed. It seemed like such a silly question. The detached penis lay on the table beside the cadaver's shoulder so she only had to make a small gesture to point out the nearly empty body cavity. The internal organs placed in clear plastic bags like leftovers.

"But this is a *penis*," Marlene said. "You're doing it like other people carve fucking snowflakes out of paper, just looking concentrated."

Jane searched the anatomy room, she didn't know for what. For the first time in a while she was conscious again of its smell, the greasy yellow sweetness.

"Come on," Jane said, "you've found this easier than me

the whole time. You managed it from day one. Now I've got it. It was really difficult but I can finally do my job." She was surprised at the anger in her voice. She used to be such a placid person, she used to be someone she could predict. She inhaled, rubbed the heel of her gloved hand along her forehead, blinked several times.

Marlene was silent. Apparent in the pause was how different the experience of the class had been for the two of them. Marlene jerked her chin at the penis. "Yeah," she said, "well, you might as well keep going."

Jane turned back to the dissection. The organ lay dark and shrivelled as an old mushroom. To hide her expression she bent closer to the material, watched her hands saw carefully across its spongy shaft, trying to maintain a straight line. She remembered Bertie holding her hand like this around himself, a circle with the thumb and forefinger, him teaching her how to slide her fingers up and down. She had concentrated just as hard on doing that right.

DAY SIXTY-SEVEN

In Histology class she noticed Michael watching her from across the room, staring at her, no more emotion on his face than when he studied his books. She looked away from him, down to her arms, smooth, with these new muscles becoming apparent. When she glanced back at him a few minutes later he was just turning away. She blinked, looked down. He had not smiled at her at all.

During class she sometimes rubbed her knees now, their smooth revealed shields. It was like having someone else's body to touch all the time, someone who could not go away, someone much thinner than she'd ever been, more athletic, muscles she'd never known baring themselves more each day. The skin was somehow smoother, more firm. Running the pads of her fingers over her knees, she glanced up, caught Trent watching the movements of her fingers.

She stared back at him. His tilted stare, mouth open. He did not blink. After a moment, she turned away.

Walking down the hall, she was more conscious of the muscles and bones in her that had been so buried. As she walked she felt the way they moved, the way they swung and clenched and balanced on their pivots. She swayed more than she used to, rolling her legs out further, feeling her body respond so smooth. She did not think that much anymore about the jerk of her limp. It's even possible her limp didn't jerk as much, with her decreased weight, with her different walk. She thought instead of the torque of her hips, the bones rolling forward, the way she could touch their outline at any time.

She was also more conscious of threat, of other people and corners, watching for them to come up unexpectedly, a table catching at her outlined thigh, or Claudio and Burpie racing down the hall toward her, feet thumping, yells echoing. She stepped back then, her fingers pressed into the new flat spot between her breasts.

The middle finger of Sarah's cadaver turned up in Dean Craigy's chili, pointing up from beneath the orange cheese. The first Jane knew about it, the first she guessed most of them knew about it, Craigy was standing in the doorway to the student cafeteria, red-faced, screaming at Walker Rice that he was expelled from this school as of this moment. He chose Walker because Walker happened to be laughing fairly hard at that moment and because he was sitting next to the entrance to the faculty lunch room. Once Walker realized what had just happened to him, he apologized profusely for making too much noise if that was the problem, suddenly dead serious. He was a third-year student, had only one more year to go. Craigy didn't listen, stepped fast from the room, the napkin pressed to his lips. Walker followed, pleading, his voice echoing back down the hall into the complete silence of the cafeteria.

There were only ninety-six students in the whole school now. Keefer said this was at least five less than normal by this point in the year. He said that meant almost a half a million dollars difference to the school this year alone.

DAY SEVENTY

In the hallway after Physiology, Marlene made fun of Jane about Michael. Trent was with Marlene and he stood, one hip canted forward, his head to the side, watching. Marlene ran the back of one finger along Jane's jaw, smiling wide, almost angry. Her fingers cold even in this heat. The gesture reminded Jane of someone else's gesture from a long time ago, she couldn't remember whose.

Since midterms Jane had caught Marlene watching her sometimes during class, watching Jane with eyes very flat and still. Marlene didn't look away once Jane spotted her staring. Each time it happened Jane tried to smile back, uncertain what else she could do.

"You know," Marlene said, cupping her hand round the top of Jane's shoulder, the way a buddy might, or perhaps a policeman, holding her out for inspection by Trent. "I'm real proud of our little girl. Doris here got herself a boyfriend."

Jane turned from Marlene to Trent. When he looked at someone straight on, he seemed a bit like Jonah, his face so very still, his eyes centered, the white sheen of his teeth.

Marlene tightened her grip on Jane, her thumb running over the newly visible bump at the clavicle's end. "Does Michael," she asked in a relaxed tone, "ever do you like a dog?"

In horror Jane turned her gaze back to Marlene. She noted the fixed smile, the overly bright shine in her eyes.

Marlene's hand on her shoulder lay motionless now. Jane stared at her so hard she forgot she herself existed. She began to glimpse for the first time the depths of Marlene's needs.

DAY SEVENTY-ONE

Jane sawed through the bone while Marlene held the knee and ankle still. The class was removing the right legs of all the male cadavers. Jane's leg rolled back and forth beneath her handsaw, the rest of the body shifting only stiffly. The exposed flesh, in spite of all her efforts to keep it wet with the formalin, was dried out as beef jerky, tasseled and fissured.

Jane couldn't seem to find the most efficient angle for the saw and the last bit of bone took her a while, head down and arm pumping, standing there between the splayed and rocking legs. As the bone finally separated, the limb jerked in Marlene's arms and she took a half step to the side for balance. Jane traded the saw for a scalpel and began to cut carefully through the last few nerves and blood vessels connecting the leg to the rest of the body. She held each structure with the tips of her fingers, cut with a flick of the wrist. She didn't realize Burnett was there until he spoke.

"Exactly," he said. She flinched, turned to see him standing a few inches away, looming inside the V of the splayed legs with her. Glancing back down, she noticed although she had jumped, her fingers had stayed still, holding on, the knife unmoving. She exhaled. Sometimes, these days, her hands actually scared her.

Burnett bent a little closer to her shoulder to examine her work. She could smell his old man's breath, hot and with a closeted sourness like the odor of cheese. "With amputations in the last century, before anesthesia, the whole point was speed. Get the patient drunk, tie him down and go. The doctors used to time it, compete. A minute, half a minute. To get through bone in that time takes strength, skill."

His head jerked hard to the side. He pursed his lips patiently, straightened up, looking around the room. "Of course that's changed now." Jane could not tell what he thought of this advancement.

"You still want," he said, "to be relatively fast so the patient is under for the least amount of time. But now in operations you've got to be gentle also, with the internal tissues. So gentle it's almost as though no fingers were ever inside." He turned back to her. "You've got the touch, fast but delicate. If you can do this with living bodies you'll make a great surgeon."

She did not know how to respond. She stared up into the height of him, into his slow eyes and red loose lips. "Thanks" seemed somehow inappropriate. She didn't like him this close. Because she could think of nothing to say, she nodded instead, made the final cut and stepped into the place where the leg had been connected. Pushing it aside like a subway turnstile in Marlene's arms, she took two steps up the body, away from Burnett. She could breathe now. She knew he still watched her but she could breathe. She rested her elbows on the body and pursed her lips, as though just surveying her work from another angle.

Burnett reached out then with his long long arm and touched her on the back of the neck. She froze. His large fingers at the base of her skull. She stood there completely still in the cold room, thinking this was the place cattle were hit to kill them. She dared not move her head. She could hear Marlene shift the leg nervously in her arms, adjusting the weight.

Jane noticed at this point her left elbow was resting on the cadaver's face, in the dip between the nose and mouth. Under her elbow she could feel the cartilage of the nose as well as the soft tissue of the lips, could feel this through the bandages wrapped round the head. She thought if this body were a living person, she would be interfering with his breathing, she would be pressing his lips closed, squishing his nose. She would be suffocating him.

Burnett took his hand back slow, walked away. Jane closed her eyes, breathed out. Kept her eyes closed for another moment. Her elbow felt comfortable where it was, she didn't bother to move it. She was too tired.

That night Jane dreamed she was losing more weight, that it was just dropping off of her. Her knee fell first, then her hand and part of her shoulder, the slack thump of meat onto the cafeteria floor. Visible in the holes created was not the cross-sectioned slice of bone and muscle she was used to, but only more skin or something close to skin, smooth as white plasticine, like there was nothing else within her, just layer after layer of undifferentiated exterior.

When her left ankle fell to the floor with the soft plop of ripe fruit, everyone congratulated her on her svelte streamlined body, on the loss of her limp. Strangely enough, her parents were there also, packing the old parts of her away into a garbage bag as fast as they fell, wiping their hands clean of any sweat or stains. Burnett stepped forward, traced one finger along the smooth flat of Jane's new face and said, "Less complex biological systems are generally more successful."

Marlene had to pick her up to hug her, pulled her hard to her chest. Jane felt fear of being held up in the air without arms to catch herself if she fell, but she found herself smiling out of confusion at Marlene. She had no limbs to do anything else.

Nineteen

‿‿

One afternoon Trent began to cut his cadaver up all wrong.

Jane stood beside Marlene, watching her sponge out the stale urine left in the recently opened female bladder. She thought she was probably the first one to notice. She heard the sound above all the other noises in that room, the awkward cutting and cracking, the slaps of wet flesh. The sounds were too even, too repetitive. She looked over to Trent two tables away and saw his slow motions, methodical as a man cutting up bread. He made level transverse slices through the uterus, completely destroying it as an organ. His head down, she could see no part of his expression. His motions appeared relaxed, almost drunken. He reached the base of the uterus, paused and began to work slowly and carefully up over the pubic mound, the crunkling of hair now added, the deeper scrape of knife against bone. Jane stared at him. Noticed his wide bony hands, the tenderness with which they cut and held. She stared at him as though she'd never seen him before.

Megan Quigly noticed next. She was at the table just behind Trent. She glanced over, then looked again. Straightened up slow, staring. Randy Nally followed her gaze. Other students noticed, looking over confused, then watching, their knives hanging forgotten in their hands. More people turned at the increasing silence behind them or followed the stares of the others.

Bending over, Trent cut his careful bread slices down between the legs, through the clitoris and labia and anus. Earlier during this class the legs of each of the female cadavers had been spread apart, the tendons grinding and cracking, then a board jammed between the feet to allow the students access to the external genitalia. When Trent's knife reached the bottom of the anus, he straightened up, touched the curled fingers of his hand to the small of his back like he was tired. He sighed and then bent back down to it, evenly slicing across the top of both widespread thighs, taking care that the cuts from one to the other lined up straight. The incisions were about half an inch apart. He didn't look up at any of the other students in class.

Bent low over Ned's cadaver, Burnett was inspecting the ovaries. He slowly straightened up, glanced around. "Class," he said. "Don't forget the integrity of the perineal body is critical in childbirth. Learning its anatomy well can help to avoid prolapses." He pulled off his gloves with crisp snaps. "Twenty-six more days until exams." He didn't hear their complete silence, didn't notice their stares, perhaps because he'd always expected this absolute a silence when he spoke. "Class dismissed." He dropped his gloves into the garbage near him and walked toward the exit.

Trent brought his head up from the body to watch Burnett go. The knife swayed lazily in his hand as though in a wind no one else could feel. There was a shred of something stuck to the blade. When the doors swung shut behind Burnett, Trent's eyes moved slowly past the doors to follow the line of the wall, before turning back to the body. He started the next cut. His mouth hung open.

No one said a word. Chris Martell moved first, stepping

backward toward the doors still holding a spray bottle of formalin, her head slightly tilted as though thinking of something else. The rest of the class followed silently, no one turning their back on Trent, no one speaking. Like there was a baby asleep in the room they didn't want to wake.

Even Marlene, or perhaps especially Marlene, made no noise, said nothing, not to Trent, not to the others. Not a joke, not a swear. She stepped away from Jane, keeping silent, walking backward, glancing over her shoulder as she went to make sure she wouldn't knock anything over, sending it clattering into the peace. Her face very still, her mouth open in concentration.

And maybe it was the very silence in that room, the drip of the faucet, the muffled creeping movement, the rhythmic rasp of Trent's blade against the bone of the knee, maybe it was all this that made Jane uncertain about when she should move, at what point she should join the line. Maybe it was the way she watched Trent so closely, like with the bonfire, almost hypnotized by the destruction, his hands, his bent-over position, watching for what he would cut next. Her own self forgotten, just his movements existing. Her eyes starting to close, tired for so long now, like she might just lie down here and sleep, sleep in this cold, sleep deeply, as she had not been able to do in so long.

Once the last student left, a much deeper silence settled. Her eyes closing more, a great peace inside. She watched Trent, his cutting, his hands moving sure and tender across the body. She placed her own hands flat on the steel table in front of her for balance, to hold herself up from that sleep rising through her bones. Her head started to droop.

Someone's arm slid smooth around her neck and pulled her away. She went with it that easily, her eyes shut, paced along backward, her shoulders against the man's chest. Raised one sleepy hand to his elbow, and at the first touch of the bony joint, knew it to be Keefer.

She opened her eyes in surprise. Thin but stronger than she would have thought, he pulled her so silently out of the room and up the stairs, out into the heat and the sun, back into the noise and the people, set her down on the steps among the crowd of them and eased her back gentle to lean against his warm chest. Holding her there, he rubbed the chilled flesh on her arms until she was almost breathing normally again, until the warmth of the sun and his body had worked their way into her. She felt his lips silently rehearsing their words against her hair until he got them right.

"Come back, Doris," he said. "Come back to me."

She lay slack against him, held in his arms, staring straight up into the white sun, her body shivering less and less.

Trent came up, five minutes later. He stepped out through the doors, into the sunlight, into the waiting circle of them. He was laughing hard. As one they backed up, but now he was without his lab overalls, his gloves, the knife. He looked again like the Trent they knew. His teeth were white and bared, his throat jerking as fast as if choked, his face red with pleasure. He seemed so normal in his shorts and tank top, laughing at all of them. And not one of them moved toward him or away, no one said a word, as he jolted into his walk around them down to his moped.

That laughter was how a lot of the students decided to take it in the end, as a joke delivered completely deadpan. Burpie, Claudio and Susan got hysterical with laughter each time it was mentioned. They held their sides, shoulders shaking. Gasping, they described to each other again and again that moment when they had all begun to back up, their faces, their fear. The three of them acted it out, exaggerating different people's reactions, Randy's half-stumble, Ned's facial twitch. They said as people moved toward the exit, they could smell them, sweet as freshly opened beer. Burpie began to hiccup with the giggles, tears came to Claudio's eyes. Susan slid to the floor, gasping there weakly with her legs pressed tight together.

Others believed Trent had—at least momentarily—been out of control. They stayed far away from him, in The Bar, in the cafeteria, in the hall. If it had been any other student than Trent, someone would certainly have talked to him afterward, asked him how he had intended it, made sure he was alright. But with Trent, even those who thought he'd been joking did not clap him hard on his long stooped back, did not bring the incident up with him to laugh about it together. Instead, they hesitantly talked with him about other things, awkwardly looking up into his waiting tilted stare, stepping away after just a few labored minutes.

At least on the surface, Marlene's reaction seemed to be somewhere in between. She stared at Trent a lot when he was not looking. She examined his arms, his legs, his gestures, as though these might answer some unasked question. Her expression was not loving or fearful, but something else, very absorbed. In general Marlene spent less time with Trent, but she still did spend time with him, every few days. Whenever she got back from seeing him, Jane could tell where she had been without even asking. Marlene glittered then more than ever, her eyes open, shining, her lips a little swollen, and she laughed easy and high, punchy. She laughed, dropping her fingers casually to her jerking neck, the delicate cords and tendons. Tracing them tenderly.

The students decided to read Jane's reaction as pure paralyzed fear. They said it was lucky Keefer had been walking by, had gone down for her. They said she was not good in emergencies, asked if she fainted a lot. She could see they thought paralyzing fear a fundamental part of her character.

Even those who were pretty sure Trent had been serious didn't tell Burnett what he had done. None of them were sure enough. By and large, they were not the kind of students who easily ran to authority.

DAY SEVENTY-THREE

That next anatomy class, after Trent cut up the body wrong, he pulled back the sheet from the cadaver, inhaled in surprise and called for Burnett. Burnett paced over, looked down, taking it all in, then moved his slow eyes up to Trent. Trent stood there, his eyes still on the sliced body, his mouth open, blinking.

"Mr. Maddocks," Burnett said, and Trent brought his face up. Burnett watched him, his head to the side, judging him.

With them standing this way, Jane could see clearly how much taller Burnett was than Trent, three or four inches easy. Burnett moved his chin higher. Trent did not shift under the inspection, his eyes did not shimmy.

Burnett turned to the class slowly. "I can see my previous punishment strategy is not working." He narrowed his eyes, looked off at the ceiling.

"In the manner of scientific experiment," he continued, "I will then try a new one. I no longer care who is responsible for these jokes. You're all just as guilty to me. All of you. Next joke, I will expel the first alphabetical person. Is that clear?" He paused, looked around the room. "That would be, ahh, little Jenny Custule, yes? Think about that. You have your little fun and she leaves. As you probably all know, Jenny's been getting quite good grades, working hard. Jenny, why don't you wave hi now. Wave hi to the class." Jenny looked around at all of them, her face slack, still holding a half-opened package of gloves in her hand.

"Jenny," Burnett screamed, spittle spraying from his lips. "I said wave hi."

Jenny jumped, waved the hand with the gloves hard, at all of them.

"You got that?" Burnett said. "I don't care what kind of grades Jenny's been getting or her whereabouts for the last twenty-four hours. I don't care if everyone else in the class confesses. She gets on the next plane. A second joke and the next alphabetical person goes." He inhaled and bellowed out with a space between each word, "*I—will—not—stand—for—this*."

He paused, stepped closer to Trent, just the table between them now, the sliced cadaver. "Your cadaver is ruined," said Burnett, leaning forward, almost whispering. "We have no extras until next term. You will have to work with someone else for the rest of the semester." Burnett looked around the room, into the face of each of the students. Even before his pale eyes reached her, Jane realized he already knew his choice.

"Work with Guy," Burnett said. "She is getting quite the touch." He faced her, still speaking smooth and careful. "You'll learn a lot from her."

Trent twisted his lazy head toward her, Burnett smiled and Jane took a step back.

That afternoon she was sitting on Jonah's dock, looking out at the endless sea leading all the way home.

She thought of asking Dean Craigy to allow her a little time away from the school, in view of her good grades. Not too long, she thought, just a week or so. Just a week or so back at her home, out of the heat, where she could eat. Just a week at home in her bed, away from the books, away from The Bar, away from her friends.

But she knew she couldn't ask for this, she knew he'd never say yes. She realized she couldn't stop any of this because it was what she'd asked for.

Twenty

Keefer kept his hair shaved off, said hair made him sweat more. He ran his fingers absentmindedly over his skull during class, repetitively.

Being bald felt like skinny-dipping, he told Jane down at the dock, the skull so sensitized without its habitual covering. Even with his eyes closed he could sense someone else's hand held a half inch off his scalp. He said he could feel the warmth, he said he could feel the *presence*. Jane tested him again and again, her finger shivering so close above different positions: his left temple, the base of the occipital plate, the sagittal suture. His pale scalp stretched tight over the smooth shell of bone beneath, an almost bluish tinge. She held her finger motionless, near. He waited, concentrating. His eyelids trembling, his pale mouth pursed.

On this island, the humidity had an effect on everyone's hair. It affected different people differently.

In her parents' home, back in the States, Jane's hair used to lie quiet and shiny, brushed out so smooth you could see vague reflections in it, an open door, the lit TV, her father's smooth skull. It had swung heavy, obedient, a gentle whisper along her back.

Each day, here, by midafternoon Jane could see oil streaking down Marlene's hair, darkening the color in stripes. It angered Marlene. She washed it twice a day and brushed it roughly each evening so the slap and whisk of hair filled the bungalow.

Trent's hair got curlier, a little more, it seemed, each day. Heavy shining ringlets, wavy at the top like the hair of heroines in old vampire movies, the curls spilling down his neck, sometimes falling forward to obscure his expression. Simply looking at those curls, Jane knew what they would feel like in the palm of her hand, weighty, solid, shifting slightly like something alive. When Trent pushed his hair back with two bent knuckles, Jane felt the weight of it in her own palm.

Holding her finger above Keefer's head, she thought his bared skull was as beautiful as a piece of art, like Japanese pottery, elegant and stark. It seemed to get more beautiful each day. She wanted to have armed guards nearby, surveillance systems. She liked imagining the shine of his smooth skull bobbing down the stairs to the autopsy room to get her away from Trent, to lead her out. No one else would have gone down those stairs for her. She imagined his panic as he ran, his breath high in his mouth, his hands grabbing at the railing. She told herself she was the sister he'd never had. She told herself she was his best friend. Sometimes now when she looked at his head, it almost hurt, like looking at the sun reflecting off the waves. She had to move her eyes away. Even growing up with the austerity of her mother's stripped-down body had not prepared her for the simple curve of Keefer's skull.

On this island, Jane's hair grew wide. Each morning Jane washed it. It stayed visibly wet into the second class, the shoulders and back of her T-shirt stained at least into lunch. Hours later her hand pushed into her hair, the fingers came back wet, the nails gleaming. In the afternoon and night the curls frizzed out into the air. Her hair occupied space. It spread in a cloud above her head. Looking out from under her hair, people appeared cut off at the neck. People leaned forward and down. They peered in to see what she really meant.

Eyes still closed, Keefer snorted, reached for her finger abruptly, directly, clasped it in his thin boy's hand. For a moment she let her hand go loose in his. His beating narrow flesh.

But each time he opened his eyes, each time, she exhaled and pulled her hand away.

DAY SEVENTY-THREE

During the first autopsy with Trent, Jane and he began work on the back. They hefted the body up onto its side, then rolled it forward onto the belly, the toenails of its remaining leg scraping across the metal. Its face made the soft thud of meat. Both she and Trent reached for the scalpel. Their hands hit. His fingers surprisingly hot, like something fevered. She thought of a snake she'd once found partially run over on the driveway at home. The snake had twisted and jerked against the seal of its own flesh with the road, its moving belly making a soft rasp. Impulsively she'd reached down toward it—perhaps to free it, although she didn't know how— only to jerk her hand back from the cooking heat of the road and its jumping hot body.

She pulled her hand back, holding the scalpel. Did not look up at him. She had vowed she would not get sleepy again. She made sure to breathe evenly, slowly.

They moved together round the cadaver, her cutting delicately along the back, him tugging the opened skin away to expose the muscles. The damp cold of its flesh was apparent even through the gloves. They didn't say much. Once the dermis and epidermis was out of the way, he read her the instructions from the lab workbook. She uncovered each structure, he leaned close to look at it. She felt that warmth again, stepped away.

Sometimes she had to put the scalpel down to separate a nerve from a vein with forceps and scissors. She hid the knife each time, in behind her hip, on the table. Afterward they both reached for it, his hand brushing in around her. Each time she got to it first. The third time this happened he looked at her, at her wide eyes, her hand clenched around the knife, her mouth tight with her breath.

He paused for a moment. Then smiled so wide his cheeks creased in, the way a dog smiles. He stepped back.

One of the last things they did that lab was cut open part of the spine, sawing through the vertebral canal. Handsaw rasping, she could feel herself get red in the face, feel her arms flapping, her neck straining. He watched, smooth, waiting. When she began to huff, he reached out and grasped the handsaw, his hot hand against hers. She watched the saw twist away from her, point facing back toward her belly. She did not fight. He stepped forward, around the table toward her. She stood there, waiting. He matter-of-factly bumped her out of the way with his hip, put the handsaw back into the cut and sawed, his eyes screwed closed against the bone chips, his lean arms rolling. Still she stood there, arms slack at her sides, understanding what would have been her acceptance of any move he made.

Jane sat on the dock beside Keefer as he picked a fish out of the pail and lowered it into the water, holding it just by the tail. Jonah swung its slow weight by, sucked the fish from Keefer's fingers with a thick roll of its head.

When Jonah's fin was right in front of her, Jane leaned forward and touched it. Lowered her hand into the water, following its flank, letting it run by against her fingers, her palm. The shark did not flinch at all, just slid easily along, as though expecting her touch, as though it could see into her mind and know her future actions. Through her hand she could feel its wet muscles turning slow and strong, a snake's smooth side, the muscled tightness of a heart. Not slimy at all, she realized, not like a dead fish. Its tail pushed her hand away.

She pulled back her hand, turned it over in front of her, examining both sides. Cautiously she smelled her fingers for anything that might be considered shark. Nothing there at all but the salt of the sea. She hadn't thought before she would touch it, hadn't recognized what she wanted. Her hands had become something new. Her hands round a drink in The Bar, or sliding a scalpel into the cadaver, or tracing and retracing the outline of her new hips. At night, now, she sometimes imagined Michael pulling her close, overwhelmed by her new body, his soft fingers scraping with power, the salt of the sea. Afterward she hated herself.

Keefer looked her straight in the face, his chin tucked into his neck, shocked. "Wh-wh-what?" He reached out to touch her hand, stopped only at the last second. His fingers hovering above her skin.

A silence fell between them. It used to be the silences between them were one of the main reasons Jane came down here, the silences so calm. Both of them would sit on the dock, as busy as they wanted to be in looking at the shark, at the sea, in listening to the waves on the beach. Talking only when they wished. In the last week or so she'd begun to notice a change.

Three days ago Claren had screamed at Keefer, in the cafeteria during lunch. Everyone watching. Things had seemed normal before, the clatter of cutlery, plates scraping, conversation—maybe Claren and Keefer's table was a little louder, Jane did not know, she hadn't been paying attention to them. The first she noticed Claren had just started screaming, screaming loud enough to silence her table, silence the tables near her, silence them all, screaming she didn't want his rice pudding, screaming she didn't want him to get her any iced tea. She screamed stop being so nice. She screamed he was hers for all . . . She suddenly quieted, midsentence, staring at him, breathing harsh between her teeth.

After a long minute the others started up again, sipping their drinks, using their forks, going about their business again, after a fashion. Their eyes pointed away. Everyone moving but Claren and Keefer. He was still sitting there, hunched. Claren staring.

Now Keefer took his hand back from Jane, kept his head down, leaned forward to dabble the fish blood off his fingers into the water. He flicked his fingers about quickly, as though he had some appointment to get to. Even the splashes of the water sounded harsh.

She thought this was her fault. These days she sometimes caught even Marlene looking at her with surprise in her eyes, standing there, a little back. She thought of the time on Keefer's moped, holding his beating heart in her hand.

He reached back into the bucket for the next fish and with his head down like that, away from her, asked roughly, "What is it you talk to Michael about, a-a-a-a. Anyway."

She looked back down at her hand.

DAY SEVENTY-NINE

Jane was getting thin enough she could trace some of Burnett's lectures on the skin of her body. No longer was every structure softened by fat, losing its edges and articulation. Along her legs and arms, in places along her ribs and neck, she could now feel the outlines of muscles, bones and veins baring themselves, the shifting of tendons.

"Small saphenous artery," Burnett said at the start of class, "posterior to the lateral malleolus. Nears the surface at the medial dorsal aspect of the knee, and again just inferior to the inguinal ring inside the femoral sheath."

She ran her hand down behind her ankle to the neck of the fluted Achilles, the lumps of old scar tissue still there. Pushed her fingers forward to the pulse of the artery, ticking and precise. Tracing her fingers up her leg, she found the blood vessel again at the back of the knee, then in at the cup of her thigh, the femoral artery. Even through her shorts and underwear she could feel it beating in there. She ticked her head to the side, surprised at the determined pulse of her body.

She heard clothing rasp against the table behind her, felt the heat of him through her back. Trent must have just arrived, must be standing in close. She took her hand back, from between her thighs, took a slow step away.

She'd discovered how to study on her own body. She'd learned so much. In The Bar after her second beer (after her body began to get heavy again and her head light, so she sat there motionless in order not to initiate complete separation between the two), she could look over at Marlene's bared sternum, at Keefer's inner wrist. Her friends. She knew the muscles beneath, the bones and nerves, the delicate veins which ran close to the surface. She knew just by looking how hard she would have to press to cut.

DAY EIGHTY-THREE

On her weekly date with Michael she no longer tried to start anything. While she was with him she was grateful just for the cuddling, that someone would touch her. They lay facing each other, the cap of her skull tucked into the curve of his neck, the soles of her feet cradled along the tops of his feet, his hands along her back. They both breathed slow, thinking of other things. She noticed he didn't sweat much, his skin almost cool. The dusty feel of a newt, she imagined, his plump child's fingers and patient old-man movements. His walk, so straight, his head carried high. He was the best student in the class. She could not imagine why he was at this school at all.

She lay against his body, nestled in the cool of his arms. Rested her lips against the methodical beat of the jugular in his neck. She tried to match her breathing to his—inhale, exhale—hoping her heart would just fall in sync, her mind. After a minute of trying, her breath blew out ragged from the wait, her heart pounding, and she had to pant before she could start all over again.

Frequently she fell asleep in the safety of his arms, sleeping deep and hard as an exhausted child. She knew danger would not dare to exist near him and she was so low on sleep. When she awoke, no matter after how long, he was lying there motionless, waiting.

One time, after her eyes had opened fully, he apologized and pulled his arm out from under her to shake it. "It fell asleep," he said.

She watched him, his hand flapping slack as cloth in the air. "Why didn't you wake me?" Her mouth felt heavy, her words slow.

He turned to her surprised, his hand held out, all wilted. "You looked too tired."

Touched, she pulled him close, running her hands obediently only over his back, his arms, pointing her face upward to secretly breathe the air from his lips. She wanted to suck his brain inside her, she wanted to have it for her own. On this whole island, he was the only person who did not scare her in one way or another.

Each date he told her when it was time to go. She got up off the bed, obediently smoothed her clothes, her hair, pretending for him they were all mussed. She looked back at him, sitting up on the bed, slow and tall, his hands checking each of his buttons. She wanted to stay inside his arms forever, bring a pillow, canned goods, camp out. She thought if she could stay here, if she were always in his arms, perhaps everything would still turn out alright. She got so many urges these days, so many thoughts. Her mother would not even recognize the inside of her mind.

She was the number two student in the class now.

DAY EIGHTY-FIVE

During autopsy class she tried to stay away from Trent. She was more and more sensitive to his touch. Flinched at even the brush of his sleeve, as though it was not the cadaver's skin they had been removing section by section, but her own, baring the nerves beneath.

While they sketched out the tendons of the calf, she stayed on the other side of the table from him. She kept her weight back, her feet spread, as though she might have to break into a run. Somehow, in spite of all this, they still always touched. Her head down labelling a tendon, she reached out at the same moment as Trent to test the tendon's effect. Expecting the slack chill of death, her fingers touched his hot moving hand. She pulled her hand back, fast as if slapped. He looked up at her, his face still, studying her. The smile grew out slow from his eyes. She turned her head away, to date the sketch, pretend absorption. Resettled her feet. He hooked the probe into the tendon, pulled. The gray toes trembled and curled.

She ended up touching Trent no matter what. She tried not to. She tried to keep a distance between them, to always be conscious of how close he was. She got so good at this she sometimes knew how he was standing even when her back was turned. Clear to her mind came an image of the knuckles of his right hand on the steel table, his face cocked over toward the clock on the wall, his wiry torso angled over his right hip. If she looked around to check, he turned his face slow from the clock to stare back at her.

Whenever she reasonably could, whenever she remembered, she moved away. While Burnett lectured the class on an interesting anomaly found in Randy's cadaver, a dual nerve supply to the hamstrings, she took two or three steps closer to the demonstration, away from the area of the body she and Trent worked on. She tried to concentrate on Burnett's words. Her right arm felt cold, Trent no longer close to her. Her neck got tense knowing he was behind her, perhaps watching. She imagined his dark eyes on her hands, on the small of her back, on her butt. She could feel his disinterested eyes on her fear. Her neck hurt. She rolled her head to the left, rubbing her wet plastic glove into her neck muscles. She rolled her head back, at the same time Burnett pointed out the dual nerves. Trent took a step forward, to see. His head rising too close, just behind her, a mushrooming expression. She snapped her head upright, stepped away.

Later, near the end of Burnett's speech, she forgot again. She crossed her hands backward, yawning. Trent reached forward. He touched her. Through the skin of her hands she heard him smile. She blinked and stepped away.

Standing there, silent, in that moment before she would have to go back to the cadaver, to pick up the scalpel and move in by Trent's side, she looked around at her friends in the lab, some still standing up straight listening to Burnett, others already bent back over the lumpy piles that lay on their autopsy tables. She couldn't remember a time when she wasn't here on this island, when she didn't know these people. When she didn't have to study. She thought of her life in the U.S. as a vague dream. She could no longer remember what ice cream tasted like, what her favorite songs sounded like, what it felt like to fall into a deep afternoon nap with the blankets tucked up tight round her neck. The exact purr of a Lincoln Continental cruising down a highway at sixty. Her parents' house with its hall clock ticking sedately on, the hum of the air conditioner through the thick wood walls, the TV mumbling to itself in just the next room.

Each night she stayed awake for a little longer, staring upward, listening to the sound of her breath through her mouth, the whining heat, the crash of waves. Things rustled slow beneath the house.

Twenty-one

On December 12th Keefer threw a Christmas party, ten days before final exams. On average, a seventh of the class flunked out of first year, were asked to repeat the failed courses all over again or leave. After first year almost no one flunked. They had all, finally, been taught how to study.

By this point in the semester, everyone was tense. There was less drinking at night. Most people, especially the first-year students, spent all their spare time at the library, and the few who still went to The Bar didn't talk as much anymore about what they used to do when they lived in the States or what they would do first thing when they returned. Instead they listed the telltale signs of a lymphocytic infiltrate, numbering the signs off on their fingers, eyes closed to memory. For the last few days even Marlene's skin had appeared a little dull, a little gray at the edges.

So people strode into the party around the corner of Keefer's bungalow with harsh grins on, before they saw the decorations, before they talked to a single person, even before they started to drink. They moved down the beach with their voices already louder than normal, calling out "Hallooo" and yelling "Merry Christmas," their gestures wide and almost angry.

The party was on the beach in front of Jonah's dock. From a distance it looked magical, transformed from the beach they knew so well. Keefer had set out a hundred candles, each in a paper bag, around the dunes and out onto the dock, the light flickering and muted. Three separate bars were set up with islanders mixing drinks. A baby palm tree had been dragged down here and propped up in the sand in the center of the beach, decorated with candles and what at first looked like real Christmas ornaments. Only when Jane had walked down to within fifteen feet did she see it was all stolen medical equipment. Autopsy gloves were inflated so they looked like bloated udders waving gentle in the breeze. Forceps, hemostats and probes hung from lines looped into the tree, the instruments glittering and twisting and sometimes ringing musically against each other. The empty foil wrappings of scalpel blades shimmered, cut into outlines of stars and snowmen. Candles balanced out on the handles of scalpels which were jammed deep into the tree at even intervals, like shiny silver stairs ascending for tiny feet.

And in the last yard or two of Jane's approach, she saw other things hanging from the strings on the tree, ornaments twisting dully white. It wasn't until she closed her fingers upon one to hold it still that she identified the metacarpal of a human foot strung up with dental floss. Other bones twisted lazily nearby.

Keefer was clearly excited. He ran up to her stuttering. "Mm-M-M-M-Mm."

She could see his tongue spasming in his mouth. Impulsively she reached out and touched her fingers to his lips, calming them, taking her hand back slow. His tongue stilled, he closed his eyes, breathed deep. He whispered,

"Merry Christmas," and pulled her into a tight hug, his arms clapping in around her sides.

Surprised, she hugged him back, her arms tightening for a large portion of their arc without touching his sides, so for an instant she thought she must have missed his body somehow, must be hugging empty space. Only then did her arms close in tight enough to reach his nervous beating chest, as miraculous as life inhabiting some quivering sticks. Out of surprise she exhaled, holding him, wanted to rest right there, her head cocked to his different body. Instead he kissed her three times fast about the cheeks and pulled away abruptly, laughing hysterically.

"And a happy New Year," he called, handing her a martini in a paper cup and leaving her there, upon the beach.

She took a gulp of the drink. It went down so cold it seemed the liquid escaped her esophagus and cascaded down along the inside of her ribs, making her exhale a little. Michael was not here at the party. He had decided he could not spare the time from studying and Jane was glad. She would not have to stand still and downcast by his side. She took another gulp of the drink, threw her head back there beside the tree, and laughed hard for no real reason she could name. She felt the laugh push and pull at her lungs, her diaphragm clenching and rocking inside. Not a single person standing nearby looked over at her laughing all by herself.

Marlene appeared, grabbed her hand and pulled her away across the sand determined. Trent strolled along behind. Jane saw through the crowd Claren, head thrown back, suckling from an upheld rum bottle. Marlene dragged her over to Randy and Burpie who played the bongos while trying to sing what they thought of as songs that should go with bongos, things with Spanish rhythms.

"Aye yi yi yiii," Burpie wailed high-pitched as a dog. "I am the Frito Bandito." His arms flashed in the candlelight. He was sweating, bare-chested, his legs curled protectively round his bongos. He hunched up his shoulders between verses and howled.

"Yi yi yoop," sang Randy at points in the song that seemed appropriate to him.

Marlene made Jane and Trent dance with her, doing the twist, calisthenics and the bump around the bongos. Other people joined them, five people, then fifteen. Nina Sheiffer brought her flashlight over and tried to turn it on and off fast enough to get a disco effect. Instead people would glance up blinking at the light, caught off-balance. Then disappear.

At first Jane danced a little self-consciously. This was not dancing where the music throbbed so loud she couldn't help but feel the beat, lights strobing above so all movements were fragmentary enough to seem purposeful. This was dancing where the dance alone had to fill her, where the movements had to be just right, where she could hear the sand shuffle beneath her feet and clearly see each awkward movement of her arms. It was only after a while, with Marlene hooting like a monkey, up on one leg, and Trent swaying lean-hipped all by himself, with Claren doing the hustle round and round the dance area and Bob Feldington trying to shimmy—it was only after a while, Jane began to really dance. Or it might be more accurate to say her body began to really dance, her new body, the thin one. Her exhaustion began to dance, her fear of exams. Her body swayed down from her neck, each of her muscles rippling, these new muscles, this thin skin. She did not care anymore who might be looking. She didn't glance up even at the bursts of the flashlight.

Someone held out another martini toward her; this drink filled the paper cup to the very lip. She looked up to see Trent holding it, to see him watching her. As she reached for the drink she bent forward for a gulp so it wouldn't spill, breaking his stare. Femoris, she thought, vastus. She threw back her head again and laughed, swung her hips around. Her face felt numb.

"Go, girl," Marlene yelled. "Boo-*tay*."

Each time the wind blew, a paper bag or two would crumple in over its candle and explode into flame, burn down to the sand and go out. The beach slowly darkened, people harder to see. At one point Jane spun low to the ground as a crouched thing and as she turned she saw what looked like two men standing up to their ankles in the sea inside Jonah's fenced-in area, whipping stones purposefully into the deeper water.

Somehow it seemed natural that after the dancing, a footrace would start around Jonah's dock. People running, pushing at each other, taking the corners with slipping feet. A paper bag was knocked over, a candle hissed in the waves. Went out. The black water swallowed it, calm. Nina scanned the waves with her flashlight, beneath the surface the sliding glimmer of white sand, twinkling shells. No one saw an answering movement. A second race lined up, thudded off round the first corner, the winner from each race receiving a drink.

It must be understood they were all imagining the shark down there, lying on the bottom, breathing through its mouth, looking up at all the light. It was only a matter of time before they went further.

At the point when the jungle was no longer as loud as during the true night—some of the birds had quieted, and the monkeys—but before dawn had clearly started, at the point when the dark if anything seemed darker from the light about to break, the twenty or so students remaining at the party sat or lay around the dock, looking down into the water, quiet while they thought of the next thing to do, not yet ready to let the party die, not yet ready to return to studying. Marlene sat abruptly up, stuck both her feet into the water inside the circle of Jonah's dock and swirled them around for a second. She jerked her feet back out with a harsh laugh. "Dare any of you," she called. "Dare all of you."

Trent, on the far arm of the dock, sat up casual but without a pause. Slipped his legs into the water up to his knees, kicked around for the count of three, pulled them out slow. He looked back into Marlene's face from across the water. Jane could see they'd played this game before, with other things, in another context. Neither of them smiled. It was not a friendly game.

Soon people were kicking their legs clear off the dock, sinking hip deep into the sea while holding on to the dock with their hands, then hefting themselves fast back up and out, rolling back far from the edge, awkward and breathing hard. Their shorts were as soaked as though they had wet themselves in their fear. Laughing, sharp-edged and hysterical.

Jane had reached that stage of drunkenness where this all seemed to have the crystal-clear beauty of genius. She'd realized about an hour ago she'd started breathing through her mouth, like she'd been jogging. She hadn't bothered to try to modify this. Lying on her stomach on the dock, she leaned her head and shoulders over the side, watching for the shark, to see if it was near any of them. She wanted to know if it was scared. She found herself empathizing with Jonah, loud drunken louts swishing their articulated limbs clumsy through the surface of its home.

She could not see anything through the candles' shimmer on the water, shaded her eyes with her hands and leaned further out. Nina's flashlight turned nearby, bounced over the waves. Below in the swinging column of light, for a single instant, she saw the gray striped side of the shark silhouetted, starting a slow turn along the very bottom. She saw its dark eyes looking up into the light.

"Hey," she called out with sympathy, to where the shark had been. "Hey, poor Jonah." She held out both hands toward it, leaning over, remembering its skin.

Her sudden fall. The slap of water against her face. Warm as the inside of her lungs. Like diving into blood, so calm, so salty. All sound was gone, her classmates, her drunkenness. She had returned to a simpler world, one without abrupt movements, without teachers, grades or breathing. Without vision, just dark water all around as she spun downward, headfirst, hands outheld like for a hug.

The watery line of the flashlight bobbed frantically by, gliding across the black eye of Jonah watching her from below, floating gently closer. The recognition between them clear as a smile. Then darkness again.

She remembered her fear abruptly.

Flapped back. Turned unwieldy, slow. Arms pumping. Up toward the rippled quicksilver surface. Her legs kicking, her calves and tender knees, her narrow ankles, thrashing through the water. The soft digits of her hands pulling. The surface was still four feet away, three. Her body's clutching thump in her ear, her clinging life.

Marlene was the one to pull her out, heave her up. The water swirled black behind Jane from her passage. Nothing moved below.

She didn't cry when she got out, didn't scream in terror. Instead as soon as she stood on the dock again, she sat down, as fast as if she'd lost her balance. She was swept over with the need for sleep; the exhaustion of the last three months filled her entire body in a single moment. Lying back slow on the boards, she was heavy, as slack to gravity as a fish. Noticed distantly everyone clustered around her, asking questions. She could barely hear them through the continuing thump of her heart, the hiss of her breath in her throat. Her eyes closed. She felt someone's hands travel fast down each of her limbs, thorough, checking that all was still there. Heard Marlene's persistent questions from a great distance.

"Yeah," Jane whispered thick-lipped. "I'm fine." She had

not yet bothered to figure out if it was true. Opened her eyes through an effort of will.

Marlene, Keefer and Claren's faces were clustered over her. Others were in the background. Claren asked if she'd intended to do that, if she'd intended to jump in. Jane stared at Claren's talking mouth. It wasn't that she meant not to answer. It was just she was busy, listening to her body. It seemed so very loud. The drip-drip of water off her hair, her blood rustling through her limbs, the solid hum of each tender muscle settling down lower against the dock.

At this moment she'd never felt more alive.

And it must have seemed to her classmates that she was so calm there, smiling sleepy on the dock after swimming with the shark. Perhaps this was when they decided they finally understood why Marlene hung out with her.

As the excitement died down and people got one more drink before disbanding, while Jane lay draped flat and wet across the dock, her mouth open, listening to her heart, she realized Trent had sat down just two feet away, was watching the water. She looked up to the distant fading stars, her hands against the rough dock, and with all the heightened awareness of her body, knew the heel of his right hand to be within reach of the tip of her middle finger.

Her finger stretched out, half an inch, three quarters, touched him. The very corner of his heated skin. He looked down at her. Dawn was coming. The trees gray with it. Water dripping off the dock beneath her and down into the sea.

Twenty-two

⌒

Trent and Jane were working on the cadaver's arm now. Trent was holding the arm out at a ninety-degree angle from the body, the elbow up, like he was helping a drowned victim from the water. This made the muscles loose so she could slip her fingers into the newly opened area beneath the shoulder blade. The shoulder blade was freed from the back entirely, connected only at the arm and in the front by the collarbone, the gap underneath for her hand quite wide. Her fingers moved inside, over the muscle, across the smooth underside of the bone, the side she'd never touched before, ancient in purpose as the inside of a seashell. She stared down at a tendril of yellowish fat. Since her fall into Jonah's pool, colors seemed much more vivid, so saturated, especially yellow. Any yellow seemed to vibrate in her eyes; even the smallest patch almost made a noise, a high hum in her ears. She didn't know why. A half-hidden flower, a pale band of yellow in the sunset, her highlighter. She came to a slow stop in front of each, mouth open. She wanted to be able to swallow the color, keep it in her lungs. Sometimes through her mind went what could have been the different possible first touches of the shark, a sharp tug on one leg, pressure tight as a hug round her middle. At each thought, her body jerked, slightly.

She liked to breathe now, had never been conscious of it before, not like this, the sweet slide of air down her throat. She didn't have as much of a problem standing near Trent, actually tried to stand closer to him because she could feel her life beating so clearly then. She could feel each erect hair on her arms.

She exhaled slow, looked down at the white shell of bone, the frayed stringy white of the muscle. She ran her fingers across its secret inside curve. Below it, on the table, lay the scalpel. The light shivered along its edge. She no longer felt so tightly in her own body. She could be anyone.

She looked up and Trent still held the arm out patiently for her, watching. She took her hand back from the shoulder slow.

A muscle in her neck jumped. She was so much more relaxed except for this one muscle in her neck. It felt as though things inside of her had changed: broken or settled, she could not tell. She had found in the two days since the party she could sleep sometimes now, not for much more than an hour or two at a time, but still she was sleeping deeply. Then she shuddered awake hard, sitting up fast, as though at a loud voice, or like someone had just shaken her. The pillow stained with drool, her head hurt. Heart beating, she was all alone. Lying back down slow to watch the ceiling for hours before she could sleep again.

The muscle at the right side of her neck, just beneath her ear, jumped again. She didn't know what muscle it was. This was one of the few areas of the body left unknown to her. Her map of her body had changed over the semester like maps of South America over the last hundred years. First, it was a wide-open continent drawn only as an outline, hesitant towns speckled along the edge, the hazy path of rivers wandering off into the unknown, an understand-

able belief in inexhaustible resources. Gradually that
changed to things charted, known, the exact edges of rivers,
fault lines, the height and metallurgic composition of the
interior mountains. She couldn't suck in a deep breath now
thinking only in a hazy way about her health or the smooth
magic of her body. Instead she saw the SA node enervating
the independent squeeze of her heart, the pulmonary artery
gushing its contents into the arterioles in her lungs. Three
fifths of the weight of her living lungs, she knew, was made
up of blood and blood vessels. Oxygen from the lungs was
carried down to the cells, mitochondria building ATP bonds.
Carbon dioxide carried back to the lungs, osmosis and
exhale.

In the slow dismemberment of the cadaver she learned
of all the small changes that could stop these processes in
herself. A tiny puncture in the lungs and all the blood
would come rolling out, her breath abruptly wet and foam-
ing. Or the SA node would start signalling irregularly, her
heart pounding out of control. Or the lung's alveoli could
fill up with pus from an infection, and she'd drown to death
on land.

She inhaled, slow and hungry, sucking in until the air
pushed at the back of her throat. The pressure made her
stand up straight. Still holding her breath, she walked
around the body to Trent, to switch positions so he could
put his fingers beneath the shoulder blade. He watched her
walk toward him. His eyes slid down to her hips, resting
there. Through his level eyes, Jane knew for sure her limp
was no longer apparent, no longer what others noted. Her
hips so much more limber in this heat, in their pared-down
state, her ribs. She moved with her ankle now, rather than
against it, swaying along its knotted strength.

She stopped beside him, took the arm, standing close.
Across the back of her neck she felt what the push of water
in front of the shark's jaws would have been like. The muscle in her neck jerked. She looked back at the scalpel, the

light so different now, from this angle. Nothing bothered her that much anymore. Trent stepped around her. She breathed out, touched the muscle in her neck gently, the filament jerking tight, an alien life-form trying to get out. It bounced delicate against her wet glove.

She knew soon this unknown muscle's mystery would be gone. It would have a name, a purpose, an origin and insertion. They had only the neck and head left to dissect. The head, the area of the body thought of as most human, saved for last.

Eight days before final exams, she woke up in the evening nestled deep in Michael's arms on the couch. She'd been sleeping solidly, dreamlessly. Her affection for him seemed suddenly limitless within her. He was the only one she trusted. He was the only one who held her. She pulled him in a little tighter, but not so much he would mind. As she shifted she noticed her face where it rested on his shoulder was wet. She brought one hand up, her damp cheeks rubbery. Just sweat, she realized. For an instant she'd worried about blood. She wiped her hand off on her shirt.

This morning she'd found herself staring for some time close up at the skin of an orange, its tiny living pockmarks. The color so deeply pure—as if internally lit—that she'd begun to doubt the reality of the fruit in her hand. She'd begun to see the orange floating partly up toward her, weightless with its own purity. Until Marlene slapped the back of her head as they were late for class.

"Why're you at this school?" Jane asked Michael, still thinking of the orange. She hadn't planned to ask him the question. In a conciliatory way she added, "You're such a good student." She didn't breathe fast at her question, didn't blush or look away. So many things seemed simpler. She lay full against him, breathing slow.

Michael also didn't seem taken aback at the question. He

seemed almost to have expected it. He swept her hair back gently from her face, ran his hands over her shoulders, slow circular strokes. Jane remembered this was the way, as a child, she'd always imagined her mother would touch her, when she was sick, when she needed comfort. She closed her eyes under his touch.

Michael spoke, his voice quiet but straightforward. She wasn't sure if it was his trust in her that made him tell. Perhaps if anyone had asked, he would have given the same honest answer.

"I was found. With a boy. I'd been baby-sitting for him and his younger sister."

She opened her eyes. Noticed there was yellow in his shirt, humming narrow lines of it against all the blue. Distantly she realized Michael had spoken with his normal low voice. He'd spoken at the same deliberate pace he would use to explain the metabolism of the pancreas, using some of the same words: "was," "with," "a." She found her mind going through the words one by one again, to see if there were other duplicates. Not "baby-sitting," she thought, not "boy."

Jane realized she was probably supposed to say something at this point. She couldn't imagine what she could say. Her whole head felt heavy. She loosened her hold on him, shifted back.

"What exactly were you doing?" she asked, forcing her eyes up from his shirt.

Michael's brow creased a little as though she had gotten the wrong answer to one of his study quizzes. His proud face continued to talk without answering her. "My parents settled out of court, but it made newspapers. My family is well known. I didn't make it into schools in the States."

She nodded, staring.

The image came to her of Michael pulling the little boy in close, bending down to smell the sweet part of his hair, cupping the small chin, rubbing the back. The image, she found, didn't surprise her that much. She looked down at her own body, its soft breasts under the T-shirt, its hips, its scent of a woman's sweat. She imagined the narrow practicality of a boy, his hairless body smelling of earth and child, his delicate shoulders held out with the blocky confidence of a grown man's stance. The bones of a bird poised along the edge of his chest, all set to unfold into change. She could see what would be attractive in that.

Michael pulled her back gently against him. After a moment of resistance, she settled into his touch, her muscles loosening. For the first time she understood their relationship. She realized with a mild surprise this needn't affect anything she felt for Michael. Not what she expected from him, nor how they would interact. Her hands slowly slid around his back, to hold him almost as before. These last two days she hadn't seemed to worry as much, about anything. She wished she hadn't asked the question in the first place, wondered where it had come from, gently touched her forehead. Her skin felt hot. She stared at his yellow stripes. Things would continue on as before. She wanted them to.

And at no time did she imagine herself to be any better than him. She thought next time she would wear a looser shirt.

A long silence fell between them.

"What about you? Why are you here?" he asked. "You're a good student too." He sounded suspicious.

She pulled her fingers back slow from her head, her brow creased. She could feel the truth in her mouth, just at the back of her tongue. She could feel him looking at her. She kept her eyes down.

"I guess," she said, "I guess I'm just bad at writing those application essays."

DAY NINETY-ONE

"Another fifteen minutes of studying and let's catch a quick brewski," Marlene announced into the silence of the people studying near her in the library. She sat up tall, stretching her arms out until her shoulders popped.

For the last five minutes, Susan had been pacing the floor near one of the doors, listlessly braiding and rebraiding her hair. "You think?" she asked and turned in the direction of Jane who stood by the water cooler drinking glass after glass of water. Jane looked back at her blankly, only figuring out after a moment Susan hadn't turned in her direction by chance, but was asking her opinion.

Jane blinked in surprise. Since the party she'd noticed people looking at her more. They asked her questions, waited for her response. Dana Bork even seemed to be imitating Jane a bit, wearing her hair fluffed out, pausing sometimes for the count of two before she answered a question, brow creased. Jane wasn't sure how to deal with this. She thought it strange it came so late. She wanted to tell them that for the first time in her life, she didn't care if she were included.

"Sure," she said and nodded her head. Behind Susan was the glass-paneled door to the hall and Jane saw a full-length reflection nod back at her from the dark glass. Each of the sections of the reflected body was separated and slightly tilted off from the other panels, fractured. It was a montage of a woman more than an actual female form. A single limp hand, the bony sternum, a narrow thigh.

The reflection's face froze looking back at her, dark eyes open. Wide hair was spread across three panels. Staring, the blackness all around her, the face pale and so surprised with bone.

She had begun to walk at night, when she couldn't really sleep. It was better than just lying there. She did not try to

walk fast or get anywhere in particular. She no longer cared
about exercise. She wandered, her mouth open, turning in
midstride toward anything that interested her. She still felt
amazed to be alive, amazed at her body. It moved so well
in its walk, smooth, like when she'd danced on the night of
the Christmas party, like her new muscles were moving
themselves, her bones, her skin. Not her moving them, not
anymore. She breathed deeper than she had to, sucking in
the moist jungle air. Walking along the beach, she listened
to the hiss and sigh of the waves, like the sounds of someone sleeping deeply. She wandered by the bungalows, looking in, sometimes trailing a single finger along their rough
white sides. Once she scared a snake. It slid fast off a window ledge, fell with a thump to the porch, rolled into a gap
in the boards to spill away, smooth as water. She closed her
eyes afterward to remember the swirl of its crimson scales,
the grace of its fear.

Mostly inside the bungalows there was nothing to see,
dark, silent. The occupants still at the library or autopsy
lab, or inside the bungalow sleeping. One night she
stepped onto a porch, paused by the window to find Dana
Bork curled up on her bed just inside, sleeping naked,
her fists clenched beneath her chin. The position in
which, Jane imagined, squirrels hibernate through the
winter, the way fetuses wait, busy, for birth. In sleep,
Dana breathed deeply, harshly as if in some intense
labor. From outside Jane looked down at her, laying her
fingertips against her own cheek, skin papery with
exhaustion.

Sometimes Jane walked round and round Jonah's dock.
Ambling around its area more than fifty times in a row; the
stars above her had shifted to different positions by the time
she left. She wanted to feel tired, the healthy feeling of
tired she remembered from childhood, from long afternoons
sledding where afterward, inside, her hands still burning
from the cold, she could fall asleep in the front hall, leaning

back against the wall, mouth open, only one boot pried off. The exhaustion she reached now was different, it made her feel too tired even for sleep. Lying in bed, it made her blink dry-eyed up at the ceiling.

At the first sound of a person's feet on the dock, Jonah would appear, its smooth fin splitting the water, its unseen bulk below. It expected food, meat offered out by a human hand. Lazily it matched her pace, three feet away. For a moment she thought of walking a dog.

When she stepped onto the beach part of her circuit, Jonah continued in the water to follow along. She noted with surprise the ease with which it could swim through such shallow water, the heft of its side passing silently through water barely a foot deep, half its smooth back exposed, its tail swaying behind, curved up heavy and sail-like into the air. Submarine—she thought at the slope of its back—snake, buttock. She remembered hearing of a Native American belief that the person who saved your life became your slave. She wondered then what about the creature who did not kill you. She could see its head so well through the water, see straight into its dark eye.

She felt a wave flicker in over her toes. Looked down to find out she'd been walking closer, into the water, toward that eye.

The shark's mouth opened, scenting, working. She remembered that moment in the water with Jonah, the moment before the fear. Nothing, she found, scared her all that much anymore.

It no longer surprised her that since then she couldn't study her books.

After following her around the corral eight or nine times, Jonah would realize she wasn't going to feed it. It gradually sank back down then, disappearing into the shadows of the deeper end.

DAY NINETY-TWO

Using the metal probe, Trent tugged on the circular muscle round the eye, to demonstrate how it worked. What was left of the face, skinless, gray, tattered as beef jerky, twitched its eye open at Jane. She found herself, for a brief moment, glimpsing what this man would have looked like alive, if he'd been looking at her. The pupil of his eye bemused with the milky film of death. It was focused permanently on middle distance, his jaw firm, mouth tilted habitually to the right. Perhaps he'd laughed a lot.

For so long she'd managed to forget that this had once been human. She looked down at what remained of his body, bloodless, gnawed down to the bone, only one leg and the upper part of an arm still connected. In the empty bowl where the guts used to be lay four fingers of one hand and the lab book. Everything else—limbs, tendons, organs— was piled around the edge of the table or in plastic bags underneath. It reminded Jane of the unconnected pile of bones and bits of flesh left on the plate after a chicken dinner.

Four days after she'd fallen into Jonah's pool, colors were fading for Jane, losing some of their shimmer. Breathing no longer a conscious pleasure in her throat. This morning she had lined up all her yellow pencils, all twelve of them, sat staring at them, tying to savor what was left of the hiss of their color.

Trent let go with the probe. The eye, dried and hard, stayed open like an old cupboard door. Until Jane, shivering for the first time in weeks, pushed it shut with one finger.

DAY NINETY-THREE

On a walk, she went up to Keefer and Claren's bungalow, looked in the main window, the one with the light on. She saw the suitcase open, partially packed on the floor. A bunch of T-shirts came flying in through the bedroom door to fall scattered about the suitcase. It was only at this point that Jane noticed Keefer rocking in the corner. He was so silent, on his heels, rocking and rocking. He was so small and folded up he could have been a wastepaper basket, he could have been a stool. He had a fist jammed tight into his mouth, as though if he removed it all his words would finally come pouring out, without impediments. Because of his bare skull, the expression on his face seemed to expand to cover his whole head, the mottled heat written everywhere.

She stood there mesmerized. She could feel his pain swelling under her skin, filling her completely. Her shoulders softened, she made a certain involuntary *huh*. She started to turn, started to hurry right around the house, to the front door, to him. There was no one else she cared about more. Her head hurt.

A closet door slammed in the other room. The sound stopped her dead.

She looked back slow to Keefer. As simple as that, she could feel only her heavy face. She was alone in her skin. Colors completely gone. Her mouth held tight. Everything like before she fell in with the shark.

A shower of Claren's underwear was tossed into the room, falling across the suitcase and the floor. Jane was suddenly so bone-tired she wanted to sink down right there onto her knees to sleep on the sand. She didn't bother, for she knew sleep wouldn't come.

One pair of underwear landed on Keefer's head, caught on his ear, slid off, casual. He didn't seem to notice. Jane wandered away then, so tired, rubbing the jumping skin on her neck. She concentrated on breathing deeply enough. Felt like she wasn't getting enough air. Didn't make another sound. There was nothing she could do. For him or for herself.

As she walked she found herself humming a tune from childhood, the one that ended ". . . and they all fell down." She hummed it over and over again, could not remember the rest of the words. She was not conscious of thinking of Keefer. Her voice was thin and quavering slightly on the high notes like a child's. She wet her lips a lot, rubbed them with the back of her fingers. Her head hurt.

Late that night sleep was shallow again.

For weeks now she'd lie in bed each night for four hours, five at the most. Much of that time she was awake, listening to the waves outside, the monkeys. She watched the way the moonlight moved across the floor. Sometimes she even dreamed that way, with her eyes open, tiny figures moving silent upon her wall.

She wondered if this lack of sleep was bad for her. No one really knew why sleep was important anyway, at least not for so many hours each day. One man she had read about in Physiology had lived for months without any sleep at all, not napping even when the doctors put him in a dark warm laboratory bed, when they played lullabies, sang to him. She imagined the doctors clustered, barbershop quartet stance, humming softly of rocking cradles. The man had died in the end from something they assumed was unrelated. She could not remember now what it was. This lack of memory surprised her, for it seemed she could forget no medical fact these days, not even if she wanted to. She thought his death might have been from liver cancer.

She remembered back in Connecticut she used to sleep nine hours a night, luxuriously nestled under her thick quilt. Now lying in bed, she could see the frail outline of her bones pressing up through her hands, the internal structure, the frame of her body off which everything else hung. Each day this frame was closer to the surface, more prominent, lighter of anything holding on. The color of the bone visible now through the flesh, along her shoulders, her knees and wrists. She knew one day this frame would just slip free of the softer flesh.

She'd begun to spend a lot of time staring at herself in the bathroom mirror, from the side or straight on, tilting up her chin. She no longer recognized herself, the elegant face, wild curling hair, the expression distant and transfixed as that of the dogs that roamed the island.

Near dawn, still unable to sleep, she got up slow, pulled on shorts, a shirt, walked heavy up to town. The ghostly white houses loomed out of the dark, the chickens lined up in the trees twitching their startled heads round in her direction, the lingering smells of hot peppers, incense and rice. The dark carved god clasping his zigzagging sword stared at her. She stepped cautiously closer to the carving, looked up into his crazed half-dog face, reached out to touch a single wood tooth. The town around her so motionless. He continued to grin at her. She backed away.

Standing near one of the windows of a house, she heard breathing inside, occasional rustles. There wasn't even a mosquito screen in the window frame. How many islanders, she wondered, got malaria? It was possible no one had ever counted, not the islanders, not the medical school. She heard a child inside sighing in the midst of sleep, breathing faster now, catching in its throat. Jane took a step closer. She wanted to crawl into the window, curl up inside, with them. Maybe then she could sleep. She was almost skinny enough now to pass for an islander in the dark. Not quite a medical student anymore, she realized.

She continued to stand there, just outside, all alone.

The child's sharp exhale, a jerking movement. Complete silence, then a woman's sleepy clucking. A hand was rubbed across flesh. The child breathed again, slower, the sound of limbs resettling.

Jane stood just outside, wrapped her arms round her ribs. She could have leaned in and touched them both.

Most nights when she went on her walks she would en-

counter one of the dog packs on the island. These dogs
looked like what she remembered of dogs from home. They
had dog-faces, dog-bodies, they ran like dogs did and slept
curled up. But they were not dogs, not the dogs she knew.
They did not wag their tails, they didn't bark excited. They
loped in silent packs together, tails down, bony as coyotes,
dangerous as rats.

Standing by the window, she saw a group of them trot
busily into town, six of them, seven. She stepped back, almost flat against the shadow of the house. They saw her
movement. Narrow skulls turning, tracking her with bright
eyes. The trot of all seven faltered simultaneously, like in
ballet.

Adrenaline, she thought, released by the adrenal medulla.
Heartbeat up, increased breathing, glucose floods the system. Arousal of the senses. The lenses of the eyes actually
flatten, allowing the whole scene to be viewed more easily.
For a moment she felt herself vividly inside her body again,
as though she was caught up on sleep, as though she hadn't
seen Keefer that night. She could hear the hiss of their
yellow eyes, see every fawn hair along their backs, the dark
pupils in the center of their eyes, black noses twitching.
One dog led the curve in, toward her. Like with the shark,
she could feel her hands again, her face, sympathy.

She watched herself take a slow step forward, to meet
them, raised her arms in welcome.

They jolted to a stop, stiff-legged. Eyed her. They
wheeled, scattering into the jungle.

Twenty-three

Trent finished the cut across the scalp. Jane grasped the cadaver's hair and used it to peel the scalp down out of the way while he reached for the saw. She tugged the scalp down until the pale inner shell of the skull was bared for the saw, until the face was completely hidden by its inside-out sock of skin. At the bottom of the flap, around the chin, the man's head hair stuck out, like a thick straight beard.

She looked down at the face masked this way. She wasn't quite sure what was so disturbing until she realized the facial features were clearly outlined through the pulpy sheath. This silhouetted face even had a beard but lacked any detail, the flattened distortion of a robber's stockinged stare. This outlined face stared up at her without eyes, nostrils or lips, almost thoroughly erased.

Once again she imagined herself in the States as a surgeon, long hours, so much importance and money, her scalpel slicing casually through living flesh. How happy her parents would be bragging at all the parties, her smile turned on each new person as slack as though anesthetized. Her usefulness so clearly defined.

This morning she'd had a vision of a coffin shipped home, the end of the argument absurdly clear. The image had been small but surprisingly real, projected on the bathroom mirror in front of her, in color like a slide. She could see the three brass handles along the side. For some reason the image had struck her as so funny she sank down onto her heels giggling. Basically she had thought, all this effort for *that*?

After a while she stopped laughing and turned away from the image, toward the sea. But the coffin followed her everywhere she looked. She worked to change it to a boat, a plane, to a suitcase with her holding the handle. Still she saw the coffin, if anything more realistic, more three-dimensional, the detail of the wood trim, the hinges, the sheen. She watched it float by the window, heard the waves lap against its sides. She stood there, staring in the end, too scared to move.

Jane had not studied in almost a week.

She did what she could to get more sleep. She lay down on her bed, forced her eyes closed, breathed slow and regular through her mouth. Hoping to trick sleep through imitation. She felt brittle in the wake of what had been days of such beauty. After a while she would notice her eyes had popped open, her breath become shallow and fast. Last night at that point she had cried, shaking, her eyes completely dry.

DAY NINETY-SIX

It was two days before exams. Even Michael felt the pressure. He had chewed the skin round one of his thumbnails until it bled. He disinfected his thumb every hour or so with alcohol, examined it closely, put on a new sterile bandage.

"The tropics," he told Jane, "are just one giant petri dish of bacteria waiting to transplant onto you. Infections can grow like that." He moved his hand as though to snap his fingers, stopped at the last second, looking down at his thumb.

She sat beside him at his desk in the library, head down over her books, hoping his quiet concentration would rub off on her, hoping she could manage to concentrate, to read, for half an hour. Hoping she could remember again for an hour what it was like to care what happened to her. As always he had a schedule of what he was supposed to study; when to quiz himself in physiology, when to review the structures of the human eye. His schedule lay on the top of his desk, the thirty-minute time allotments shaded in different ways so it was easy to read. Two days before exams Jane watched his schedule break down. He studied the eye for five minutes, then flipped to the physiology quiz he had made for himself, scrubbing the back of his head, the rustle of his flat brown hair, his lips moving silently around his answers. Abruptly he turned to his histology textbook.

She looked up from her flash cards, reached out curious for his physiology quiz.

He moved back from his textbook fast, jerked the paper away. She looked down at her empty hand.

"How's your studying going?" he asked, looking at the quiz as though reading it through again, as though busy with it and that was why he'd grabbed it from her. He was number one in the class, but she was now ranked number two. Over the last few weeks he had gradually stopped lecturing her on how to study, no longer gave her efficiency hints. His hair was out of place. One flat strand stuck straight up, like a giant splinter through his brain.

"How is it," he asked, looking back up at her. His eyes were red, she saw, and smaller than she remembered. "How is it you study anyway? What exactly is your system?"

She had thought him telling her about baby-sitting the boy wouldn't change anything between them. She hadn't considered his shame. She moved her hand toward his hair, to brush back that one strand, to touch him. He jerked away, looked back to his books. She watched him, her hand still outheld, missing more than she could say his warm touch, the unthinking confidence of his skin. He sat in front of her, looking so small. Perhaps this was the final straw.

"Michael," she said, "I cheated in college. Got caught." The truth came out so quick. She exhaled afterward, looked away, over his shoulder, like at a sudden sound there. The words didn't seem all that big.

"That's why I'm here at this school," she added, raising her fingertips to her temple. Her head felt empty without the secret, a huge open space. She could move a couch in there now, a dinette set, remodel. She turned back to him, reached forward again, to touch just the back of one hand.

He drew away from her, like she might leap over the desk toward him baring her teeth. Like she might do any thing. He blinked twice.

"You what?" he asked, his righteous voice shocked into a whisper but rising. "You did what?"

Jane was sitting on the dock when Keefer came down to feed Jonah. Her head hurt just at the sight of his slow bony walk. She wanted to feed him nourishing soups, whole cakes, cornstarch. She wanted to hold him close. She looked away. With Claren gone he spent a lot more time down here by himself.

He didn't say hi to Jane, just yanked the bucket out of the shed, reached in for the food. He hardly ever said anything anymore, to anyone. Jane was the only one he even sat near. He plopped down beside her, fish in hand, splashed the fish about in the water enough to get the smell in there, the blood. Then—she watched him do this—he picked the fish out of the sea and dropped it back into the bucket. While Jonah swung in close to the dock looking for the fish,

Keefer kicked his feet about in the water, making the sea almost foam.

Jane watched, confused. He had had Jonah a long time. She figured he knew how far to push it.

Jonah circled, scenting food, unable to find it, eyeing Keefer's dancing feet. It swam in a tight circle, then another. Keefer kicked on, seemed so determined. Jane turned to him, opened her mouth. She was going to say something, she didn't know what. Out of the corner of her eye she saw Jonah twist.

Jonah hit Keefer's calves. Keefer's whole body rocked with the power. He yanked his feet out, ran his hands down them. He giggled, his whole face relaxed. His feet were still there, their narrow ankles, their browned tops. He spread them out complete, on the dock beside Jane, wiggled the toes.

"Punched me," he explained.

Jane saw this was not the first time this had happened. It took her a moment to get back her voice.

"Why . . ." she asked, holding her hand out, empty. Knowing. "Why . . ." She couldn't finish her sentence. She wanted to pull him close, slap him, protect him. Did nothing. Around him, all her new bravery gone.

Keefer looked at her. Only his lips smiling. He spent so much time now, down here in the sun alone. His scalp was red and peeling, the stubble growing in along what had been so smooth. He sat stooped.

Claren lived two hundred feet down the beach now, in Penny's bungalow. If Claren was home, Jane knew, she'd be able to see them from the living-room window. She could be standing back in the shade, her arms crossed, her chin forward, stare unwavering.

"Why do you care?" Keefer asked. His voice cold. "You have Michael."

"Keefer," she started but he just looked at her. "Keefer," she said more quietly, almost whispering. She saw if she tried to stop him from kicking his feet in the water he'd do it even more. She'd do anything to protect him.

She licked her lips, closed her mouth slow. It was so hard.

Sometimes, this last week or so, while she sat on the dock with him, he hadn't spoken, not once the whole time. This silence now so far from restful. Her head hurt. She lowered herself back onto the dock, her head last, lay flat, breathed out, inhaled. She could hear the rhythmic slop of waves against the boards beneath her. She could smell salt and seaweed, the sun on wood, a touch of formalin from her hands or hair. She could feel the beat of blood in her neck.

Keefer was the only one who could still pull her back into her head. Her eyes closed in weariness and after a moment she heard him move, felt the heat of his hand near her right cheek, but no actual touch. Without opening her eyes she knew exactly where his hand was, how it was held. The back of his index finger closest, extended, the others curled partly in. She could have reached up to lace her fingers right in with his on the first try. They had switched roles, powers, she realized. She felt his hand withdraw so slow.

The water slapped against the dock. She exhaled.

After this afternoon she began to cut down on visiting Jonah when Keefer was around. She missed him even more than she would have thought.

After this afternoon, several times a day, she stepped out on the deck of her bungalow to look across the beach in Keefer's direction, to stand there, concentrating. Concentrating as though, if there was anything wrong, she would be able to sense it from clear around the island's point.

DAY NINETY-SEVEN

Late in the afternoon, the day before final exams, she sat in her room, forcing herself into an attempt at studying.

Tongue heavy, words blurring. Epididymis, fibrinolysin, bulbourethral glands. She rubbed her eyes, looked up at the ceiling, tried to repeat the first word. Her ability to memorize new things gone, without warning, without a trace.

Epidermis, she thought. No, epiglottis, epicenter. Epiphany.

Before she finished the first paragraph, she got up to take a walk. Outside the door she breathed deeply, her head back. The sunset was over, the sky just turning to night. While she walked, she swung her arms around, flapped them about trying to get the blood moving. Her feet stumbled. She started sweating before she even reached the jungle.

She entered town at dusk, hoping her pale skin and hair would be muted some by the approaching darkness. That the islanders might not notice her as much.

Dusk was when the women set out their sacrifices by the shrines and on the paths and corners of their houses, tiny intricately woven leaf plates of food, a spoonful of rice, a piece of chicken, a slice of fruit, incense. Turning the corner into town, Jane saw three different women kneeling down, lighting incense. Many other sticks already lit. The smoke billowed out, thick columns rising slow into the growing darkness, fifty sticks of incense, one hundred. In the heavy unmoving air beneath the trees the smoke hung in soft blue walls, creating a fog around the entire town, the air thick, sweet and enclosed. The light at dusk became more tricky, the smoke shifting gradually into night. Distances and colors were impossible to judge.

Five children played in the relative cool of the evening, pelting down the street, twisting along the path of a house, laughing and calling, an intricate game similar perhaps to Tag or Follow the Leader. Jane realized at this point she'd never seen any of the islander children cry. She'd never seen them scream in rage, punch each other or run home bawling to their mothers. They generally ran about like tiny limber adults playing kindly with each other. When one of the group—a pot-bellied three-year-old girl—spotted Jane, she uttered a single startled, "*hhh*," and stopped dead in her tracks. They all turned. They didn't yell then or throw twigs or giggle soft behind their hands, but instead stopped, quite serious, watching Jane go by. Once she was a few feet ahead the children trailed patiently after her, down the dirt street, their grave round faces watching intently. She seemed a problem that demanded much consideration.

When she reached the edge of town the children stopped at the last house, clustered in the growing dark, the incense rising behind them. Against the whitewashed houses their small forms were silhouetted, solemn as priests, watching her pale limbs swing off into the dark.

An hour later, maybe two, on the way back down through town at the end of her walk, in darkness now, the night creatures already shrilling, she came around the corner of the first house and almost walked into Trent coming out of the Red Door with a bottle of whiskey. She stopped abruptly. They stood there for a moment motionless in the night, facing each other, his hand slung down by his side holding the bottle with one long finger hooked on either side of the neck.

He reached out his other hand and led her away, like they had had an agreement about this meeting for quite a while. Like she was right on time.

She did not take her hand away, did not drag behind, didn't object at all. Instead her fingers gradually relaxed into his, holding on, the heat of his flesh loosening her muscles like a sauna. Her vision widened as in danger, her breathing slowed. She walked after him, following his scent. She had never allowed herself what she wanted.

"Trent," she said, speaking his name aloud for the first time that she could remember. "I cheated during college, on my organic chem final." The repetition felt good.

He looked back at her, irritated that she had broken the

silence. He shifted his hold on her hand, tighter. Strode on. She thought about that for a while, following him. Began to smile.

"Trent," she said, "my mother's had a breast tuck."

He did not even turn.

"My father," she added to his back, "has been sued for malpractice, four times."

Outside of town now, Trent stepped off the road and into the jungle, walking fast and confident, following a path she could not see. Leaves slapped at her, her feet stumbled on roots. She kept her free hand up by her face, her mouth closed, head bowed a bit. Still she could not stop smiling.

"Hey," she asked, "Where are we . . ."

He looked back at her again, the narrow oval of his face. His expression was flat. She didn't finish the question.

They reached a dense thicket of bamboo, two-inch-wide trunks straight as the bristles in a hairbrush, heading up, pale bone, into the darkness somewhere above her head. Somewhere up there were the leaves. Each trunk rose smooth and knuckled as a finger. Here he let go of her hand and pushed his way into the thicket with his arms sweeping the hard stems aside in the motion of swimming. He disappeared from view with the second step. The trunks swayed, the hard wood clacking far above.

She followed, no longer held by him. Walked into the thick wood curtain, like pushing open the ribs to move forward into the area of the lungs, the heart. Above a bird flapped off, calling loud and enraged. It was difficult to find places between the trunks for her feet. It was difficult to follow Trent, to hold a straight line through the bamboo, to keep the stalks from slapping back against her face.

She stepped abruptly into a clearing, a private room. The straight fingers of the thicket all around. Trent stood there waiting, a few feet back. She walked right into his arms, breathed out like she'd been holding her breath. She could feel every millimeter of flesh against him, his shoulder, his chest, her face against his neck. He laid her gently down, one hand on the back of her head to protect it. Her limbs heavy, her head thick with blood. He laid her on her back like a cadaver.

He took off her shirt, each button opened one at a time with a snap she could almost see. He pulled the sleeves gentle off her shoulders. The tie on her shorts loosened completely, rasping. The strings were draped away neatly to each side before he slid the material down over her hips.

He looked her over only once she was completely nude. She looked down too. A pretty stranger's body, she thought, pale, narrow, the ridges of her hips pressing up like the twin keels of a boat.

She turned back to him, Trent kneeling beside her still completely dressed. So used to Michael, she didn't think of starting the touching.

He leaned over and placed the tip of his tongue just once against her right nipple like a child might touch his tongue to the fogged glass of a car. She reached out now to cup the back of his neck just above, the heavy crinkling curls, the shifting cords of his neck. She ran her hand down his lean back, paused to make sure this was OK with him. He exhaled into her breast. She smelled garlic and the rich digestion of meat, the half-pant of a dog. She felt desire loosen every muscle of her body.

Drawing back, he opened the bottle of whiskey, the iron rasp of the cap against glass. He took a swallow, then dribbled the liquid from his lips down into the cup of her belly button. The cold was deep as novocaine, the ache the way rubbing alcohol chills the skin. She'd been sweating before. He filled the belly button to capacity, the liquid brimming slightly over the edge. Then he dribbled more whiskey in a line up her belly, over her ribs and around both breasts, ran his finger after through the splatters. The cold followed just behind, evaporation making her shiver. She looked down at his moving finger from a great distance, like watching the start of a surgical movie, the hand tracing the line the knife would make. She watched her nipples harden with the cold. She thought this was probably the first time her nipples had done that since she'd arrived on this island. She waited for his next move with interest. She found herself hungry in ways she would never have believed before this. She found herself curious. For a single moment she saw her body dead and cold and stiff.

Rather than tasting the liquid with his warm lips as she wished, he flicked a match out from somewhere in his hands, a lit match. She saw the flame, the shimmer lighting both of them up. It hit her belly button dead center. Heat. The ball of flame ran up her belly, round her breasts, fast as a scuttling creature searching for a hiding place.

Her automatic reaction. She turned sharp and frenzied onto her side, slapping at the liquid while the fire flickered across her hands, her fingers, her side and then was gone. Without leaving a mark, like something dreamed. Not even the smell of fire left, not even the stench of flesh.

In the sudden darkness after the flames she found him gone from her side. Sitting up she caught the ghostly outline of his face turned back to her disappointed as he pushed into the bamboo. The clacking of the shafts so far above the only sign of his passing.

Twenty-four

Christmas day Jane's parents called at five in the morning. They asked her why she hadn't been calling, said they'd tried to call her many times, at all sorts of hours.

Holding the sweating metal receiver against her ear, Jane imagined the phone ringing while she walked round and round Jonah's pen, while she lay naked on her back in the bamboo thicket. She found that the thing she wanted to do most at this point was get off the phone.

"There have been," she said, and for a moment lost her train of thought as a parrot fluttered yellow-eyed by her window. "There have been," she roused herself again, "some phone problems here." She tried to think of a specific problem to make the lie more believable. This took effort. In the end she just added, "Developing country, you know." She scrubbed her knuckles slow across her forehead.

"Oh yes," said her mother.

"It's to be expected," added her father. They understood perfectly, imagining America to be the only country with efficiency, with modern conveniences and the right set of values. Jane remembered vaguely how when they'd travelled to Europe her father had brought a refrigerated bag of his own blood. Just in case, he had said. Since then she'd learned the U.S.'s rate of AIDS was higher than most of Europe's.

"How're both of you?" she remembered to ask. Her voice sounded distant and tinny in her ears. They didn't seem to notice. It was so difficult to remember how she used to be.

"I'm thinking of starting a flower-arrangement school," said her mother. "Nothing big. No more than ten students at first. I think there's a need."

"Keep her busy," added her father. "Give something back to the community."

Jane looked out at the sea while her parents talked at her, the waves licking the shore in the heat. Her parents, she realized, existed in a completely different season from her, not in the same hour, not on the same day. They stood on the far side of the globe, their heads pointing out in the opposite direction. All that remained for her was their voices, faded through all the wire.

"Sounds great," she said at a pause in the conversation, not sure anymore what was being said. "And you, Dad?"

She found she was timing each question well, slipping her words into the long-distance lag. She could feel her parents' mouths tighten long before they opened. Could tell when their sentences would end. She didn't know why she'd had a problem before. Finally she'd found a way to speak as they'd always wanted, asking questions as she was supposed to, as easy as falling. She thought this took no effort at all.

Slow and deep, she breathed through her nose. Ran her hand gently across the tips of both breasts. She tried to listen. She could hear in the distance the plane making its approach, to drop off supplies. It stuttered down. It would take away any student who wanted to get on it. The school never put up a fight. All you had to do was get on the plane. All you had to do was say you'd had enough.

Nobody had left for a month.

She knew that later, when it took off—engines roaring—wherever she was on the island she'd turn to watch. The silver glint of it slipping away into the sky like a city disappearing in the rearview mirror. Like something magical being buried back into the earth. Within two hours it would land in Jakarta, the capital. Theoretically she knew she could get on the plane, if she just walked to the landing field. Theoretically, she knew, she had more than enough money to pay for years of life in a country like Indonesia, or Vietnam, or Malaysia. She would not have to go back home until she wanted to.

The plane puttered into sight in the frame of the window. Trailing it with her eyes, she took a step forward. The phone cord jerked her to a stop. Her parents were still talking.

". . . vacation plans," said her father's tiny voice.

"Maybe Tahoe," murmured her mother.

Jane took the receiver away from her ear, looked at it. Distantly she remembered a time she used to talk on one regularly, when she used to come running at its first ring. At the moment it seemed completely foreign to her, an object she had never seen.

"It's just I need," whispered her father's voice, "some time off."

Ever so gently she put the receiver down on the table. Loosened her fingers from it one at a time. Walked out on the balcony to watch the landing.

After a while—she was not sure how long—the phone began making high beeping noises, distracting her from the sound of the plane, so she shut the door to the balcony completely.

Christmas day celebrations started late, everyone still exhausted from exams. Around two o'clock Keefer drove by on his scooter to give Jane one of his sketches of Jonah, the only one she'd ever seen him not tear up. It was a close-up of it turning, as simple as a Japanese sketch, the outline, the motion through the water. Its dark eye seeking.

At 3:30 Marlene gave Jane one of her shirts. It was blue silk with a print of what she said were little sea cucumbers wearing sunglasses. Jane pulled her own T-shirt off her head, saw Marlene eye her body in surprise. Jane realized belatedly she'd never undressed in front of Marlene before, ashamed of the lumpy hang of her own body. Now she felt clean as a skeleton, no more fleshy than a door. She shrugged the new shirt on, began to button it, Marlene still watching. It fit Jane, perhaps a bit loose. Even her bones felt smaller, like she was reverting to childhood. Soon her height would diminish also, her head curling down over her unformed hands like a fetus's.

At five Michael stopped by to give her a small diamond pendant. He said it was actually from his mother. He said he'd told her that Jane and he had been going out all semester. His mother had sent this to give to her. The pendant, he said, had been in his family for generations. He seemed to have a problem looking her in the face.

After each gift Jane stepped into her room, looked around, picked up something to give back. Whatever caught her eye. Her linen safari outfit went to Marlene because it was the first thing Marlene had seen Jane in. Her high-school ring went to Michael, jewelry for jewelry. Her picture of her parents' piece of skin she gave to Keefer. When her gifts were given there was clothing left on the floor, books, but her room was stripped of the objects she'd considered valuable, as neatly as if she'd moved.

Michael tried the ring on, but it wouldn't fit even on his pinky, so he dropped it into his pocket instead. Bent forward to kiss her awkwardly on the forehead, said he hoped she forgave him for being such a bear before exams.

"Tension," he said. "You know I'm not like that normally.

"Don't worry," he said, "about the . . ." He looked away,

out the window. ". . . about the cheating. We won't speak of it again."

She watched him, realizing he would not ask her one question. She preferred, she understood at this point, to be around even Claudio's company over Michael's.

So she pulled him close then before he left, pulled him tight into her arms, for the first time without his lead. He stood there stiffly, then wound his hands slowly around her. She sighed once, breathed his smell in deeply, held it in her lungs. Stepped away.

He seemed small as a boy walking down to his moped.

Marlene held the safari outfit up, starting to laugh. "Gawd, Jane, you were such a dork." She laughed hard, her face all crinkled up. She looked so young, her eyes beginning to tear from the giggles. Jane realized it was the first time Marlene had called her by her real name.

Then, as Marlene's face continued to jerk with laughter, her mouth began to stretch, down at the edges. She turned her twisted face, fast and startlingly clear on Jane, as though at something just said. Her wet eyes blinking. She strode away into her room.

Jane stared at the slammed door. Blinked around at the room.

Marlene didn't come out for the rest of the afternoon.

Keefer took the picture, looked at it. He cupped it in against his chest, standing so close to her. "Parents?"

She nodded and noticed for the first time a jagged rip across the back of his right hand, the stitching uneven and awkward.

"How'd you do that?" she asked.

Keefer glanced down at his hand as though he didn't know what she could mean. "Oh," he said. "Stole the sutures. Got drunk before." He touched the swelling of it with the fingers of his other hand, added smoothly as though it went with the rest of the conversation, "Don't love Claren a-a-a-a." He closed his eyes, his lips moving through his words once silently before he opened his eyes again and spoke. "Anymore. No matter what I do.

"Jane, I . . ." he said. "I studied too hard for Egren. Flunked Parasitology instead. Know it. Couldn't answer more than half. Can't stay back again. C-c-c. Can't."

She stared at him, her face flat as a plate, no response anywhere inside her.

He looked away, breathed in. In some ways she preferred his anger. "I can't handle this," he said suddenly low. His voice was stammerless now, clear. He didn't rehearse his words.

"I can't," he repeated.

She held out her hands, looking at the backs of them for something to stare at more than his face. Folded them in.

"Keefer," she said. "Don't forget the plane," she said. "You can still leave here." Got the courage to look up. The existence still in her mind of the plane.

His expression.

Her hand moved out to his chest, to feel him close, to hold him back. Noticed her so dependable fingers shaking.

"I love you," she said. She spat it out in a burst like a threat, heard its echo in her ears, surprised. Remembered the way her mother touched her father.

Through her hand on his ribs, she could feel Keefer inhale. It made her shut her eyes. His breath on her face.

"Don't touch me," she barked.

For a moment neither one of them moved.

She ran from him as fast as she could. Left him blinking at the place where her face had been.

Twenty-five

Two days before Christmas, when she'd taken the final exams, she hadn't risen out of her body.

She'd sat heavy and filled with weight, firmly contained within her head. She looked down at the exam and it was there, a foot from her face. It didn't move. Her hand gripped the pencil. She stared at it. Her perspective didn't rise. After a while with nothing else to do, she read through the first question. She found, surprisingly enough, she could answer it. Hepatic portal hypertension, she thought. She knew this to be the answer. She looked up slow to Krakow, the start of a wide grin on her face, the first real grin in such a long time.

He was already watching her, determined, unblinking. His mouth tight. Bitter.

The phrase "Wipe that expression off your face" ran harsh through her head, in her mother's voice. She saw where the two small cuts would go, at the base of his ears, the facial nerves so delicate. The expression slackening smoothly, utterly, as in sleep.

For the first time she understood how completely she

hated him. How that hatred carried over to hepatic portal hypertension and the functioning of the liver as a whole. She sucked in her breath with the power of it. Perhaps the sound was loud. Several people turned to look.

Quickly and with anger she wrote out Hepatic Portal Hypertension, read the second question, filled in every answer as fast as she could, accurate and mechanical as a Teletype. Pressing so hard with her pen the paper ripped a little, twice. At no point did she move an inch out of her head.

Afterward she turned her chair to the window, folded her hands, and for the rest of the hour watched the gulls circling easily in the heat.

Twenty-six

She searched for him everywhere the morning after Christmas, after Keefer, didn't find him in town, not down at The Bar, not in the bamboo thicket. She went to his house, sat down square on the steps of his porch, in sight. There was nowhere else she wanted to be. There was nowhere else she could be. She sat heavy, her hands in her lap. She had never wanted to want anything more than the life her parents had decided on for her. She kept brushing the fingertips of her hand against her shorts. She kept seeing Keefer's expression. People drove by occasionally on their mopeds, Dana, Burpie, Randy Nally. Their heads jerked clear around to see her there. Before dinner the whole school would know where she had waited today.

Trent himself arrived after an hour, walking down the road, his hair still wet from a swim in the sea. He stopped in the dusty road when he saw her. Regarded her, sitting so small on his porch. He turned silently to the jungle, made no gesture toward her or away, moved away through the trees long-legged and jolting. She got up and followed without a word; just watching him move, she could feel her fear loosening momentarily in her chest.

He stopped in a glen twenty feet from The Bar. They were shielded from people seeing them by the underbrush but she worried someone might hear. She could hear all the voices from The Bar, calling for beer, laughing hard, so much noise to be let out in a single week between semesters. Only occasionally did the silences fall, everyone staring out at the sea or at their hands, these disruptions all the louder for the noise before and after.

Against the noise of The Bar, she could hear herself and Trent, leaves rustling, sticks crackling, their heavy half-breaths. He lay on top of her, slammed into her hard, backing her up every time into something sharp along the ground: part of a root, a rock? She didn't try to move away, didn't seek to protect herself. She ran her hand hungry over the bared socket of his hip. She wanted this, the pain, the danger. She pressed her fingers hard against him, trying to erase any other feeling, any other memory. His body stretched out solid tendon and bone, hard and functional, as different from most hips as wood was from flesh. Her fingers moved over the stretched plane of his lizard's belly, higher to his chest and tender nipples. She exhaled, feeling the back of her head loosen like a muscle. She traced the propped spider stance of his hands on the ground. She could feel every hair, every muscle and ridge. She could feel the jolt from his hips all the way up into her lungs. Alive, she thought, alive.

He leaned down to cup the side of her neck in his mouth, he cupped the carotid artery. He peeled back his lips a bit so she could feel his teeth gently there like one dog demanding obedience from another. Then he closed his mouth another degree so she could feel the hard pulse of her flesh against his teeth. He moved inside her. Pushed in, paused, pushed in, pushed. She felt every movement.

Pumping faster, he clenched his teeth in excitement.

She felt the constriction. Her vision began to blacken along the edges. At the same time she felt this heat swelling up within her from the base of where her tail would be if she were an animal. She slowed down her movements to listen to it, opened her eyes to see. It rose up her spine to her neck to exit out her lips like a little creature fighting free. In a silence from The Bar she heard her own voice in a child's breathy cry.

This was when the second vision came to her, with her mouth still open. Not the coffin. Instead a photo of herself, a photo she hadn't seen in ten years at least. She'd wedged her whole child's body into the confines of a flowered pillowcase, only her head visible. She was surprised at the tight bundle of herself. Small, contained, alive. Back when she doubted nothing. Not even herself. She couldn't have been older than five. Her face so sly with pride it was turned mostly away.

She was not sure when he let go with his mouth. She did not care. No one came out of The Bar at her cry.

After he had rolled off her, long after he had left, she looked down and saw the skin of her hip mashed from a broken root. The skin was purple and oozing as if she were already dead and did not know it, decomposing fast in this tropical sun.

She stared at it for a long time. Saw so much within. Perhaps it was then she rethought things. Got up after two tries, walked home slow and raw for the disinfectant.

She realized, with regret, she would not seek out Trent again.

She remembered the feeling of being curled inside the pillowcase, held so tight. She remembered back then loving the idea her parents might not be able to tell the difference between her and their own pillows, the image of them resting their heads against her, every night. The three of them so tight together.

DAY ONE HUNDRED THREE

That night, walking on the beach, she spotted Keefer, his back to her, moving down to Jonah's dock. Lately, each time she'd spotted him, she walked the other way, while they were still a fair distance apart, as though she hadn't seen him, forcing her arms to swing relaxed by her sides, making herself not look back. She did not want to know how he reacted; if he trailed after her for a few feet, mouth half-open to call, or just stood there looking smaller with each of her steps.

Through the dark, she watched him walk ahead of her, head down, hands in his pockets. His feet as silent through the sand as a ghost. She trailed down after him, unseen, watched him lie down on the dock, on his chest, slide the whole of his arms into the water, out to the shark. Jonah appeared immediately, must have been moving already, just beneath the surface. Its fin turned tight, fast, water streaming off it. So much energy, she thought, so alive. It circled smooth, moving closer, passing once, then twice. Keefer's attention fixed on its mass. She wandered closer, thirty feet away, twenty, sat down behind a rock, able to see the flicker of Keefer's white arms underwater in the wake of the shark.

She hugged her ribs, could remember now at will the smell of the pillowcase, clean and crisp, mixed with the sunbaked heat of her own child's body. She sidled half a foot closer. If he could stay there long enough, she thought, if he could stay there absolutely still for days, she would be able to creep right up to him, until her arms snaked around his chest. She knew him; from the moment she touched him he would not say a thing. They would sit there, motionless in the night, pressed up tight against each other, watching the shark.

Jonah punched Keefer fast, high up on one arm.

Keefer's whole body twisted so hard with the blow the

side of his head hit the dock. She jumped to her feet. He jerked back his arms, out of the water, obviously surprised to see both, held them smooth and whole above him in the night. Twenty feet apart, Keefer and she stared at them, transfixed by their narrow beauty. She sat back down slow. Looking at them, she understood now why Keefer teased the shark this way. She had never understood the miracle of arms so clearly as at this moment, never seen his arms so exact, the smooth pale skin, the spot he probed gently where the bruise would be.

She wondered if Keefer were feeding Jonah at all anymore. She didn't remember it being this alert, swinging its long body through the water, moving this strong and fast. Strange, when it must be getting weaker every day.

Twenty-seven

She was walking along the beach, working to remember, piece by piece, life as a five-year-old. Sometimes she smiled involuntarily, feeling the pulse of her stubborn heart. She could remember loving to run, back before the operations, back when her body was all her own, one predictable piece, what she'd been born with. She remembered that back then her body, if flawed, was still as smooth and solid as anything she'd ever imagined.

Grades would be announced tomorrow. Classes would start again, tomorrow.

Near dawn she came around the corner of Penny's porch, heading down toward Jonah's dock.

Down by the water she saw him on his side on the sand. At first she thought he was sleeping, but his limbs were too awkwardly sprawled, like he'd been dropped from a great height. Like the cadavers the first day. Even understanding then, understanding so clearly, she ran fast toward him.

The bottom side of Keefer's face was sticky with vomit. He had bled out from his nose. His hands clenched and small. An empty bottle of pills was spilled over beside him.

It hadn't been painless, she could tell that. Sand was kicked up all around, on his bare legs and in his clothing, stuck to his cheeks and tongue. So lonely, he had died by Jonah.

She'd never seen the open eyes of someone she knew after he'd stopped blinking, after the eyes dried out, dull as rubber.

She sat down beside him, as hesitant as though they'd just been introduced, looked away, then touched his narrow chest, in the same place she had last time she'd talked to him. His chest had always shivered, his heart beating, his breath struggling. Now his ribs were clenched, rigid with the effort of his departure.

Cautiously she lay down beside him. His skin a whole different set of colors. His face smaller. Every part of him appeared fake, wrong, an inanimate dummy made to resemble him. It wasn't him she looked at.

An ant walked into his left nostril. She stared into Keefer's dry upturned eyes.

Systematically then—it seemed the only thing she could do—she began to touch him, starting with his fingertips, his hands, moving up over his forearms and elbows. It would have been hard for her to say why. This all seemed so unlikely. She needed to make sure. There was nothing else for her to touch but his body. Except for that she was alone. She ran her fingers slow over his biceps and shoulders, into his armpits and down his sides, pressing, probing, measuring, learning by touch, by smell.

She traced through his thin skin every bared bone and tendon, fingered each surface vein and the frizzy hazing of his hair, checked the origin and swell of each muscle. In her head she heard not a single name for this anatomy, not one word of vocabulary. Not for this body. There existed only the feel of his tight skin, the clamped tension of his stomach muscles, the slabs of his hipbones, what remained of him.

She twisted her finger gentle in his belly button, pushed

her hands up the back of his shorts to learn of his narrow buttocks, slid her hands down his front to cradle his cold penis. She ran her hands thoroughly down each of his thin thighs, circled her thumbs slowly round his outsized boy's kneecaps, traced the outline of his delicate anklebones. She turned back to his head to touch her finger to the muscled white of his eye, hefted his skull between her hands. Just ten pounds of bone and soft tissue, she realized, no more movement than a rock. She'd always thought him stronger than her.

She started down his body again, touching it all, trying so hard to learn the real anatomy of death, a single death, the death of Keefer. Trying to memorize the knees of it, the hips, groin and belly, its bared arching ribs and spread shoulders, the narrow neck and smooth smooth skull.

A wave splashed warm against her feet. She'd slept somehow, she'd slept of course. Deeply, easily, stunned, wrapped tight around his body. Pressing her fingers into her lips, she felt pins and needles, the feeling coming back. His face still stared up from beside her, the same expression, neck stretched back to see the dawn. She sat up slow.

Looking down she noticed Jonah waiting just below in the water, so knowing, so patient. Its nose barely three feet from her toes. Its mouth scenting. The tide was coming in. Already Keefer's feet lay in the water, shifting slightly with the slap of each wave, the roughened sand under the heels being smoothed away, hollowed out, becoming a slide straight down. Jonah's fin pointing.

She touched him one last time. Ran her hand down his chest, yanked one button from his shirt, slid it between her lips. The next wave went as high as his knees; the hair on his calves waved, then flattened. She stood up slow, staggering twice, almost drunk, straightened her legs.

A moment passed. The sea hissed along the sand. A bird called *Kiii* in the distance. The surprise she felt was like a hand passing over her face.

Keefer's body continued not to breathe.

She looked all around her, the sea, the dock, Jonah, the distant spire of the school. Everything distinct. She inhaled salt, dirt, sun, the slight copper of his blood, moved her hands across her own ribs. She could feel everything, her mobile fingers, her ribs rising, their fall, the taste of air in her lungs, the blood beating in her ears.

Jonah shimmied impatiently a little closer, its gills fluttering just underwater. Its nose two feet from Keefer's toes.

Abruptly she turned and jolted away, up toward the forest. Walking, she pressed the button between her tongue and the inside of her lips, moving it all around. She didn't look back, didn't listen, didn't have the strength. Only now did her hands begin to shiver, her legs shaking, her breath. On the button she could taste his sweat, the smooth enamel of his fear, the binding threads. She felt she'd never tasted anything before this. With the heels of her hands she scrubbed her face, her neck, her chest, her whole body tingling.

She paced through the jungle, climbing up the hill toward the landing field. Looking around at everything, the leaves, the vines, the rich crumbling earth. The plane would arrive soon enough. Everything appeared so clear, the leaves as sharp as if cut from glass. She would leave, of course, was leaving. There was nothing left for her here.

Carefully she placed her shaking feet, stepping up the hill, determined, keeping her pace down. She knew enough not to run until the end.